I0669282

THE PATH
ARIEL TACHNA

Published by
DREAMSPINNER PRESS

5032 Capital Circle SW, Suite 2, PMB# 279, Tallahassee, FL 32305-7886 USA
http://www.dreamspinnerpress.com/

The Path
© 2014 Ariel Tachna.

Cover Design
© 2014 Paul Richmond.
www.paulrichmondstudio.com
Cover Photo
© 2014 Ariel Tachna
Cover content is for illustrative purposes only and any person depicted on the cover is a model.

ISBN: 978-1-63216-222-9
Digital ISBN: 978-1-63216-223-6
Library of Congress Control Number: 2014944013
First Edition September 2014

Printed in the United States of America

Readers love ARIEL TACHNA

Chateau d'Eternite

"A story so captivating that you just want it to continue!"
—Sid Love Reviews

Under the Skin

"Romance, danger and thrills, this one's an m/m must read."
—Sinfully Sexy Books

Testament to Love

"… a sweet story that addressed a number of serious topics in a short period of time without feeling rushed and featured some appealing characters and spins on religion and love while never crossing the line into sappy."
—Joyfully Jay Reviews

"This was just a fast, fun, sexy read. … It was so sexy and sweet and added a depth of feeling that set this story apart from other similar stories. Definitely recommend this read."
—MM Good Book Reviews

"This was just a short, sweet, little story, a lot of love, and some beautiful angel sex! I can count on Ariel to give me a fantastic story, she does wonderful things with big intense novels, and sweet little ones like this."
—Love Bytes Reviews

"I love angel stories and this one that completely enthralled me with its premise. … I totally adore this story about the true meaning of love, and the ultimate message that love takes many forms and may not always be what we expect."
—Rainbow Book Reviews

By Ariel Tachna

All For One (with Nicki Bennett)
Best Ideas
Château d'Eternité
Checkmate (with Nicki Bennett)
Fallout
Her Two Dads
Highland Lover
In Search of Fireworks
The Inventor's Companion
The Matelot
Music of the Heart
Myths and Magic: Legends of Love (Dreamspinner Anthology)
Once in a Lifetime
Out of the Fire
Overdrive
The Path
Rediscovery
Revelations in the Dark
Riding Double (Dreamspinner Anthology)
Rose Among the Ruins
Seducing C.C.
Stolen Moments
A Summer Place
Sutcliffe Cove (with Madeleine Urban)
Testament to Love
Under the Skin (with Nicki Bennett)
Why Nileas Loved the Sea

The Exploring Limits Series (with Nicki Bennett)
Exploring Limits • Stretching Limits • Refining Limits
Breaking Limits • Transcending Limits • No Limits

Games Lovers Play
Amorous Liaison • Best Behavior • Ride 'em Cowboy

Hot Cargo
Hot Cargo (with Nicki Bennett) • Something About Harry (with Nicki Bennett)
Healing in His Wings

Lang Downs
Inherit the Sky • Chase the Stars • Outlast the Night • Conquer the Flames

Partnership in Blood
Alliance in Blood • Covenant in Blood • Conflict in Blood • Reparation in Blood
Crossroads in Blood
Perilous Partnership • Reluctant Partnerships • Lycan Partnership

Available at Dreamspinner Press
http://www.dreamspinnerpress.com

To the Llama Lovers, who hiked the Inca Trail with me last year.

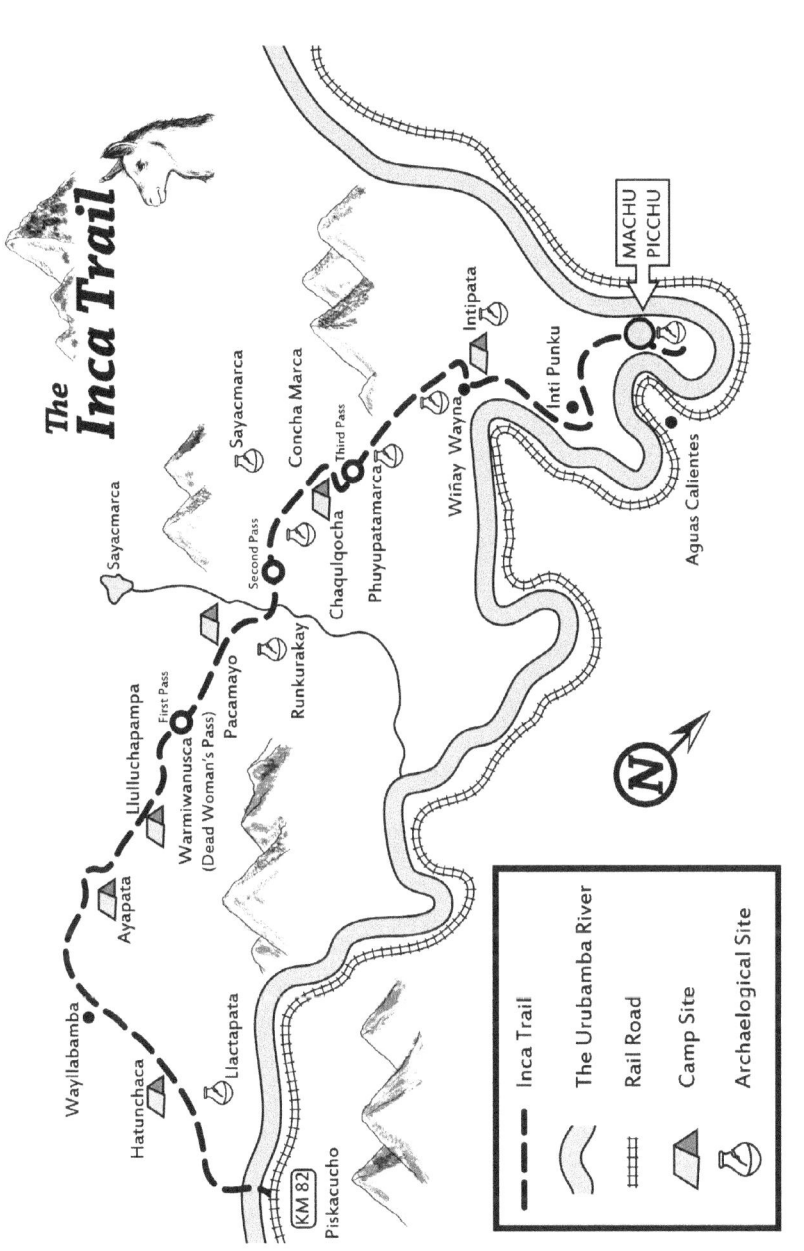

The
Inca Trail

MACHU PICCHU

Piskacucho
KM 82

Hatunchaca

Wayllabamba

Llactapata

Ayapata

Llulluchapampa

Warmiwanusca
(Dead Woman's Pass)

First Pass

Pacamayo

Runkurakay

Sayacmarca

Sayacmarca

Second Pass

Concha Marca

Chaquiqocha

Third Pass

Phuyupatamarca

Wiñay Wayna

Intipata

Inti Punku

Aguas Calientes

Inca Trail

The Urubamba River

Rail Road

Camp Site

Archaelogical Site

small, but it's mine, not something I ever had at home, and it's not expensive, so I can live there and still have money to send home to my mother."

"It's not too overwhelming, being there?"

"Some days it is, but I'll be out on the trail more days than not before long—at least, I hope I will—and that will be more like home."

"We have a very busy winter," Miguel confirmed. "We have at least two groups every week from now until Christmas, and some weeks, we have three or four. You won't lack for work, although you may want to take a week off once a month to give your knees a break. Hiking the Inca Trail every week is hard on the body. We can use you in other ways during those weeks, either doing local tours or in more of an organizational capacity. I like for my guides to be familiar with the full spectrum of a group's visit, even if they focus primarily on one aspect."

Benicio did a quick calculation. It was only May. If he could indeed count on steady income from treks between now and December, he ought to be able to buy the solar generator he'd read about online for his mother so she would have electricity for the first time. Of course, then he'd have to save up for appliances or the generator would sit there unused, but he could do that. Not during the rainy season when fewer tourists wanted to risk bad weather to visit the sites, but next winter for sure.

"That makes sense, and it lets us keep working even if we aren't on the trail one week."

"Yes, exactly." The door opened behind them, drawing their attention. Benicio turned to look at the new arrival. Alberto, if it was indeed Alberto, was the epitome of Quechua handsomeness, with his round face, distinguished nose, wide cheeks, and narrow-set almond-shaped eyes. His skin was dark from a life lived outdoors but not weathered like Benicio's older brother's skin already was. Most of all, though, the man had a twinkle in his eyes and a smile flirting around the corners of his mouth that made Benicio take an instant liking to him.

"Ah, you made it, Alberto." Miguel shook Alberto's hand and gestured for him to take the chair next to Benicio's. "Alberto, this is Benicio, the new guide I was telling you about. You're ready to take another first-time guide under your wing, and I know Benicio will be a good student."

"Hi." Alberto offered Benicio his hand. Benicio shook it, meeting Alberto's eyes with more confidence than he felt. He wanted to make a good first impression even if he had to fake his way through the meeting to do it.

"Hi," Benicio replied. "It's a pleasure to meet you. I'm excited to get started."

"Do you speak Quechua?" Alberto asked.

"Yes," Benicio replied, switching languages. "That's all my grandparents spoke, so I didn't learn Spanish until I started school."

"Good." Alberto didn't take Benicio's reply as an invitation to switch to Quechua, but he had clearly understood. "That'll be useful on the trail. Not all of the porters speak Spanish well. It'll be nice having a guide who can translate for me instead of having to rely on the head porter. I know some Quechua, but I grew up in Urubamba. Most people don't speak it here anymore."

"I'd noticed," Benicio replied. "Some people do in Pisac, but not many here unless they're like me and have just come down from the highlands."

"No, and it's sad, but I guess it's the way the world works."

Benicio wasn't sure he agreed, but it wasn't worth pursuing right now. "So besides talking to the porters, what else do you expect of me while we're on the trail?"

"That depends on what you're comfortable with. We have a group of twelve, so there have to be two of us, but you don't have to actually do much. Twelve isn't that different from eight. If you want to just follow along and listen this first time, you can bring up the back of the line and get a feel for how things go. If you want to give one segment of the tour, I can certainly let you do that."

"I don't want to be deadweight." Benicio had spent too many years listening to his brother complain about him being lazy because he stayed home and helped his mother take care of his ailing father rather than working in the fields. He didn't ever want to give Alberto, or worse, Miguel, a reason to say the same.

"You won't be. Even if all you do is stay with the slower hikers and make sure they get to camp safely, you'll be doing your job. I remember what it was like to be new and nervous. I'm happy to give you anything you feel comfortable with, but I'm also perfectly capable of dealing with the routine of the trail. If you need to sit back and observe this time to see how we work around here, I can give you that time."

Alberto's words made sense, but they didn't alleviate that visceral need to avoid censure. "Can we see how it goes? Maybe I can mostly observe the first day and then take on more as the hike goes on?"

"We can do that. Is there a stop along the trail you're particularly interested in or fascinated by? You could give the explanation for that one, and if you know ahead of time, you can even go back and brush up on those details specifically."

It was a generous offer, to give him the choice instead of assigning him a group of ruins. Not wanting to appear greedy, he chose one of the smaller ones—still interesting, but not as elaborate or important as Wiñay Wayna or Machu Picchu. "I could talk about Runkurakay. By the third day, I should be comfortable enough to do that."

"It would be toward the end of the second day," Alberto corrected. "I guess Miguel hasn't given you our schedule yet. We don't camp at Pacamayo like some of the other companies do. I know it's the dry season, but if we get unexpected heavy rains, we'd have to deal with the risk of flooding. We push farther on the first two days so we can camp near Phuyupatamarca on the second night at the Chaqulqocha campsite. It makes for long days, but it's worth it not to have to worry about the weather as much. Plus, we get to Wiñay Wayna early on the third day, so everyone can relax a bit and spend more time in the ruins if they want. They're by far the most interesting with the exception of Machu Picchu."

Benicio could hardly argue with that when he had resented how little time they spent at Wiñay Wayna during his tour. He could have spent nearly as much time there as he had in Machu Picchu. "That makes sense. You'd think if there was a risk of flooding, more companies would push on, but I guess there are only so many campsites."

"And not all companies are as scrupulous about safety as we are," Miguel interjected. "I'm not saying they're careless, but some companies are satisfied with following the regulations and nothing more. We don't do things that way. The regulations are a starting point, not an ending point. If you ever have concerns about any aspect of what we do or see any way to make the trip safer and more enjoyable for our guests, I expect you to tell me, or at least to tell Alberto so he can tell me."

"I will," Benicio promised. He would wait until he saw how everything worked before he said anything, but the offer touched a chord in him. He would not simply be a drudge here. He would be a contributing member of a team dedicated to showing the best the Andes had to offer to people from all over the world.

"Good. I'll leave you two to go over plans for tomorrow night's meeting and the hike. If you need me, I'll be in the other room answering e-mails."

Benicio's nerves returned with a vengeance when Miguel left them alone. Miguel might own the company, but Alberto would be the one reporting on his progress over the next two months. If Benicio had to impress anyone, it was Alberto.

"So we have a meeting tomorrow night with the first group to go over everything, right?"

"Yes, at the Casa Andina Cusco Plaza. We're meeting them at seven. Someone else from the company will be there with their gear, as well, for the people who rented sleeping bags, walking poles, or porters. Once that's all passed out, we'll go over the trip, what time we're meeting on Wednesday, and answer any questions they have. I'll introduce you, but I'll probably do most of the talking this time. After a few weeks, when you're more familiar with the routine, we'll see about having you do some of that presentation."

"I don't mind just listening," Benicio said. "I know I'm new at this."

"They don't need to know that." Alberto's face was so serious Benicio nodded before he even had a chance to think about it. "We need them to trust us, and we don't want them doubting your advice because this is your first trip. You grew up in the mountains. You know how to survive in them, what to watch out for, what's safe and what's not. The fact that this is the first time you're using that information on the actual Inca Trail is irrelevant."

Benicio wasn't completely sure he agreed, but he didn't argue. Alberto had far more experience. "What if they ask?"

"If they ask, we'll tell them, but we'll try to keep the conversation on other topics for the first day or two. They're far more likely to ask if you have a girlfriend or are married. That's always what people ask the first day."

"I don't," Benicio said.

"There's no law that says you have to," Alberto said. "I'm single too, but they do ask, especially since we always take pains to remind them that the porters are supporting their families. It's easy for them to forget to look at the porters as people instead of just worker ants scurrying around. Hearing about the porters' families helps with that."

"And since you bring up their families, they ask about yours. Makes sense. I can tell them about my mother and my brothers still in Cancha Cancha, and I'll have a niece or nephew before the season is over, so there will be a baby to talk about too."

"You don't have to give a lot of details either. They're curious, but they'll usually respect whatever boundaries you set. We'll meet them at the hotel Wednesday morning at 4:00 a.m. If you bring your gear here tomorrow, it can go with the porters the next morning, so all you have to bring is your day pack. Make sure you get a duffel bag from Miguel or the receptionist before you leave so you can pack in it. It's easier for the porters to carry that way."

"I don't need much," Benicio said. "A change of clothes, my sleeping bag, and my toiletries."

"The porters will appreciate that. Do you have somewhere in Cusco to stay so you don't have to try to get here that early?"

"I have a cousin here," Benicio said. "I stayed with him when I came in to take my guide's test. He won't mind if I sleep on his couch once a week. Cusco is too big and too expensive. I couldn't live here full-time."

"It doesn't ever get less expensive, but you do get used to the size," Alberto said. "I grew up in Urubamba. It's larger than Cancha Cancha, but it's nothing compared to Cusco, but I don't even think about it now."

"How long have you lived in Cusco?" Benicio asked.

"About six years," Alberto said. "I got tired of the early mornings or sleeping on friends' couches on tour nights, and by then, I was earning enough to afford a small place here. You'll get there too. It may take a few years, less if you find someone to share an apartment with."

He could do that, Benicio supposed, but he found he rather enjoyed having a place entirely to himself after having shared a room with his brothers all his life. Even after his older brother had gotten married and moved out, he'd still had his younger brother in the room with him. "We'll see how it goes. For now, I can stay with my cousin. After I'm sure everything will work out with the job, I can look at other options. Is there anything else I need to do between now and tomorrow night to help make sure everything is ready?"

"No, Miguel and his staff will make sure all the equipment is ready for the porters," Alberto said.

"Then I'd better get back to Pisac and pack my gear," Benicio said. "I'll see you tomorrow night at the hotel."

"See you then." Alberto headed toward the office where Miguel had gone, so Benicio took that as a sign he could leave. He walked back outside, flinching a little at the noise of the traffic going by. Despite Alberto's reassurances, he doubted he'd ever get used to the sheer number of people and cars in Cusco. They didn't have any kind of mechanical equipment in Cancha Cancha because they had no way to get it there. They rode horses and used llamas as pack animals to transport in goods they couldn't produce on their own and to transport out the wool and the surplus food they grew.

He headed toward the Plaza de Armas and the bus station where he could catch the bus back to Pisac. One left the station as he was crossing the plaza, but they ran approximately every fifteen minutes, so he wouldn't have too long to wait for the next one. His thoughts raced as he took a seat on a bench and waited for the next bus to board. He knew his first hike as a guide would be as much a learning experience as the hike as a tourist had been, because he would be seeing a different side of the journey. Where before he had gone with the idea of experiencing what his guests would, now he would be seeing it from the point of view of the people running the trip. He would learn that side of things over time, but he refused to sit and do nothing this first trip. At least he spoke Quechua and could help Alberto that way. He was determined to meet the head porter first thing on Wednesday morning and to learn everyone's names as quickly as possible so he could work with them directly. If he couldn't help Alberto, maybe he could help them while they were in camp together. After all, the more he knew about the way things worked, the better he would be able to assist later.

He also had to go back over his notes on Runkurakay. It wasn't the most complicated of the ruins they would stop at, but it was an interesting one, and its function would give him the opportunity to talk a bit about the communications network of the Inca Empire. Benicio wanted his information to be as complete as possible, if only so Alberto would trust him with more presentations on future trips.

The bus rumbled into the station, drawing Benicio back out of his thoughts. With his resolve fully in place, he paid for his ticket and climbed on the bus to head home.

TWO

ALBERTO KNOCKED on the door to Miguel's office but didn't wait for an invitation to enter. It had been years since the door was last closed to him.

"Finished already?" Miguel looked up from his computer with a smile.

"Yes. Did you have to saddle me with another beginner?" Alberto flopped down in the chair with a halfhearted glare for his mentor.

"You're so good with them," Miguel said. "You have a flair for helping them to understand not just the actions that go into being a good guide, but the heart of the people and the trail we want our guests to leave understanding. Besides, you haven't found your partner yet, the one you don't even have to talk to for him to know what you're thinking."

"Kind of hard to develop that kind of rapport when you switch out the person I'm working with as soon as he begins to get his feet under him." Alberto knew he sounded sullen, but Miguel knew him well enough to know he was letting off steam, not really complaining.

"Yes, they were getting their feet under them, but you were with them all long enough for that to have developed if it was going to," Miguel insisted. "You made them into good guides, but none of them were good for you. If they were, you wouldn't have come back from the hikes looking so worn out."

"It's a forty-five kilometer hike in three and a half days. Of course I'm worn out." It didn't matter how many times he hiked the Inca Trail. Getting up at three thirty in the morning on the last day so they could make Machu Picchu at sunrise always left him exhausted.

"You were tired at the end of the trip when we worked together, but you weren't worn like you are now," Miguel insisted.

"That's because you did all the work." Miguel had taken Alberto under his wing back when Miguel's father was still running the business and Miguel was on the trail most weeks. Alberto freely admitted he'd learned everything he now taught to other guides from the man sitting across the desk from him. "All I had to do was show up."

"That's not true and you know it," Miguel said. "Maybe it was true the first hike or even the fifth. By the time I retired, though, you were doing most of the work. I was on paper as the primary guide, but we worked as a team, and that made it easier on us both. You'll find the person you can work with that way, and when you do, the difference will stun you. You just have to keep looking."

"Yeah, okay," Alberto said. He ran his hand through his short black hair. "So what do we know about the new kid?"

"He's twenty-six, so he's not a kid. He's from Cancha Cancha. He speaks Spanish and Quechua fluently and his English is passable. You should encourage him to practice any chance he gets because your next several groups are from the US."

"Breaking him in hard and fast?"

Miguel smiled apologetically. "I can't control who reserves tours when. You know that. If I'd had a Spanish-speaking group available, I'd have given it to you, but I don't. I have two groups from the US, one from France, and one from Sweden, all English speaking. Since neither of you speaks French, the only choice is an English-language group, unless you want a week off."

"You could send me with someone else."

"I could, but then Benicio would have to work with a different guide, and I'd rather he stay with you until he gets familiar with how things work. You really are the best I have, Alberto."

Alberto scoffed, but this wasn't the first time Miguel had told him that. Alberto didn't know how that could be. He just did his job.

"And that look on your face is exactly why I know you haven't found the right partner yet. Go out tonight. Go to that club you like so much. Have a few drinks, dance with some cute thing who catches your eye. Get lucky, even. You need to let off some steam before this hike. You're wound too tight, and that's dangerous out on the trail."

"You do realize how awkward it is when my boss tells me to go find a piece of ass and fuck it, don't you?" Alberto said.

"I'm not just your boss," Miguel reminded him. "I like to think we're friends."

Miguel was more than that. He was like an uncle to Alberto, especially since Miguel knew about and accepted him when Alberto's family still preferred to pretend he was single because he was too busy on the trail to meet a nice girl and settle down, rather than acknowledge he would never get married unless Peru legalized gay marriage. "We are. I'm not sure that makes it less awkward, though."

Miguel grinned and shooed Alberto toward the door. "Get out of here. I don't want to see you before three tomorrow afternoon, and you'd better have a smile on your face when you come in. A real one, not the one you plaster on for the tourists."

Alberto left, but he turned toward home rather than toward the Queen. He would do as Miguel suggested, up to a point anyway, and go out dancing, but he'd call Joaquin and see if he wanted to go with him to the gay dance club. They always had a blast, even if it never led to anything other than letting off steam. That's what Miguel said Alberto needed to do, so he'd do it and tell his boss he'd followed orders when he came into the office tomorrow afternoon.

ALBERTO LEANED against the bar and sipped his Pisco Sour. If he'd really wanted to get drunk, he'd have chosen something stronger, but he didn't want to be hungover tomorrow even if he wasn't expected at the office until three or to deal with tourists until the evening. He hated feeling that out of control, even if Joaquin insisted he wasn't a wild and crazy drunk.

"What's that scowl for?"

Alberto turned to face his friend. "Thinking about something Miguel said."

"I thought you loved your boss," Joaquin said. "Did something happen?"

"No, nothing like that. He's worried about me. Told me to go out tonight and relax."

"So why are you scowling? That isn't relaxing."

Alberto didn't reply. He didn't want to open himself up to Joaquin's teasing. Another night, he'd give back as good as he got and it wouldn't matter, but he was already feeling raw tonight. Having to listen to Joaquin, however well-meaning, would only make it worse. He drained his drink and set the glass on the bar. "Let's dance," he said, dragging Joaquin toward the space between tables that had not yet filled up with bodies. By the time the night—or morning—was over, it would be so crowded they'd hardly be able to do more than grind against the people in front of or behind them, but for the moment, they had space to pick up the sultry rhythms of the salsa.

Even before they cleared the last table, Joaquin had pressed up against Alberto's back, his feet and hips moving in time to the beat, enticing Alberto to join in. Alberto closed his eyes and leaned back against his friend, letting Joaquin's hands on his hips guide him. Here, now, with the music pulsing around them, he could let go. Joaquin would not let him fall.

As the beat took over, Alberto felt his stress fade away and a real smile form. He lifted his hands over his head, hips shimmying as he turned in Joaquin's arms. Joaquin's smile answered Alberto's own and Alberto backed away, enticing Joaquin to follow. Joaquin strutted after him, reaching out to catch his hand and twirl him back into a tighter embrace. They undulated together for a moment, eliciting catcalls from the men sitting at tables around the dance floor. Alberto grinned at Joaquin before looking coyly over Joaquin's shoulder at their oglers. They would take his invitation or not; it didn't matter. The music had hold of him now. He would dance until he dropped and then maybe he'd feel better.

He spun away from Joaquin again, expecting his friend to follow, but before Joaquin could reel him back in, another dancer had stepped into place. Alberto changed partners easily enough, enjoying the spark of arousal that came with knowing he'd enticed one of the spectators onto the floor. The man wasn't anything special to look at, but he danced masterfully, leading Alberto through the steps and into his arms with ease. The sparks leaped along his nerves as his new partner pulled Alberto against him, grinding their hips together. The hard ridge of the man's cock felt so good against his ass. He pushed back and shimmied harder before breaking the man's hold and twirling away. It made him a tease, but he didn't care. Despite Miguel's admonishment, Alberto wasn't there to fuck. He just wanted to dance.

Another partner took the place of the one he'd abandoned, better looking but not as good a dancer. Alberto laughed and took a little more initiative with this one, brushing their bodies together each time they got close enough. He reveled in the look on the man's face each time. He wasn't a freak of nature here in this club. He could flirt and dance and be himself without worrying about who was watching, about how the tourists or the other guides or the porters might react. He could pick someone to take into a dark corner or the back alley, or he could stay on the dance floor and tease them all. He had choices here instead of the great empty gulf that was the rest of his life, devoid of passion except for his passion for the trail.

Another man cut in, and Alberto stopped keeping track, moving from partner to partner as the whim took him, sometimes finding himself in the middle of a group of dancers, sometimes the sole focus of one man or another. Sweat beaded between his shoulder blades, across his forehead, and under his arms, but he kept dancing. His pulse pounded with the exertion and his ever-growing arousal. All these men to grind against, to tantalize himself and them… it went to his head, leaving him feeling like he was floating on the scents of sweat and musk and all the mingled colognes. Little by little, the knot of tension at the base of his skull began to loosen with the sheer bliss of hands on him and strong bodies against his own.

Sometimes he thought he could come from the frenzy of dancing alone, but Joaquin always pulled him back before he lost himself that completely. He hated his friend each time in that moment but always thanked him in the morning. Dancing was enough of a release on its own without adding sex to the mix, any more than the intimacy of dancing already did. He hadn't reached that point yet tonight, though, and he wanted to. He wanted to fly, so he worked his way toward the center of the floor to the most crowded part and insinuated himself into the middle of the press of bodies. They made room for him, hands wandering over his chest, back, and ass. He lifted his arms, revealing a strip of skin below the hem of his shirt. One bold man took the movement as invitation and hiked his shirt up to his armpits. The crowd hooted and Alberto smiled wider, meeting their gazes flirtatiously, one man at a time before moving on to the next, daring them to reach out and touch. Some did, fleeting caresses in most cases, the rhythm of the dance keeping them from lingering. One particularly temerarious man grabbed his hips and pulled him close enough long enough to tweak his nipples. Alberto pushed him away quickly, ignoring the spike of arousal. He was there to dance, not have sex on the dance floor.

He nearly jumped out of his skin when he felt hard hands close around his arms, bringing his gyrations to a halt. "Time for a break."

"Fuck you," he muttered, but Joaquin's grip was implacable. Alberto followed him off the dance floor and back to the bar.

"Drink this," Joaquin ordered, pressing a bottle of water into Alberto's hands.

"I'm supposed to be getting drunk," Alberto replied sullenly.

"I ordered another Pisco Sour for you, but drink the water first or you'll be sick in the morning."

Alberto glared at him but drank the water obediently. It was icy cold, almost burning his throat in its freshness as he guzzled it down, but as his head cooled off, he could admit the wisdom of Joaquin's words. He hadn't realized how parched he'd gotten. "How long was I dancing?"

"Over an hour," Joaquin replied. "Are you sure you're all right? I haven't seen you get lost like that in a long time." Alberto took so long to consider the question that Joaquin poked him in the side. "Talk to me."

"When my father was my age, he was married with two kids and my sister on the way," Alberto said slowly. "When my brother was my age, he was married with his fourth on the way."

"I hate to break it to you, but even if you moved somewhere you could get married, the whole 'kids on the way' thing isn't happening."

"I know that, but this just seems… pointless, I guess. I mean, we all come here and we dance and maybe we hook up and get off, but then we all go home to empty apartments and empty lives. It's depressing."

"You hardly have an empty life," Joaquin retorted. "I've listened to you talk about your hikes, and I've watched you devour every new archeological discovery and anthropological paper you can get your hands on. You don't have time for a wife and kids even if you wanted them, because you're too in love with that damn trail to spend any time with them."

"I spend all that time on the trail, learning about it and staying abreast of all the latest developments, because I have to do something to fill my time or I'd go crazy," Alberto replied. "If I had someone to come home to, maybe I'd spend more time there."

"If you spent more time in Cusco, maybe you'd meet someone."

They'd had this discussion before. Alberto would lament the lack of a significant other in his life, Joaquin would give the same reply, and nothing would ever change. Alberto might spend less time on the trail if he had someone to come home to, but he had to meet someone first, and not just anyone, but someone who would understand and accept that the Inca would always be his passion and that hiking the trail was in his blood. He might do a week on and a week off instead of hiking every time Miguel called him, but he would still be gone four days at a time. He could earn a living doing city tours in Cusco or Sacred Valley tours in Pisac and Ollantaytambo, but it was the Inca Trail and Machu Picchu that nourished his soul.

"If I spent more time in Cusco, I'd be miserable, holed up in my crap apartment by myself with no one to talk to."

"You can always talk to me."

"I know." And he did know that, but it wasn't the same. Joaquin would always listen, would always kick him in the ass if he needed it or provide a sympathetic shoulder if that was what he needed, but the emptiness went deeper than Joaquin could fill. Alberto wanted the bond his parents had shared, not a few random fucks just to let off steam.

"But I'm not enough, am I?"

"Not for this," Alberto said. "I wish you were. I wish…." He couldn't finish the sentence. He couldn't tell Joaquin he wished they could be real lovers instead of friends with very occasional benefits. It seemed too final, like he was closing a door that couldn't be reopened. Maybe he would never want it open again, but he still couldn't make himself shut it.

"Yeah, I know," Joaquin said. "Me too."

THREE

BENICIO ARRIVED at the Casa Andina twenty minutes before the scheduled time. He had been afraid of delays with the bus and with getting from his cousin's house to the hotel, so he'd left earlier than necessary, but he would rather be early than late. At least the men and women hawking their wares to the tourists left him alone, approaching the gringos instead. Benicio would put money on his mother and sister-in-law making better quality textiles than the ones on display here, probably selling for less money. His uncle certainly had a finer hand with jewelry, when he could be persuaded to work on that instead of in his fields. If Cancha Cancha were less remote, Benicio would try to bring some of their products into town to sell, but getting home was a trek. He could take a bus as far as Calca, but then it was a two-hour hike up into the mountains.

A bus pulled up in front of the hotel and a group of tourists piled out. Benicio wondered if this was the group he and Alberto would be working with. The bus did not have the Huaman Travel logo on it, but that didn't mean anything. A lot of the tour companies rented buses as needed instead of buying and having to maintain the vehicles themselves, and Benicio hadn't thought to ask which way Huaman Travel did it. The group was young, for the most part, probably close to Benicio's age, although he noted a couple of slightly older faces. If this was his group, he hoped they were prepared for the rigors of the trail. He'd seen too many people struggling as he hiked his first time to take it for granted that people would come prepared for the demands of the climb, much less for the altitude.

"You're early."

Alberto's voice started Benicio out of his contemplation. "I didn't want to be late."

"That's a good quality to have. You didn't have to wait outside, though. There's a sitting area inside where you could have waited."

"But it's so interesting out here, watching all the people go by. You never see anything like this in Cancha Cancha, and even in Pisac, it's not this busy. Well, maybe on market day, but I don't live near the market and don't usually go out then because it's too many people. Besides, the market is geared toward the tourists. I can get the same quality sweaters or hats from my mother for free."

"Does your family raise alpacas?"

"Yes, along with sheep and guinea pigs. My brother has some chickens too, but they don't do as well at that altitude. Still, a few eggs are better than none."

"There's Domingo. He'll have all the gear for our group. Shall we go meet them?"

Benicio followed Alberto into the hotel, watching as he greeted the hotel staff by name. He introduced Benicio, but it was too many names too fast for Benicio to remember them all. Next time, he'd come in and meet them without waiting for Alberto to show up.

"And this is Domingo," Alberto added. "He's the group's liaison with Huaman Travel. He organizes all the transportation, gear, and trips for his groups."

"Nice to meet you, Domingo," Benicio said.

"And you. Give me ten minutes to get the gear passed out and to introduce you, and then you can get started." He handed Alberto a piece of paper. "I don't imagine you need this anymore, since nothing's changed, but here's your official itinerary."

Alberto glanced at the paper and then handed it to Benicio. Benicio paid it more attention than Alberto had, but he expected to hear it all again during the briefing so he didn't linger over it, watching instead as Domingo passed out gear to the gathered group. It wasn't the people he had seen come in, but the tourists all seemed friendly and excited about the trip, talking in lowered voices to each other as Domingo called names and handed out sleeping bags, walking sticks, and duffel bags for personal gear. When he had finished checking everyone off, he called for their attention.

"Amigos, I'd like to introduce your guides." Domingo's English was accented but smooth, far smoother than Benicio's own, he was sure. "Alberto Salazar has been with Huaman Travel for ten years now, so I'll leave you in his capable hands, but I'll be around when he's done if anyone has questions I need to answer."

"Buenos tardes, muchachos." Alberto stepped into the place Domingo had stood with a swagger and a cocky grin. Benicio's stomach flip-flopped at the sight, and he had to look away for a moment lest he embarrass himself. "I'm Alberto, as Domingo said. I'll be leading your hike, along with Benicio, here, on the Camino Inka, or Inca Trail. Is everyone ready to go?"

A chorus of affirmations greeted the question.

"Good. Domingo left maps for you on the tables if you want to follow along, but first, does everyone have good boots for hiking? The trail is very rough in places, and tennis shoes won't be enough protection. If you have light shoes, though, you might want to bring them for the campsites. After hiking all day, getting out of your heavy boots will feel very good and will help refresh you for sleep and for the next day. Everyone has a way to carry water as well, *sí*?"

Again the positive response. Benicio would certainly be adding light shoes to his pack when he got to his cousin's tonight. He hadn't thought of that on his first trek, but he had wished for something to change into when he hiked the trail before. He wouldn't make that mistake again.

"There will be opportunities to buy water or snacks at most of our stops the first day, but once we leave Pacamayo on the second day, there won't be anywhere to buy anything until we get to Machu Picchu. We'll provide boiled water at all the meal stops, of course, so you can refill your canteens. We will provide snacks each day as well, but if you prefer something particular, you should get that tonight or at the stops the first day."

Everything was overpriced in the little villages, as far as Benicio was concerned, but he supposed that was the advantage of a monopoly. He had a bag of nuts to munch on while they hiked in addition to whatever the company provided.

"Also, you should make sure to have a waterproof poncho of some sort," Alberto continued. "It's the dry season, but the weather in the mountains is unpredictable. We could get light rain even now."

It wasn't that far into the dry season, Benicio thought. He'd known it to rain, even quite heavily, into early June, but he didn't contradict Alberto. Alberto had the experience, not him, and he didn't want to do anything to antagonize his mentor before they even got on the trail.

"Any questions about equipment and supplies before we talk about the trail?"

Everyone shook their heads, so Alberto picked up the map to illustrate what he was saying. "The bus will be here to get us tomorrow at four." Everyone groaned, not that Benicio was surprised. He wasn't looking forward to the early morning either. "We'll load up and drive as far as Ollantaytambo, where you'll be able to get breakfast and buy any last-minute supplies you didn't find tonight. From there, we'll get back on the bus and head to Piskacucho, better known as kilometer eighty-two. We'll have a few minutes there to get everything ready, mosquito repellent and sunscreen on, packs arranged, and all that before we head out on the trail. You will need to show your passports as we cross the checkpoint there. The INAC, the National Institute of Culture, limits the number of people allowed on the Inca Trail at any given time, and tickets are nontransferable, so you must show your passport before you can begin the hike. Benicio and I will keep the tickets that you show at each of the other checkpoints so they don't get lost while we're hiking, but you should keep your passports with you."

Benicio reached automatically for his wallet to make sure he had it so he could show his ID when they went through the checkpoint. As a guide, he had a different kind of ticket than the tourists, but he still had to prove he was who he claimed to be. He'd been warned of the risk of his group not being allowed to hike if he forgot his guide card. It would be just his luck to screw up on his first trip and get fired. He breathed a little easier when his hand closed around the familiar leather bulk of his wallet.

"We have twelve kilometers to hike the first day," Alberto said. "We'll pass Salapunku and Huillca Raccay before lunch. Salapunku is across the river, but we'll be able to see it and I'll tell you about both when we get to Huillca Raccay. We'll have lunch soon after that, and from there, it's on toward Llactapata and our campsite at Ayapata."

Benicio hadn't stayed at Ayapata the last time. They'd stayed at the campsites in the village of Wayllabamba. Ayapata was another hour to two hours beyond Wayllabamba, depending on how fast the group hiked.

He studied them as they listened to Alberto describe the campsite. Most of them seemed in good shape. Certainly none of them were overly large, but that was not necessarily an indicator of fitness. He had seen slender people struggling on the trail too because of the altitude.

"I won't go into detail about the rest of the trip. There will be time to do that each evening at dinner," Alberto said, "but are there any questions about tomorrow?"

"You mentioned lunch and a couple of ruins we'd be visiting, but are there other stops along the trail?"

"There are two places before lunch and two places between lunch and dinner where we schedule short rest stops," Alberto replied, "but you can hike at your own pace. I'll be in the front and Benicio will be at the rear of our group. If you want to stop to take a picture or to rest for a minute or two, you can do that. You don't have to keep moving constantly between stops."

For Benicio, being at the end of the line would be a blessing this time. He could stick with a slower pace and not worry about whether he was walking fast enough for Alberto or making good time for the porters. He would arrive when the last tourist arrived, and his contribution would be ensuring that person was as safe as a person walking right behind Alberto.

"What about campsite facilities?" another person asked. "I know we'll be sleeping in tents, but beyond that, what can we expect?"

"All of the campsites, by which I mean places where our porters stop and set up our dining tent, have running water for washing and restroom facilities, although perhaps not up to American standards. You should bring your own toilet paper, though, because that isn't supplied once we leave Piskacucho. There are shower facilities at most of the sites, but the water isn't heated. It also isn't purified, so you shouldn't drink it until it's been boiled by the porters."

Benicio hid a chuckle at the shudders that went through the tourists at the mention of cold showers. With no electricity in his house growing up, he'd never taken a hot shower until he moved to Pisac, but he had listened to the shrieks from the few people who had dared the cold showers on his trip before. He suspected this group wouldn't be any different. At least it was heading into winter and wouldn't be as hot on the trail, especially at the high altitudes of Dead Woman Pass and Runkurakay Pass.

"Is there anywhere to get a beer?" one of the men asked, eliciting a laugh from the others.

"There used to be a bar at Wiñay Wayna, but it closed a few years ago," Alberto said. "You can get a beer when we get to Machu Picchu, but it will be expensive. Ten or twelve soles for something that would cost four or five in Cusco. If you can wait until you get down to Aguas Calientes later in the afternoon, the prices will be a little more reasonable. Maybe six soles instead of four, but at least not ten or twelve. Any more questions before we leave you to get ready for the morning?"

Everyone shook their heads, so Alberto bid them good night. Benicio echoed his words and followed Alberto outside. "You didn't go over the whole trip with them. I thought we were expected to do that."

"We are, for the most part," Alberto agreed, "but the most important part is tomorrow's schedule, and we went over that."

"Why didn't you go over the rest?" Benicio was sure Alberto had a reason, but Benicio could not figure it out, and Miguel had told him to learn everything he could from Alberto. This was as good a place as any to start.

"Did you see the tall guy in the back?" Benicio took a minute to pick out which one Alberto was talking about. "Just with the detail I'd already given, he was getting restless. He wasn't going to hear much more of anything I said. That might not matter since we'll go back over everything each night anyway, but if we lost his attention too completely, he might not even remember everything we said for the first day, and that part is important, especially the passports and the gear they need to bring. We'd be in far more trouble if we got to Piskacucho and he didn't have his passport than we'll be in if anyone complains about not knowing the full route tonight. It was in the itinerary Miguel sent them all as part of their trip, and it's on the map, and we'll go over it as we hike. We hit the important points, and that's what matters."

"Is he going to be a problem?" Benicio asked.

Alberto shrugged. "We'll have to see. Some people do better with structured trips than others. He is probably one who would prefer to see things on his own instead of with a group and a guide. That's fine in Cusco or even in the Sacred Valley, but there are too many variables on the Inca Trail for that. We'll have to watch him and make sure he doesn't get himself in trouble, but most groups end up spread out enough that hopefully he won't feel like we're hovering over him every second of the day."

"I do remember occasionally feeling smothered by my guide when I went out," Benicio said. "Not so much the first day, but by the end, when I felt like I knew more what I was doing."

"I try to give them as much space as I can without compromising anyone's safety," Alberto said, "but there are limits to what's possible. And then, some groups and some individuals prefer a more structured visit, while others prefer to wander the ruins more on their own with a minimum of explanation from us. As long as they're happy at the end of the tour, it's not terribly important which option we choose. We can give them a lot of information, but some get more out of it by observing themselves and then asking the questions that interest them on the next section of the hike."

Perhaps it had been the depth of his knowledge that had tipped the scales for him, but Benicio had definitely been in the latter group. He would keep that in mind as they hiked and try to look for signs to indicate where the members of this group fell. If they tended one way or another as a whole, Benicio would let Alberto take the lead, but if he noticed a split, he'd offer to work with one group or the other so everyone would feel like they had their needs met.

"We talked about me doing the presentation at Runkurakay, and I'm ready to do that, but if we need to divide the group in two so everyone gets their questions answered, I can do more than just Runkurakay. I won't be as smooth at it as you would be, but it's better than you having to try to do two things at once."

"We'll see how it goes."

The answer was less than Benicio had hoped for, but it made sense, he supposed. Alberto had no idea what he knew or was capable of. He had no reason to trust Benicio with giving the archeological and anthropological lessons that added such depth to hiking the Inca Trail. The scenery needed no elaboration, but the ruins themselves took on a whole new meaning in light of a good explanation. Benicio would just have to prove himself to Alberto so that, next time, Alberto would trust him with more responsibility.

FOUR

BY THE time they piled off the bus at Piskacucho the next morning, Benicio had given up on trying to be useful to Alberto where the tourists were concerned. Alberto had them all perfectly in hand, even the restless one from the night before, and was giving them directions about sunscreen and mosquito repellant and restrooms. Refusing to stand around and do nothing, Benicio picked out the head porter from among the group of men working on the supplies.

"*Napaykuykin*," he greeted as he approached them.

"You speak Quechua?" the porter asked.

"I grew up in Cancha Cancha. I only spoke Spanish at school," Benicio explained. "I'm Benicio."

"I'm Arturo. It's good to have you here."

"It's good to be here," Benicio said. "What can I do to help? Alberto has the tourists under control and getting ready, so he doesn't need me."

"He's a good guide," Arturo said, "but the porters will appreciate having someone who speaks their language. Not all of them are comfortable in Spanish, and none of us speak more than a few words of English, just things we've picked up from tourists."

"My English isn't great, but enough that I can translate for you or for them if you need it. Don't hesitate to come find me if you need anything. How's the packing coming?"

"Almost everything is done," Arturo said. "We just have to put it in the packs. Señor Ramirez does a good job of measuring supplies out by both weight and size before we get here so we don't have to spend a lot of time dividing things up ourselves, but we still have to double-check. If we get to the control point and our packs aren't the right weight, they'll send us back, and that's a waste of time."

"I can start weighing the packs that are ready," Benicio offered. "That way you can make sure the others get packed as quickly as possible. I saw how long it took to get through the porters' control point when I hiked the trail two weeks ago. I don't want you to be at the back of the line."

"Thank you," Arturo said. "The scale is over there."

Benicio grabbed the portable hand scale and the pile of packs that were ready to go. He nodded to the porters working on the other packs and began checking weight. Regulations prohibited the porters from carrying more than thirty kilos each. Benicio wondered how they managed even that much and at twice the pace the much less laden guides and tourists hiked.

As he weighed the first pack and set it aside as within the allowance, he heard Alberto explaining the same regulations to the tourists.

"They're here working, doing their job, and a tough job, to make sure we all have the best experience possible. If you see them coming, move to the mountain side of the trail so they can pass, and be sure to speak or clap to show your appreciation. Many of them have families they're trying to support, and this is a hard job. They'll hike the same distance we do in about half the time because they have to get to our lunch spot in time to get the dining and cooking tents set up and get lunch prepared. They'll leave after we do and still get to our overnight campsite before us so they can have it set up and ready for dinner and sleeping. Most of them don't speak English, but they'll understand if you say thank you, even if you can't say it in Spanish or Quechua."

Benicio smiled and went back to his weighing. Alberto would make sure the porters got the respect they deserved. Benicio could do his part by speeding things up for them.

"How do you say 'thank you' in Quechua?" one of the tourists asked.

"Benicio is our resident Quechua expert," Alberto said, waving him over.

Benicio set down the pack he'd just finished weighing and joined them. "There are much ways to say it, but the most simple is *añay*. They all understand you if you say that. They understand *gracias* as well. We use that too."

The group repeated *añay* a couple of times, making Benicio smile. He could do this. He could be part of bringing Andean culture to life for this group of men and women. No one had blinked at his awkward English. They had simply taken his meaning and practiced the word.

Behind them, Arturo called that the porters were ready, so Alberto gathered the tourists and led them down toward the checkpoint, the bridge, and the entrance onto the Inca Trail. Fortunately the line for the porters hadn't gotten long yet, so they didn't have to wait at the checkpoint. By the time they had all showed their passports and made it across the bridge, Arturo had come up behind them at the head of the porters. Benicio and Alberto moved to the side and the tourists followed suit. The porters trooped by, stooped forward to support the weight. Alberto clapped as they passed and Benicio took that as his cue, calling out, "*Añay*" to all of them as encouragement for the group to do the same. Once the porters were clear, they began their own hike up the dusty trail. At the head of the line, Alberto explained about how this section of the trail was used by locals and was actually not part of the original trail but rather the most convenient way to join the original trail, which had once stretched all the way from Cusco to Machu Picchu.

BY THE time they reached their lunch stop, Benicio had lost track of how many locals they had passed going the other way, leading mules or driving llamas ahead of them, some of them laden with goods to sell in the markets of the Sacred Valley, others with empty packs to bring back supplies for their villages. The tourists had all kept up pretty well. None of them seemed to be struggling, for which Benicio was grateful. If even the first leg was difficult, the second day would be hellish for them.

They walked into the lunch site to find the dining tent set up and ready, just waiting for them to sit down to eat. The first arrivals had already taken off their packs and were stretched out in the sun. Benicio was tempted to do the same, but he was here to work, not relax. He dropped his pack on the tarp with the others and went to check in with Arturo, but the porters had everything under control. He looked around for something to do and noticed that Thomas, the restless tourist from the night before, was not with the others, lounging in the shade of the tents. Benicio searched the campsite until he found the man poking around the stone foundations of the camping pads.

"Is modern," he said, walking up to Thomas, "but in the style of the Inca."

"I wondered," Thomas said. "It looked like what we passed today, but I couldn't imagine they'd let us have free run of an actual Inca ruin like this."

"No, not for camping," Benicio agreed, "but is same technique. Stones, mortar. The Inca use no mortar for sacred buildings, but for houses, businesses, is less precise, needs mortar. In my village, is just like this. Stone or mud brick, mortar, slanted walls to protect against seisms."

"Seisms?"

"You know, when the earth moves."

"Oh, seisms, like seismic. We say earthquakes in English."

Benicio filed the word away in his memory.

"So the slanted walls protect against earthquakes?" Thomas asked, going back to Benicio's original comment.

"Yes," Benicio said. "Like this." He held his hands up at a slight angle inward to demonstrate. "I no know why it works, but earthquakes come, some buildings fall, others stay standing. Ones with slanted walls stay standing, so we build with slanted walls. Is like anything else. See what works and do it again."

"Makes perfect sense to me," Thomas said.

Benicio looked back toward the area where the tents were set up and saw Alberto gathering everyone for lunch. "Is time to eat. We should go."

Thomas nodded agreeably enough, and they headed down to the dining tent. As soon as everyone was settled, the porters arrived with a first course. Arturo told Benicio what it was in Quechua, leaving him to struggle to translate it into English. After a moment, he gave up and told Alberto in Spanish.

"Our first course is fresh avocado with wonton crackers," Alberto told the hikers as they passed them down to the end of the table. "There is previously boiled water as well. You should make sure to drink plenty. It's easy to get dehydrated on the trail and not realize it."

Everyone dug in as soon as the plates were all served, Benicio included. The dish was nothing complicated, but after the morning's hike, it tasted wonderful. When they had all finished and the porters brought the second course, Benicio decided they were in for a treat. The semolina soup was a familiar dish, but it had never been this good before. He told himself it was his hunger talking, but his mother's version of the soup had never been so delicately spiced. It made him eager to see what else the camp cook could come up with.

The hikers seemed to share his enthusiasm, commenting repeatedly on how delicious everything was. "Would you like to meet our cook?" Alberto asked. "We'll ask him to come to the tent after lunch."

Benicio thought that was a marvelous idea. INAC regulations required that all food on the Inca Trail be fresh and organic, but that didn't mean all camp cooks were equal. The food on his previous hike hadn't been bad, but this meal put it all to shame. He'd have to make sure to tell the cook that privately when they finished dinner tonight. He didn't want to disrupt their routine to do it now.

"During February, when the Inca Trail is closed, the adventure cooks go to special classes to help them come up with new meals and to improve their adventure cooking skills," Alberto continued telling the group.

"It certainly shows," Thomas said. "This is better than some meals I've had in five-star restaurants."

Benicio hadn't ever eaten in a five-star restaurant to make that comparison, but he'd already compared the soup favorably to his mother's cooking, and she was the best cook he knew.

"WHAT'S IT like, growing up in a village like this?" Thomas asked a few minutes after they left the first rest area after lunch.

"What's it like growing up in America?" Benicio retorted. "Was just my life. I had nothing to compare it to."

"You don't live there still, though. At least, you said you live in Pisac. Pisac may not be large compared to some American cities, but it's not a village like yours either."

"No, is much larger than home. Almost two hundred times the size of home. Was…." He paused, struggling to find the words to describe his childhood, where everything was much as it had always been and everyone knew their place and stayed in it. It was safe, in a way. He never had to ask himself questions at home, but he could never be anything other than a farmer or miner. If he stayed there, his life would be the same as his father's and grandfather's, and their grandfather's grandfathers, had been, except that he would never marry because he wouldn't ask a woman to share that hard life without the comfort of a husband who loved her. "Was simple. Get up, do chores, go to school, come home, do chores, go to bed. Get up and repeat."

"School must have been in a larger town."

"In Calca, two hours' walk down the mountain, then bus to school. Then two hours back up the mountain in the afternoon. We got up very early to do chores before school."

"I can't even imagine."

Benicio shrugged. "I no can imagine a big city, cars everywhere. Where you played? Where you ran? How you knew the gods if you no lived with them?"

"Church on Sunday, if you chose to go," Thomas said, "and we had parks and playgrounds for the rest."

Benicio shook his head in disbelief. "Is not same. Here, we are surrounded by nature. Mother Earth, Father Sun, life-giving rain, sacred rainbow… all are part of life and part of us. The snake, the llama, the condor, they are here too—the three levels of time and strength."

"Fascinating," Thomas said.

Benicio flushed. "Tonight at camp, I show you Andean Cross and explain meanings. You see again in Machu Picchu."

"Say it again. You don't say it the way I do."

"Machu Picchu."

"Machu Pic-chu," Thomas repeated slowly, finally getting the hard c before the diphthong.

"Yes, is right," Benicio said. "Is two c's in Picchu for a reason."

"I hear that now," Thomas said. "No one says it right at home."

"Now you do. When you go back, you tell them right way."

"I will," Thomas said. "So tell me more about Cancha Cancha."

Benicio didn't know what else he could say, so he launched into tales of his family and the trouble he and his brothers got into as children. Before they knew it, they had arrived at Wayllabamba and the last checkpoint before the campsite.

"Is not far now," Benicio said. "Only an hour or a little more at this speed. You need break?"

"Just the restroom," Thomas said.

Benicio pointed him in the direction of the restrooms and checked with the INAC officer to make sure everything was in order. He didn't see Alberto and the rest of the group, but Thomas had stopped so often to take pictures that they were quite far behind. He frowned a little at the thought of being so dispensable that Alberto hadn't waited, but he pushed it aside. Thomas deserved better than Benicio's black thoughts.

When he returned a few minutes later, Benicio smiled and said, "Tell me about life in America. Where are you from?"

Thomas happily reciprocated with the storytelling, and before long, they had arrived at Ayapata. The porters had done their job and the campsite was fully prepared: seven tents waiting for the six couples and two guides, as well as the dining and cooking tents.

"Restrooms and showers are at the base of camp," Benicio said, pointing to the building. Two other groups were camped in the same location as them, farther down the hill.

"I don't know if I'm up for a cold shower," Thomas said. "I think I'll just wash my face and hands."

"The porters have hot water for that before dinner," Benicio said. "I leave you get settled."

"Thank you," Thomas said. "You didn't have to take all that time and answer all my questions."

Benicio smiled shyly and brushed off the thanks. He was just doing his job. Goodness knew he hadn't contributed much of anything else to the day's hike.

Feeling sorry for himself wouldn't get him anywhere, though, so he grabbed his toiletries kit and clean underwear and headed for the showers. Thomas might not be up for a cold shower, but after the dusty trail, Benicio thought that sounded heavenly. It would get better once they joined the original Inca Trail in the morning. Only the connecting section from Piskacucho was this dusty.

When he came back to camp a few minutes later, skin still prickling from the cold mountain water, he felt much more like himself. Alberto might not need his help, but Benicio could find ways to be useful anyway. He checked in with Arturo and walked with the porters to each of the tents, letting the guests know they had hot water to wash up with and that dinner would be ready in ten minutes. The porters chatted with him in Quechua between tents, talking about dinner, complaining about the dust, the weather, and anything else that came to mind. Benicio didn't share their complaints about anything but the dust, but he listened and nodded at the appropriate times and left them at their tent feeling far more settled and appreciated again.

The last stop was the tent he would share with Alberto. The porters set two basins down at their tent as well, even if Benicio had already washed up. "Alberto?" Benicio called. "The hot water's here and dinner's almost ready."

"Thanks," Alberto said, his voice muffled. "I'll be right out."

Benicio deliberately did not think about Alberto inside the tent, possibly changing his clothes. That would be completely unprofessional, and Benicio had two strikes against him already with his inexperience and his poor English. He didn't need to add unprofessional behavior to the list. His English would improve and each trip would provide more experience, but there was no cure for a lack of professionalism.

Instead he turned to observe the tourists making their way out of their tents and toward the dining tent. He had spent most of the day with Thomas. He hoped to get to know the others a little better at dinner. Alberto had mentioned at lunch the idea of being a family, and Benicio wanted that, however fleeting it would be.

When everyone had gathered, Alberto called for the porters to serve dinner. Once the first course had been passed down and everyone was eating, Alberto turned to the couple to his right and asked where they were from.

They answered easily, mentioning their hometown—nowhere Benicio recognized—and a little about themselves.

"And how long have you been together?"

The question surprised Benicio. He would not have gotten so personal so quickly, but the guests didn't seem to mind. They answered the question and shared a little about how they met. When they were done, the next couple volunteered the same information without prompting. They made it all the way around the table when one of the guests asked, "What about you, Alberto?"

"I'm thirty-two, from Urubamba originally, but I live in Cusco now. I've been working for Huaman Travel for ten years."

"Are you married?"

"Only to the trail," Alberto said with a grin. The guests laughed.

"So no girlfriend?"

"No girlfriend either," Alberto confirmed.

Benicio didn't ask about a boyfriend. He didn't dare.

"What about you, Benicio?"

"I am from Cancha Cancha. Is small village in the highlands. Now I live in Pisac."

"How old are you?"

"Twenty-six."

"Benicio also speaks Quechua," Alberto added, "so he's very helpful with our porters. Many of them are also from small villages. They come to the trail to earn a living for their families. It is important to remember they are real people too, with children, even grandchildren, wives, homes, people who depend on them."

The porters interrupted with the second course, giving Benicio a break from the scrutiny. He thanked them and checked on the rest of dinner and the evening.

Everyone exclaimed over the food as they had done at lunch.

"Everything on Inca Trail is organic and fresh," Alberto explained. "The porters carry coolers with ice to keep food fresh. Nothing canned or packaged here."

The conversation moved on to restaurants in various cities Benicio had only read about in school. He took a moment to remember that the places that were local to him were just as exotic to the tourists as their homes were to him.

As they finished the main course and were waiting for dessert, Alberto said, "Do you want to talk about tomorrow?"

The tourists chorused an affirmative.

"Tomorrow is the longest day," Alberto said. "Twelve hours. We wake up at five o'clock and have breakfast. By six, we leave and start for Warmiwañusca, Dead Woman Pass, the highest point of the Inca Trail at a little over four thousand meters, and then down into the valley for lunch at Pacamayo. After lunch, we make the climb to the Runkurakay Pass and the ruins of the way station there. Then on to Sayacmarca and our campsite before dark."

Benicio was not looking forward to the long hike. He understood the reasons for it, but it would be physically demanding for everyone, even him and Alberto.

"That sounds like a really long day," Thomas said, echoing Benicio's thoughts.

"*Sí*," Alberto agreed, "but means we get to Wiñay Wayna early the day after and have time to rest and enjoy the site. Other groups save the second pass for the third day, and then they have no rest before Machu Picchu. Plus, the campsite at Pacamayo, where they stay tomorrow night, floods in heavy rains. Is the dry season, but with the global warming, rains come at odd times. Is better not to take chances. If the rains no come, is no problem, but sleeping in wet tents and wet sleeping bags is no fun."

"No, definitely not," Thomas's wife agreed.

"Also, the first resting place tomorrow is last place to buy any drinks or snacks before Machu Picchu, so if you want Gatorade or chocolates or anything, make sure to get them there. Once we leave there, is only what you carry or what the porters have."

Benicio had learned that lesson last time. He would have given anything to have a Gatorade when they got to Wiñay Wayna, but by then it was too late. He wouldn't make that mistake this time.

As Alberto finished, the porters brought dessert. Everyone finished quickly and dispersed, heading back to their tents to sleep so they'd be ready for the early morning. Benicio knew he should do the same. He would have to get up even before the guests because he had wake-up duty with the porters, but he didn't really want to be alone with Alberto in the small space. He had no choice unless he wanted to carry his own tent in the future, but that wouldn't help him tonight.

"We should get to bed too," Alberto said. "Morning comes early."

"I'll be there in a minute," Benicio said. "I want to brush my teeth first."

He hoped it didn't sound like a lame excuse, but it was the best he could come up with on the spur of the moment. He lingered as long as he could brushing his teeth, but he wasn't the only one wanting to use the sink, so eventually he had to return to the tent. He stepped out of the sandals he wore in camp before climbing into the tent and zipping it up again. Alberto reclined on his mat and sleeping bag, still dressed from the day. Benicio frowned a little. He had hoped Alberto would already be in his sleeping bag and ready for bed when he returned.

"You did well today with our wanderer," Alberto said as Benicio rummaged through his pack for the clean T-shirt and shorts he'd brought to sleep in.

The words were so at odds with Alberto's treatment of him all day that Benicio fumbled the bag he was holding. "Really? It didn't seem like I was much help."

"Really," Alberto insisted. "I can handle a group, the trail, the porters, but I can't be in two places at once. If I'd been by myself, the whole group would have had to wait for Thomas, and everyone would have been impatient and irritable, or else he would have felt rushed. Neither would be good for customer satisfaction. Instead, you could hike with him at his pace, he got his pictures and his answers and whatever else he needed, and everyone else had a good hike too. Do you mind walking with him until lunch again? I know you'll want to go with the main group after that so you can do the visit at Runkurakay."

"That's fine," Benicio said, still struggling to reconcile Alberto's words with a full day of feeling superfluous. "I enjoyed talking with him, even if my English isn't very good."

"No one seems to have any trouble understanding you," Alberto said as he sat up and reached for his own bag. "That's good enough, and you'll improve with practice, especially if you keep making friends with the tourists."

Benicio looked away as Alberto stripped off his shirt and tugged another on over his head, but he couldn't unsee the glimpse he'd gotten of Alberto's bare chest, all bronzed skin and wiry muscles. He heard more rustling behind him and imagined Alberto was changing his shorts as well, but Benicio kept his back firmly turned. He wouldn't stare, no matter how attractive he found Alberto. Alberto hadn't given any indication of being gay, and Benicio did not want to do anything to make Alberto uncomfortable.

The rustling stopped and he heard a click as Alberto turned off his headlamp. "Don't stay up too long. You don't want to be tired tomorrow."

Benicio shut off his lamp as well so he could change clothes under the cover of darkness. Then he slipped inside the sleeping bag and snuggled deeper into the downy warmth, hoping sleep would come quickly.

FIVE

WELL BEFORE dawn, the alarm on Alberto's wristwatch went off. He lay in his sleeping bag for a minute, listening to the sounds of the porters moving around as they boiled water for coca, tea, and washing up. He heard Benicio roll over, still sleeping, and then mumble, "Is it time to get up already?"

"Soon," Alberto said. "You can sleep for a few more minutes if you want."

Benicio grumbled something Alberto couldn't understand and then flipped on his headlamp. "I hate mornings."

"Then you picked the wrong job," Alberto said with a laugh. "This is the latest we get to sleep in. The last morning, it's up at three thirty."

"I know," Benicio said. "It's worth it, but it doesn't make me like mornings any more than before."

Alberto watched surreptitiously as Benicio pulled off the shirt he'd slept in. For a highlander from a village as small as Cancha Cancha, Benicio looked surprisingly little like a typical Quechua Indian. He had fairer skin and lighter hair—not light, but brown instead of black—and he wore it long, pulled back into a queue. Once he'd put on a shirt, he released the band that held his hair back, and Alberto allowed himself a moment's fantasy of being allowed to brush the tangles out of those long tresses. His own hair was straight as a board, and he kept it short so he wouldn't have to deal with it. Benicio's hair, on the other hand, curled loosely and looked like it would be as soft as the vicuña wool his mother had hoarded so carefully when he was a child. The shawl she had made for his half-sister for her wedding was worth as much as the house they lived in growing up. When Benicio finally looked his way, Alberto heaved a sigh and sat up. "Will you help the porters wake everyone up while I check with Luis about breakfast?"

"Of course," Benicio said as he turned his back and pulled on another layer of clothes.

It wasn't as cold as it sometimes was at Chaqulqocha, but the predawn air was still chilly. Alberto layered his own clothes and tied his hiking boots before dragging himself out of the tent. A quick glance skyward revealed a sky full of stars, the clouds that had gathered the night before having blown over. That boded well for the day. The weather could change in a matter of minutes, but a clear morning usually meant a smaller chance of rain. They'd have the usual sprinkling of mist as they hiked through the cloud forest, but nothing to slow them down if the fall weather held to its usual pattern.

He made a quick trip to the restroom, stretched his back a little, and went to check on breakfast. As he returned to camp, he could hear Benicio waking up the tourists in a cheerful voice, offering hot water and coca tea. He checked his pocket automatically for his bag of coca leaves. He would need them as they neared the top of the Warmiwañusca Pass. Even after ten years of hiking the trail, he got out of breath near the peak, and chewing on the coca leaves helped alleviate that. He'd listened to guides joking disdainfully about the tourists and their lung capacity, but Alberto had always had a great deal of respect for the people who came to hike the trail. If he still struggled with the altitude with only fifteen hundred meters difference between his home in Cusco and the peak, he could only imagine how hard it was for them, living at much lower altitudes.

One by one, the tourists stumbled out of their tents. Some of them seemed more awake than others, but as they made their way toward the dining tent, they all smiled at him, however sleepily. Another good sign. Today would be demanding beyond what most of them were used to. If they started the day with a good attitude, they'd make it that much longer before they reached the breaking point. Some people never reached it, but at least half the tourists he led reached a point where they felt like they couldn't take another step. As long as they passed Runkurakay before that happened, he could assure them it was all downhill from there, with the exception of the Monkey Steps the last morning. Of course, for some people down was worse than up, but most people still found it reassuring once they made it past the two passes on the second day's hike.

"Anything else you need me to do?" Benicio asked as he joined him near the dining tent.

"Just be around in case anyone has questions," Alberto said. "We'll eat as soon as everyone is in the dining tent. It wouldn't hurt to keep an eye on Thomas."

"He's already in the tent," Benicio said with a grin. "I told him the sooner everyone was there, the sooner we'd get out on the trail where he could take more pictures."

Alberto laughed. "Good for you. You're a natural at this."

"It's nothing special. Just paying attention to people."

"Maybe, but not everyone does that naturally. His trip will be better because you're good at it, and everyone else's trip will be better because he's taken care of."

"Then I'd better keep taking care of him," Benicio said.

"This morning," Alberto agreed. "I'll watch him after lunch so you can lead the group and present at Runkurakay. Or we may have trained him well enough that he'll keep up with the group just to stay with you. That happens sometimes with the particular ones. They latch onto one guide to the point that they break bad habits in order to stay with that guide."

"It's not really bad habits," Benicio said. "He's just fascinated by everything, to the point that making progress on the trail isn't as important as seeing everything while he's here."

"Except that he can't take forever to reach the campsites because we can't just stop anywhere we feel like it for the night."

"I know that, and he does too," Benicio said. "We weren't late for dinner last night. I had time for a shower before Luis had dinner ready."

Alberto had been trying to keep that image out of his head. He didn't need to imagine Benicio dripping wet, nipples peaked from the cold water. He needed to focus on his job.

Fortunately he was distracted by the rest of the group going into the dining tent. Alberto pulled his thoughts away from Benicio and turned them to prepping the group for the day.

BENICIO'S STOMACH clenched as they made the final ascent toward Runkurakay. He had prepared and prepared for his first presentation, but now it seemed bland in his head. He could recite the facts, but the Inca Trail was so much more than a collection of facts. It was a journey, a sacred pilgrimage for the people who blazed the trail. To reduce it to a history lecture would do no justice to their work and to the faith of the people who traveled to Machu Picchu to pay homage to the gods who gave them life.

He couldn't do that, not when he had experienced the mystic power of the trail himself. He might not be a pilgrim of the Inca people, but the hike and the wonders along the way had called to his Andean heritage. He had to find a way to give voice to that for those who did not have the same innate connection to the land.

They reached the resting place outside the ruins of the tambo, and Benicio gave them a few minutes to rest from the climb while he gathered his thoughts. His father had been a storyteller, guarding the history of the village in his tales. Benicio had grown up hearing all the legends. He would do his father and his ancestors proud.

Alberto and Thomas arrived as Benicio was about to summon everyone to the ruins, so he waited a moment longer for Thomas to catch his breath as well. They didn't want to linger, since the temperature at that elevation was quite cool and their muscles would cramp up if they waited too long, but another few minutes wouldn't hurt. He walked over to check on Thomas, pleased to see the man still had a smile on his face.

"You take some good pictures?" Benicio asked.

"I hope so," Thomas replied. "It's hard to tell for sure on the little screen on my camera, but they look good at that size."

"Good. You ready to look at Runkurakay?"

"Let's go," Thomas said. "Everything else you've told me about the Inca Trail has been fascinating, so I'm sure this will be too."

That gave Benicio the last push he needed to commit to doing the presentation his way.

"Come to the ruins." He gestured for the whole group to follow him. When everyone had gathered, he led them to where the Inca Trail reached the pass so Runkurakay stood directly behind him. "Close eyes for a minute."

He saw several surprised looks, but everyone complied. "You leave Cusco six days ago with your llama to carry supplies, but they run out soon. You are tired, thirsty. Your leather sandals leave blisters on your feet, and all your muscles hurt, but you keep going. Machu Picchu grows more close and will be worth everything. Now is almost dark. You need place to stop, but where? Is open trail, wilderness, no shelter, so you keep climbing. Other pilgrims say is place to stop at top of mountain. You reach the pass and see it. Open eyes now."

He stepped aside so the tourists could see the circular ruins behind him. "Is shelter, place for llama to rest and eat, for you to build fire and cook last of your meat. Tomorrow you must hunt or make do with meatless stew, but tonight you eat and rest in tambo. You go inside and find chasquis messengers already there, but they make room around their fire. They have messages from priests in Machu Picchu for Inca in Cusco. The Inca is king, but even he listen to gods and priests. Are many portents, they say. Dark days come for Inca people, but we are great nation. We survive what comes. You cook stew and you worry, but you already do as gods command. You make hike to Machu Picchu to worship. Your faith help you. You are strong. Inca is strong. You will survive."

He gestured for the group to advance into the ruins, hoping he had done justice to those who had used this place for shelter in times past. The complete silence as they walked into the tambo made Benicio nervous, but then he looked past them to where Alberto stood grinning at him.

"That was brilliant," he said when all the tourists were inside the ruins. "You had them hanging on every word. What made you decide to do that?"

"My father was a storyteller in our village. I learned my history from his tales far better than from any book. I can recite all the facts."

"No, anyone can list facts. What you did was far more powerful. If they want facts, they'll ask, but you drew a picture in their heads of what life was like. That will stay with them longer than a list of dates and archeological theories on why this tambo is circular. I'll have to think up something for Phuyupatamarca, because they'll protest if I go back to facts after that."

"I'm sorry," Benicio said. "I didn't mean to put you on the spot."

"No, don't apologize!" Alberto said. "Not for that. You have a gift, Benicio. When we get back, we're going to plan this out more carefully for next time, so we can build on what you just did for the entire trip."

All the tension that had built up as Benicio wove his tale dissolved at the affirmation. Maybe he did have something to add to their partnership besides speaking Quechua. Maybe he really could do this. "I'd like that. There's so much power to the ruins, even now. It seems a shame not to help people feel that."

"Most of them feel it in Machu Picchu, but it's easy to get caught up in schedules and exhaustion on the trail. It'll be more work, but you saw their faces. They were completely lost in the world you created. We'll get some good reports from this group for sure, and Miguel will be pleased."

"That's not why I did it," Benicio said, feeling suddenly worried his brainstorm would be taken as artifice.

"I know that," Alberto said. "You couldn't have put that much passion into it if it was just a ploy, but that doesn't negate the results. You'd do it even if there weren't any customer satisfaction surveys at the end of the trail. That's what makes you a good guide, and the tourists responded to that."

Their group started to filter out of the ruins.

"We'll talk more about it tonight or tomorrow when we get to Wiñay Wayna. We should keep moving. There are other groups waiting to visit the ruins, and we don't want to get to Chaqulqocha after dark. Do you want to take the lead again?"

"I didn't prepare for Sayacmarca," Benicio said. "I'm not sure I could do the presentation there."

"You know about the baths for purification," Alberto said, "and I know you know how cold the spring water is, since you grew up in the mountains. I'm pretty sure you could use that to spin another tail of drawing near to Machu Picchu and all that entails, but I won't put you on the spot if you aren't comfortable."

"Next time," Benicio said. "We'll plan it out like you said, and I'll do my share then."

"I'll hold you to that," Alberto said. He turned to the tourists. "Ready, amigos? *Vamonos.*"

BY THE time they visited Sayacmarca and Concha Marca, it was nearly dark. The tourists didn't seem bothered, though, as they pulled out their flashlights and headlamps to walk the final distance to the campsite. It wasn't far, fortunately. Benicio debated taking a shower again, but the temperature at Chaqulqocha was quite a bit lower than it had been the night before, and the trail had not been nearly as dusty once they reached the paving stones the Inca people had used to carve out the trail. The water would be even colder and the sun was already down. They would arrive at Wiñay Wayna by early afternoon tomorrow. He could shower then.

He exchanged his boots for his sandals and went to help the porters. It appeared even they had taken longer than usual to hike the distance, because they were still setting up the last tents. "Do you need help?" he asked Arturo.

"No, this is the last one, but Luis might need help," Arturo said. Benicio nodded and went to check in with the camp cook. He and Feliberto, the assistant cook, seemed to have everything in hand, though, so he wandered back out, not sure how else to help.

"Benicio?"

He turned around to smile at several of the tourists who had congregated outside the dining tent.

"Buenas tardes," he said. "Was good hike today, *sí*?"

"Oh, yes, especially at Runkurakay," Megan said. Benicio hadn't interacted with her much since he'd spent all his time with Thomas, but from what little he'd observed, she was young, energetic, and full of zest. "I'd never thought about it like that. You have a gift for storytelling."

"Is my father's gift," Benicio said. "I learn it from him."

"You should use it more often. The trail was a bunch of rocks and pretty scenery until you started talking today. Impressive rocks, but something I looked at from the outside. I could admire the engineering that went into it, but I hadn't really connected to the reason for it."

"Two reasons," Benicio said. "Messengers and, um, what is word? People who go to pray."

"Pilgrims," Megan supplied.

"Yes, messengers and pilgrims," Benicio said. "Messengers go between Inca and priests. Pilgrims go to pray. Tomorrow we see Phuyupatamarca, site of baths to purify before Machu Picchu. Very important place for pilgrims."

"Will you tell us a story there too?" Megan asked.

"I have to see," Benicio said. "I no prepare for tomorrow, only for Runkurakay."

"Oh, please say you'll come up with something," Megan said. "Even if it's just a little to help us get in the mood of the place. Alberto can give us all the history if that would make you more comfortable, but there's magic in your words."

"We'll figure it out," Alberto said from behind Benicio. Benicio jumped a little, not having realized Alberto was there. "Because you're right. He does have magic words."

Benicio felt his cheeks heat at the praise, although he hoped it would be hidden beneath his copper skin and the cover of darkness. He wasn't as dark as Alberto, but with only flashlights to illuminate the night, he hoped no one would notice.

"You should definitely think about it," Megan insisted. "It was so much more real with your story."

The others agreed so enthusiastically that Benicio shifted uncomfortably. "I have to see," he repeated.

Arturo interrupted them to tell them that dinner was ready. Benicio sighed in relief at no longer being the center of attention. Dinner was far more interesting to them than talking him into another story.

SIX

IT FELT odd arriving at Wiñay Wayna so early in the afternoon, but Benicio thought he could get used to this rhythm with another hike or two. He had given in and told another story at Phuyupatamarca, although he wasn't as happy with that one as he had been with the first one. The tourists hadn't seemed to notice a difference, and Alberto had repeated his interest in planning their speeches before the next trip, so he told himself to be satisfied with that.

"Hey, Benicio," Thomas called, "do you play bocce ball?"

"What is bocce ball?" Benicio asked.

"Come on, we'll teach you," Thomas said. "I have a travel set that I brought along just in case. This seems like as good a time as any to get it out."

Benicio shrugged and joined him, Alberto's comments about the personal touch being important in customer satisfaction ringing in his head. He didn't expect to be any good at the game, but he would make Thomas happy by playing.

"Tell me what to do."

Thomas handed him four red balls. He tested their weight in his hand, surprised by how light they were.

"The goal is to be the one to toss your rubber ball as close as possible to this little wooden ball." Thomas tossed the wooden ball onto the open sand ahead of them. "The person closest gets two points. The second closest gets one. If your ball is actually touching the wooden one, you get three points. The first person to fifteen wins."

"Sounds easy," Benicio said.

"Simple, but not always easy," Thomas said. "It's about strategy as much as anything else."

Benicio wasn't sure he saw where strategy came into it, but he'd watch and learn and hopefully have some fun in the meantime. "You start."

Thomas nodded and tossed his first ball onto the sand. It rolled toward the wooden ball, stopping about an inch away.

"My turn," Megan said. She tossed her ball as well, bumping into Thomas's yellow one and knocking it out of the way. "That's where the strategy comes in. Your turn, Benicio."

Benicio weighed the ball again and tossed it toward the others. He misjudged the distance, and the ball rolled well past the goal.

"Not so hard next time," Thomas said. "You'll get used to it."

Helen, Thomas's wife, took her turn, and then it was back to Thomas. His second throw wasn't as lucky as his first, landing almost as far from the wooden ball as Benicio's own ball had. Megan's second throw knocked her first ball even closer to the wooden one, although not quite touching, from what Benicio could see at this distance. Benicio tossed his second ball more gently. It landed farther away than Megan's had, but much closer than the first time.

"You're getting the hang of it," Helen encouraged before aiming her second toss.

Benicio wasn't so sure about that, but he grinned anyway. He was having fun, he realized, as they finished the third round and started the fourth. As they'd hiked, these people had become his friends.

Megan won the first round, with Helen getting one point. They gathered the balls and started again.

Benicio heard a murmur of Quechua behind him and looked over his shoulder at the porters who had gathered outside the dining tent.

"Do you want to play?" he asked them. They all shook their heads, but they grabbed campstools from inside the dining tent and sat down to watch. Benicio turned back to the game and hoped he didn't make a complete fool of himself.

Helen ended up winning the first game with Megan only two points behind her. Benicio had expected to have the lowest score, but he passed Thomas in the last round when he got lucky and got three points because his ball was touching the wooden one.

"Good game," Thomas said. "You want to play again?"

"Maybe someone else want to play?" Benicio said. He didn't want to stop, but he also didn't want to be rude and keep anyone else from enjoying. "We take turns."

"You play," Helen said. "I'll sit this one out if someone else wants to join in."

Benicio looked back at the porters again and asked if anyone wanted to play, but they all shook their heads shyly. He hadn't really expected a different answer after three days of observing them with the tourists. They smiled and did their best to answer any time the tourists said anything to them, but they never initiated anything because of the language barrier. He looked around for Alberto, but he wasn't in sight.

In the meantime, Helen had recruited George to take her place.

An hour later, when Alberto came to see who wanted to walk to Wiñay Wayna to see the ruins there, Benicio had managed to win one game, and the porters had clearly learned the rules by observation alone because they cheered and booed at all the right places, although Benicio couldn't decide who they were rooting for. They cheered all the good throws and moaned in sympathy with all the bad ones. Benicio figured that wasn't a bad thing. The tourists would remember the porters' encouragement the same way Benicio would remember this afternoon even if he never played bocce ball again.

He'd let Alberto take the tourists to Wiñay Wayna without him. He had seen it, and he doubted Alberto would add anything he didn't already know. If he did, they'd go over it when they met to discuss the idea of turning all the historical facts into a cohesive story.

As everyone gathered, Thomas tossed the bocce ball set to Benicio. "In case you can convince the porters to play while we're gone."

Benicio laughed and waved as they headed across the campsite for the fifteen-minute walk to Wiñay Wayna. Almost as soon as they were out of sight, Adolpho, Dario, and Severo came up to him. "Can we play with you?"

Benicio smiled and unpacked the set. "Let's go."

"I CAN'T believe it's only been three days," Thomas said as they sat down to dinner and waited for the porters to bring the first course. "I feel like I've known everyone for far longer than that!"

"I can't believe it's already been three days," Helen replied. "Tomorrow is the last day."

"It is," Alberto agreed. "It's always that way. It seems far longer than it is and still far too short."

"We should find a way to keep in touch," Megan said. "Yes, it's only been a few days, but I feel like we're friends now, and I'd love to stay in contact. I want to see everyone's pictures!"

"We could create a Facebook group," George suggested. "We can set it to private and that way no one else will be able to see what we share. We can put pictures, memories, anything we want there. I manage that kind of thing at work. I'd be glad to set it up if everyone gives me their e-mail addresses so I can send you an invitation."

Benicio kept silent, not wanting to highlight the spartan conditions of his childhood and even his current situation. He didn't have a computer, much less a Facebook account. Maybe he could create one at one of the Internet cafés in Cusco so he could keep in touch with people, but he didn't have anything to give them now.

Some of his discomfort must have shown on his face, because Alberto leaned closer to him and murmured, "You can use my computer when we get back to Cusco."

Benicio was grateful he'd spoken in Spanish. None of the tourists in this group had much command of the language, and so probably hadn't understood if they'd even heard what he said.

"Thank you. I'll do that."

The porters interrupted with trays of food, mounds of rice and lamb chops in a thick brown sauce, toasted bread, and a pasta salad full of vegetables. Everyone oohed and aahed over the quantity of food, as they'd done at every meal. They passed the trays around and filled their plates. This meal was just as plentiful and just as delicious as all the others had been, although Benicio found he wasn't as hungry as he had been at some of the other meals, maybe because they hadn't hiked as far today and so hadn't used as much energy. Tomorrow would be even easier, other than getting up well before dawn. He wasn't looking forward to that part, but the rest of the day would be worth it, with getting to spend part of the day in Machu Picchu.

As if reading Benicio's thoughts, Alberto set down his fork and asked, "Shall we talk about tomorrow?"

Everyone nodded around mouths full of food, so Alberto continued. "Our porters will leave us in the morning. They have to catch a special train in Aguas Calientes. It's the only train they're allowed to take, and if they miss it, they have to walk back to Ollantaytambo along the train tracks carrying all the gear, so we want to make sure they have enough time to make it down the mountain. We'll get up at three thirty so we can eat and have them ready to go by four thirty." Everyone groaned, but no one protested beyond that. Benicio was pleased they had taken the porters' well-being to heart enough to want them to make their train.

"They'll begin their hike, and we'll go as far as the last checkpoint. When it opens, then we'll have a five-kilometer hike to Inti Punku, the Sun Gate. We'll watch the sun rise over Machu Picchu from there, and then we'll go down into the city. Backpacks and walking sticks aren't allowed in the site, so we'll hike straight through and outside, where we'll store our gear for the visit to Machu Picchu. I'll give a guided tour of the city, and then you'll have some free time to explore the ruins yourself before you go down to Aguas Calientes to catch your train at six thirty tomorrow evening. I'll go over all the details of when and where to take the train tomorrow. There is also a market there, if you have any last-minute shopping to do. Someone from Huaman Travel, probably Domingo, will meet you at the train station in Ollantaytambo with the bus that will take you back to your hotel in Cusco. Any questions?"

"What about our personal gear the porters are carrying?" Megan asked.

"They will leave it for you in Aguas Calientes at the Pachamama restaurant. Huaman Travel has an agreement with them for the use of a storage room for the day," Alberto said. "It's also a good restaurant, if you want lunch before you take the train. I'll give you directions at the end of the tour tomorrow."

WHEN ALBERTO'S alarm went off the next morning, Benicio groaned and burrowed deeper into his sleeping bag. He knew they needed to get up. He didn't want the porters to miss their train, and especially not because of him, but it was cold and dark outside and warm in the tent. With a sigh, he sat up and pulled on his jacket. It wasn't quite as cold as it had been at Chaqulqocha, but it wasn't warm either, and dawn was still hours away.

Beside him, Alberto rolled over as well, reaching for his clothes. "No coca tea this morning, just breakfast as quickly as possible. Remind everyone to empty their tents before breakfast so the porters can begin packing up."

"I will," Benicio said as he tied his boots. His back twinged a little as he stretched to unzip the tent. He'd be grateful for his own bed tonight, that was for sure. The hike had been easier this time than when he'd first hiked the trail, but easier didn't mean easy. He didn't know if it would ever be easy. "I can help them until it's time to eat."

"I'm sure they'll appreciate that. You've won them all over this week," Alberto said.

Benicio smiled as warmth burst through his chest at the praise. He'd worried about his usefulness on the trail for nothing, it seemed.

He hustled the tourists through getting up and emptying their tents and then helped the porters take them down while the tourists washed up and gathered for breakfast. They ate quickly, the least elaborate meal of the trip, and went to make their final preparations for the hike. The group was eager to go, and when they reached the checkpoint, there was only one group ahead of them. They sat down to wait for the checkpoint to open, some of them talking quietly while others dozed with their heads on their knees.

"Will the porters make it on time?" Benicio asked Alberto.

Alberto looked at his watch. "They should. They have almost an hour and a half to get to the station, and Arturo said they usually make it in about fifty minutes. This morning is one of the reasons I spend so much time reminding the tourists that the porters are people too. They get up early and move quickly because they don't want the men who've taken such good care of them all week to have to walk back to Ollantaytambo."

"I know it's what would happen if they missed the train, but has it ever actually happened?" Benicio asked.

"Not on my watch," Alberto replied, "but yes, it's happened at some of the other companies. Guides oversleep, tourists move slowly, something goes wrong. We can control a lot of things out here, but not everything, and sometimes life gets in the way of even the best-laid plans."

Benicio knew that all too well. He'd planned on starting his career as a guide much earlier than this, but his father's illness and death had left him tied to home in ways he hadn't taken into account.

"I don't imagine porters stay with companies if that happens often," Benicio said.

"No, I'm sure they wouldn't, but it doesn't happen often. All the guides are aware of how important the porters are, even if they don't all spend the same amount of effort in making sure the tourists see it. No guide wants to have to explain why they made the porters miss their train, because ultimately we're the ones responsible for everything that goes on out here."

Benicio knew that, but hearing it repeated drove home the risk Alberto had taken coming on the trail with a completely inexperienced guide. If Benicio had messed up, Alberto would have had to answer for it too. "Thank you for taking the chance on me. You didn't have to do that."

"Miguel took a chance on me when I was just as new as you are now," Alberto said. "He's a reasonable boss. If you'd really been as bad as all that, I'd have explained it to him and that would have been the end of it, but you're not, so his faith, and mine, were justified."

Benicio had no idea what to say to that. Before he could come up with something, the group ahead of him stood up and started through the checkpoint. "Time to go," Alberto said. "Do you want to take the front or the back?"

"The front, if you don't mind," Benicio said. "Sunrise at Inti Punku was very powerful for me. I want to be there as early as I can."

"Just don't leave the tourists behind to get there," Alberto said, flashing Benicio a grin.

"As eager as they are, I don't know if I could." He would never have imagined, four days ago, that he and Alberto could joke around together this way, but he thanked whatever gods might be listening for it. It was an unexpected blessing, but one he would take full advantage of for himself and for the tourists who benefited from their positive working relationship.

They reached the checkpoint and ushered their tourists through. Most of the morning's hike was relatively flat, a good thing since they were hiking in the pitch black with only flashlights to guide their way. By the time they made it to the Monkey Steps, the sky would have lightened enough for them to put away their flashlights and use both hands to climb the last bit to the Sun Gate.

Mindful of the people following him, Benicio set a moderately rapid pace. He wanted them to be there in time to get the full effect of sunrise over Machu Picchu, but he didn't want to run off and leave them either. He'd only led the group the one time and didn't have much sense of their speed as a whole, only of Thomas's. In the dark, even Thomas couldn't take many pictures, and Benicio had talked with him several times about how important it was to be at Inti Punku in time for the sunrise, so hopefully he would keep up.

They made their way around Machu Picchu mountain, skirting the valley that separated it from their campsite the night before, and Benicio had a moment to marvel at the engineering feat that was the Inca Trail as they passed along sections of trail supported on rock walls built up from the valley to keep travelers from having to make another descent and ascent. They still had the climb to Inti Punku, but it could have been much worse.

Everyone groaned when they reached the Monkey Steps, but as they made it to the top and over the crest of Inti Punku to the sight of Machu Picchu nestled in the valley below, the complaints stopped and a reverent silence fell over the group.

Benicio stepped aside to let them find their own vantage points and perched on a rock near the arch that formed the Sun Gate to wait for Alberto and the stragglers to arrive.

The sky had lightened to a brilliant blue by the time Alberto arrived, but sunlight had only begun to touch the top of the mountains surrounding the city.

Benicio waited for Alberto to start his presentation about the Sun Gate and Machu Picchu, but Alberto appeared in no hurry. Instead he took a seat next to Benicio and simply watched the spectacle of sunrise over the mountains.

Other groups arrived. Other guides began their lectures, but Alberto stayed where he was, and Benicio's gratitude grew. This was what he had wanted the first time he stood in this place. He had wanted to linger, to take in the experience at his own pace and in his own way instead of having his attention diverted by his guide. Alberto was giving their tourists that choice.

The sun made its way over the mountain until Machu Picchu was bathed in gold. Other groups moved on down the trail to the city, but Alberto stayed where he was. Only when everyone else had gone and the tourists began to turn and look for them did Alberto rise from his perch and begin to talk about the city, its discovery, and its significance. The respect Benicio had felt growing over the course of the trail blossomed fully now. Benicio only hoped Alberto agreed to work with him again. He thought it wouldn't be a problem with the way Alberto talked about planning a story for their next hike, but he would make a point of expressing his desire for it to happen—and the reasons why—as soon as he got back to Cusco and talked to Miguel.

SEVEN

THE CHANCE to talk to Miguel didn't come until the next day, when he met with both Benicio and Alberto to go over the surveys the tourists filled out at the end of their journey.

"You, gentlemen, were a hit," Miguel said as soon as they sat down. "I don't know what you did differently this time, but do it again. I'm used to reading generally positive feedback, but usually there's something the tourists fixate on and gripe about. Not this time. Every single comment sheet was full of nothing but praise for the two of you, the porters, and the experience as a whole. I'd intended to have Benicio work with several different guides to find the best fit and to let him experience multiple styles of guiding, but I'd be crazy to do that after reading these. I clearly found the right fit the first time out."

"We make a good team," Alberto agreed. "Benicio brings a creative and human touch to the details. They're not just facts to him, and the tourists recognize that."

"It's not just me," Benicio assured Miguel. "Alberto is very in tune with the mood of the group, when they want to linger somewhere and when they're ready to move on. He was the only guide who didn't rush his group through Inti Punku to get down to Machu Picchu. The city is a marvel, of course, but there's power in the experience of watching the sunrise, and most of the guides skipped right over that part."

"I learned from the best," Alberto said with a nod of his head toward Miguel. "I might not have grown up with the same connection to Andean spirituality that you two did, but I've come to value it as an adult. It may not work for every group, but that's what made the story you told so powerful."

"What story was this?" Miguel asked.

"When we got to Runkurakay, instead of giving the usual lecture full of facts, Benicio used a story to put the tourists in the shoes of the pilgrims who would have hiked the trail when it was new. Instead of being a collection of facts and theories, it was a moment of reflection and connection with the past and the importance of the tambo. All the lectures in the world can't do what he did in a few simple sentences."

"It was nothing special," Benicio demurred. "My English is horrendous. I'm surprised they could even understand half of it."

"Don't put yourself down like that," Alberto insisted. "They all loved you. The comment cards are proof of that, if the time you spent with them wasn't enough."

"No one complained about your English," Miguel added, "and I've had groups comment about other guides' English in the past, so either your English is better than you think it is, or your sincerity and passion for Inca culture were enough to overcome any deficiencies of language. Now, you have a four-day break and then I have another group for you, an extended family this time, ages ranging from fifteen to fifty. They're celebrating the wedding anniversary of the oldest sibling. Apparently it's something the wife has always wanted to do, and so the whole family got together and organized the trip for them as a surprise."

"If it's a surprise, will they have proper gear?" Benicio asked.

"They know about it now," Miguel said. "I've e-mailed with the couple. They're very excited. I get e-mails at least once a week talking about what they've done in preparation to make sure they're ready for the distance. The only concern is one niece who has asthma, but they assure me she manages it quite well and will have everything with her she needs to take care of any problems. I would suggest carrying extra coca leaves, though, just to be safe. She may not need them, but it's better to have them and not need them."

"I always keep an extra pack for emergencies," Alberto said. "You taught me that the first time we hiked together."

"Yes, but not everyone is as conscientious as you are. I'd rather give an unnecessary reminder than have a problem because I didn't say anything."

And that, Benicio thought, was what set Huaman Travel apart from so many of the other agencies. Miguel actually cared about the people he worked with and the tourists he organized trips for. It wasn't just a business for him.

"What will happen if she can't finish the hike?" Benicio asked.

"It depends on when it happens," Miguel said. "If it happens the first day, you'll send her back down to Piskacucho. We'll arrange to have someone pick her up and get her a hotel room for the days while everyone else is on the trail. If it happens later than that, it will depend on how serious the problem is. The porters have a stretcher they can use to carry someone if necessary. If it's more acute than that, we'll arrange for medical evacuation. Obviously we want to avoid both those options if at all possible, but we also don't want to risk anyone's health. Alberto has enough experience with the trail and lowlanders to make the call at the end of the first day."

"The first day will probably be the worst for her anyway," Alberto said. "The trail isn't as dusty once we pass Wayllabamba. If the altitude is going to be an issue, it'll be an issue here in Cusco too, so if it's different on the trail, it'll be because of the dust or the exertion, and the first day will let us see how that goes."

"Is the dust bad already?" Miguel asked. "I was hoping the wet summer we had would keep it down a little longer."

"It's not as bad as it will be, but it's definitely dusty," Alberto said. "It's been a warmer than usual fall and that's dried things up. It's better at the higher altitude because of the clouds and the mist, but the first day is pretty grimy."

"I'll suggest she bring a bandana to cover her face," Miguel said. "She can choose to do so or not, but we will have warned her."

"I'll carry an extra one," Benicio offered. "That way she has the choice if she doesn't carry one to start and then changes her mind."

"Good." Miguel handed them each a folder. "Here's all the information for the trip. I'll see you in three days for a final detail check and briefing. You can ask any questions then. Other than that, enjoy your days off."

When they were outside, Alberto turned to Benicio. "Let's find somewhere to get lunch. We can look over the packet and discuss the hike we just finished and anything we want to do differently for the next one."

"I don't really know the city, so wherever you want to go is fine with me," Benicio said. "I'll eat pretty much anything."

"There's a little place away from the main square where we can get good food for a decent price, and they won't mind if we sit and work for a few hours too," Alberto said. "I eat there a lot."

"That sounds good to me."

They headed out of the touristy section of town toward the areas where the locals shopped and lived. Benicio could practically draw a line when they reached the edge of the tourist district. The buildings weren't all that different. The streets weren't any more full of potholes, but suddenly the signs were only in Spanish, the people around him weren't dressed to draw attention, although many of them still wore traditional scarves and shawls, and the number of people with fair skin and light hair dwindled to almost none over the course of two blocks. Benicio relaxed a little. This might be larger than home or than Pisac, but it wasn't unfamiliar. Everyone here was Andean just like he was. Maybe they weren't quite as close to those roots, but they had the same background, the same history. For all its size, Cusco wasn't Lima.

"HERE WE are," Alberto said, leading Benicio into the little restaurant. He didn't know what the owner would make of Benicio, or him of her, but this was the closest thing to home he had these days, not counting an anonymous apartment in the city. He was pretty sure that wasn't home, just a place to keep his things. "Hello, Señora Vargas. Do you have a table where we can sit and work while we eat?"

"Hello, Alberto," Señora Vargas said as she came toward the front of the restaurant. "Introduce me to your friend."

"Señora Vargas, this is Benicio Quispe, my new partner on the Inca Trail. Benicio, this is Señora Vargas. She makes sure I eat when I'm in town."

"Silly boy forgets he needs food when he isn't hiking," Señora Vargas scolded. "Welcome, Benicio. Do I need to check up on you too?"

"No, señora," Benicio said. "I live in Pisac, and I promise I remember to eat when I'm not working." Alberto breathed a sigh of relief that Benicio took Señora Vargas's mothering in stride.

"As long as you come here when you're in Cusco."

"I will," Benicio promised.

She showed them to a table in the back of the restaurant where they could work undisturbed and told them she'd be back with their lunch.

"No menu?" Benicio asked when she left.

"She stopped giving me one a long time ago," Alberto said, smiling at the memory of the first time she'd presented him with a meal before he'd ordered. "She just feeds me whatever she thinks is good for me today. I guess since you came in with me, you get the same treatment. For what it's worth, I've never eaten anything here that wasn't delicious. It's nothing fancy, very traditional cooking, but it's very well prepared."

"Then I'm sure I'll be a regular when I'm in town," Benicio said. "So what do we do with the folders Miguel gave us?"

"We read through them, get familiar with the names and information about the tourists, and figure out if we need to do anything special besides the anniversary celebration. We'll save that for Wiñay Wayna, probably, since we get there early enough in the day for Luis to make a cake for them. If their anniversary is actually during the hike, we'll try to do it that day, but it's not as easy on the longer days."

"That makes sense to me," Benicio said, opening the folder. "Wow, those are some names. Pisharody and Thampi and Raghavendra." He stumbled endearingly over the pronunciation.

"Fortunately we won't have to use them," Alberto said. "It's first-name basis on the trail, and most of the first names aren't as unusual. There are a lot of vegetarians, though. I wonder if that's a family thing or a cultural thing."

"I don't know," Benicio said. "They all have American passports, so I don't know what their heritage is. Is it going to be a problem for Luis to have to make two different meals?"

"He'd rather have a large group of vegetarians than one or two," Alberto said. "It's easier to cook for a group of six than for one or two. That's why I eat here so often. Anything else of note besides the woman with asthma?"

Benicio studied the folders for a few minutes before looking back up. "I don't really know what to look for, but nothing seems critical," he said.

"It could be there's nothing else to see," Alberto said. He skimmed over the rest of the forms quickly. "No, that's it this time. Sometimes there will be notes about sleeping arrangements or special requests of one kind or another, but this is all pretty straightforward. Let's go back to the story you told. It worked so well. We should coordinate it so we can tell it from beginning to end."

"It doesn't work that way," Benicio said. "It's not a matter of writing something down and memorizing it. It's.... You have to feel the story, to know it in your heart so that when you share it, your passion for it comes through."

Alberto frowned in confusion. A story was a story, wasn't it?

"Think about your family stories," Benicio continued. "Every family has them—those moments that get told over and over again. There's a rhythm to them, a familiarity on the part of both the one telling the story and the ones hearing it, but it's never the same way twice. The storyteller didn't memorize a script. They're recounting powerful, emotional memories, whether it's funny or sad or romantic. Those moments stayed with them for a reason, and that reason is what they're sharing, not the words."

Alberto simply stared at Benicio for a moment. He'd heard Benicio's story on the trail, of course, but it had been in English, broken up by his relative weakness with the language, and that hesitation had shown on his face even if not in his voice. Now, though, Benicio didn't hesitate as he leaned forward earnestly, driving home his point with the expression on his face as much as the words he spoke. Alberto's hands tingled with adrenaline as he let the realization wash through him that Benicio felt the same way about the trail that Alberto did. Joaquin had always said no one could catch Alberto's attention because no one could compete with his love for the trail, but Benicio wasn't competing.

He was completing.

"So you're saying we have to do the same with this story," Alberto said, struggling to keep his voice level and not betray the roiling emotions assaulting him. Benicio had given no sign of being gay. Alberto's interest might be snared, but that didn't mean Benicio felt the same way.

"If we want it to mean something, yes," Benicio said. "Otherwise it's just another collection of facts."

"Then let's make it mean something," Alberto said. Even if Benicio was never interested in him in return, Alberto had found a friend who would truly understand his passion and would even help him expand on it. That was a treasure beyond price.

"There are ten sites we talk about along the trail, right?" Benicio said.

Alberto took a minute to count them up in his head. "Yes, that's right. So how do we want to divide things up?"

"I think the first day is all about anticipation," Benicio said slowly. "Think about the first time you hiked the Inca Trail, about what the tourists are feeling as they get ready to go. Think about what the pilgrims would be feeling as they set out from Cusco. Who are they? What made them decide to go on this pilgrimage? How have they prepared? What are they carrying with them? What kind of conditions do they have to endure? But also, what resources are available to them? We have to carry everything with us because the Inca sites are all ruins now, but they wouldn't have been then. There would have been places to trade for food, so what have they brought to trade? Are they stoneworkers, weavers, farmers themselves? How do the villagers feel about the pilgrims who come through? Are they welcomed as a source of trade or are they viewed as a drain on the village, wanting handouts because they're on a sacred journey?"

"You realize most of those questions don't have only one answer, or in some cases any answer at all," Alberto said. Benicio's enthusiasm was catching, and Alberto's mind was already racing with ideas of his own, but he had to be the voice of reason too.

"Not definitive ones," Benicio agreed, "but we know some things and we can make educated guesses about others. Life in Cancha Cancha isn't all that different than life during the Inca Empire, after all."

"Okay, so let's think this through, then," Alberto said. "We want the story to have a thread, but we also need to get the details in. The number of people who lived in the villages, the uses of the buildings, that sort of thing."

"That's easy," Benicio said. "Our pilgrims are experiencing those places for the first time too. Anything we need our tourists to know, we have our pilgrims observe. They can estimate how large a village is, particularly since our numbers are only estimates anyway. They will use the sites for their intended purposes. Isn't that what all our facts are designed to do? Explain the Inca people's way of life?"

"I suppose it is," Alberto said. "I always thought of it as making the trail and its history accessible to people, but what is the trail's history but the history of the Inca people?"

"Exactly," Benicio said. "The only part that will be harder to work in is what happened after the Spanish came and the Empire dissolved. Our pilgrims won't know that part."

"So maybe we tell that part during meals," Alberto said. "It's not like the only time we talk to the tourists is at the sites. We're always sharing tidbits, as we hike, as we eat, as we show them who we are."

"So we tell our story at the sites and give them everything else at other times," Benicio said. "I think that's a good balance. Let's figure out who our pilgrims are, then. The rest will develop from there."

BENICIO STARED out the window as the bus wove its way along the narrow mountain roads toward Pisac, but he didn't really see the scenery that usually kept him so captivated. His mind was still firmly fixed on lunch and the conversation with Alberto.

When they'd first met a week ago, Benicio would never have believed Alberto would see him as an equal so quickly. Alberto hadn't been cruel, but he hadn't seen Benicio as an asset either. Now he was treating Benicio as a partner.

The thought warmed him through. They had lingered half the afternoon at Señora Vargas's table, debating options for the story they wanted to tell on the next trip and enjoying the truly amazing food. Benicio hoped this would become a habit, because he could get used to having a friend and a place away from home where he was known rather than being just another stranger in town. Things were getting a little better in Pisac, but only slowly. He wouldn't be home much with his hiking schedule and that would make it harder to get to know his neighbors. He had the one cousin in Cusco, but while he could call on that family relationship for a place to stay the night before a hike, he and his cousin weren't close in age or interest. Alberto was the closest thing to a real friend Benicio had right now. That would have been unsettling last week. Now it just felt right.

He'd have to get over his pointless attraction, though. He didn't want to say or do something inadvertently that would mess up their friendship. Alberto had said he didn't have a girlfriend, but with his looks, Benicio was sure that was a temporary state of affairs. Alberto could have anyone he wanted, Benicio was sure. Including Benicio himself if he were so inclined, but Benicio didn't expect to get that lucky. He'd have to find a way to live with watching Alberto meet someone and fall in love, but that was a problem for another time. For now, he'd concentrate on building a friendship that would stand up to the passage of time.

EIGHT

BENICIO STILL arrived early at the Casa Andina when it was time to meet their new guests for the briefing, but more because he was eager to see Alberto again than because he was worried about how the evening would go. They'd have to scope out the new group and see what kind of personalities they'd be working with, but Benicio knew what to expect now. He was especially excited to debut their story tomorrow at Piskacucho. He and Alberto had agreed that while the porters were getting everything ready, they would set the stage with the tourists and tell the story of why their pilgrims decided to make the journey to Machu Picchu. If that went over well, they'd build on it from there. If it didn't, they could always fall back on the traditional methods of presenting the information. He hoped it would go over, though. They'd worked so hard on creating a world that would resonate with people.

Alberto arrived a couple of minutes after Benicio did, flashing Benicio a smile as he walked in the door. "Ready?" Alberto asked.

"Absolutely," Benicio replied. "Now that I know what I'm doing, this trip will be so much easier."

"It does get easier with practice," Alberto agreed. "Shall we go see who's here already?"

The answer was no one, so they settled in on the couches to wait. Benicio frowned a little when fifteen minutes passed and no one had come in yet. "We are in the right hotel, aren't we?"

"Yes, and they got back from the Sacred Valley tour on time. I don't know where they are."

"If they have this kind of trouble with being places on time, we might want to set an earlier meeting time for the morning," Benicio said. "It's one thing to be a few minutes late tonight, but if we get a late start tomorrow, we might not get to Ayapata until after dark."

"If that's what happens, it's what happens," Alberto said with a shrug. "Not everyone is good at being on time, and it's not a trait that matters in some cultures. We'll stress the importance of being on time in the morning, but if it doesn't register, we'll deal with it. It wouldn't be the first time I've hiked in the dark."

Benicio took a deep breath and reminded himself that everything didn't have to be perfect and that the tourists would appreciate their understanding and flexibility more than their nagging.

Ten minutes later, their group finally arrived, arms full of shopping bags. Benicio hoped they had gone in search of things they needed for the trail and not just to buy souvenirs. They would have time after the hike for souvenirs without wasting his and Alberto's time now.

Alberto cornered them before they could reach the stairs or the elevator and guided them to the sitting area. Once they were all settled, he began his usual night-before presentation. Benicio sat back and let him talk, choosing to observe the group instead. Last time, Alberto had picked out a potential problem before they ever started the hike. Benicio wanted to learn that skill. He'd discuss it with Alberto after the meeting and see if his observations coincided with Alberto's.

If they didn't, he'd have to ask Alberto how he'd drawn his conclusions so Benicio could do better next time.

Unlike the last group, which had been fairly homogenous where age was concerned, this group ran the gamut from a high school student to a man who could have been her grandfather but was probably her uncle, given the range of ages among the adults. They asked far more questions than the previous group had. It would have flustered and eventually frustrated Benicio, since much of what they asked were things Alberto would tell them if they'd just wait long enough for him to say it, but Alberto didn't even blink at the disruptions.

The older generation was the worst. The younger ones—his age and younger—seemed to expect the questions and discussion without taking part. He couldn't tell if that was out of respect for their elders, because the elders were asking everything the younger ones wanted to know anyway, or for some other reason entirely, but it would bear watching.

"Uncle," the youngest said finally, "if you'd let him finish, he might answer all your questions and it would go faster."

The uncle looked surprised that she had spoken up, but he subsided and let Alberto continue the presentation with fewer interruptions. Benicio decided he liked the girl. He'd have to make friends with her and enlist her help in keeping her family in line. Alberto finished his presentation finally, and then the questions started up again, mostly asking Alberto to repeat or verify certain details. Benicio thought they'd already know the answers if they'd listened more and talked less the first time through, but he kept that opinion to himself.

Once Alberto had gone through all the details, Domingo went through the gear check. Benicio was relieved to hear that the entire group had paid for porters for their personal gear. The younger ones might have managed it, but he really didn't see the older ones carrying their gear and managing the trail. When they finally finished and sent the tourists off to get a good night's sleep before their 4:00 a.m. departure, it was already nearly eleven o'clock.

"They're going to be tired tomorrow," Benicio said as they left the hotel.

"So are we," Alberto said, "but after that, I need to unwind for a bit before I can sleep. Do you want to get a drink? We can figure out how we're going to get anything done with a group like that."

It wasn't a date, Benicio reminded himself—Alberto had made that very clear by specifying their goal for the time spent together—but oh, how he wished it was.

"Sure. Did you have somewhere in mind?"

"There's a little place down the street that serves drinks," Alberto said. "You can get a beer or a Pisco Sour or something. I don't know where your cousin lives, but that way I don't take you out of your way."

"You know the city better than I do," Benicio said. "I'm fine with wherever you want to go."

They walked down the street and into the little bar. It was dimly lit with only low, local music playing in the background—obviously a place for locals, not tourists. Benicio relaxed a little. He'd been worried Alberto would take him to some trendy place where he'd be self-conscious all night, but he could be comfortable here.

They found seats at the bar and ordered drinks before Alberto turned to face Benicio. "Any thoughts on dealing with the group? I obviously didn't manage tonight."

Alberto's comment was so at odds with Benicio's view of the situation that he had to take a minute before he answered. "I thought you managed very well tonight. I would have lost patience with them long before the one girl interrupted her uncle and got things back on track."

"Not losing my patience isn't much of a recommendation," Alberto said wryly. "Tonight it didn't matter as much. Other than being tired tomorrow, it's not that big a deal if it took us four hours instead of two to go over the details. If everything takes that much longer, we're going to be in trouble on the trail."

"I think the young one—I have to go back and look up her name—can help us with that. She and some of the others closer to her age seemed impatient with all the interruptions. If we can get them to help us herd the older ones along, it'll help. The other thing is to be upfront with them about the situation. They can do things in a timely fashion or they can finish the hike after dark and miss rest breaks, that sort of thing."

"There is more urgency on the trail," Alberto agreed, "and other than the planned stops, we can keep moving even as we answer whatever questions they have. I still foresee some longer than usual days."

"What happens if we really can't make camp, especially the second night?" Benicio asked.

"The problem is the porters," Alberto replied. "They're so far ahead of us that we can't call them back if we wanted to stay in Pacamayo the second night. There would probably be space, what with the controls on how many people can be on the trail at any one time and the number of campsites at Pacamayo, but we wouldn't have any gear, and by the time we made that decision, it would be too late for the porters to come back."

"Then we'll have to make a decision, whatever it is, when we get to Ayapata tomorrow night," Benicio said. "If we get to Ayapata."

"We don't have a choice for that one," Alberto said. "Wayllabamba doesn't have enough campsites for us to stay there if we've been assigned space at Ayapata. We have to make it there for the night. We can negotiate the second night's camp if we have to, but not the first."

"Then let's see how tomorrow goes. There's no use borrowing trouble," Benicio said. "I'm sure plenty will find us without adding to it."

"I hadn't pegged you as a pessimist," Alberto said when he finished laughing.

"I'm not," Benicio said, "but given what we do for a living, trouble is going to find us eventually. Maybe it won't be anything serious, but mishaps happen in the mountains. You know this as well as I do."

"So when did it become your job to make me feel better?" Alberto asked with a grin. "I thought I was supposed to be teaching you."

"You are," Benicio said. "Teaching me, I mean, but I'm not an inexperienced kid either. I may not be an expert on the Inca Trail, but I know the mountains. The rest is just applying that to our current situation."

"Whatever it is, thank you," Alberto said. "I don't figure anything will make the next four days easy, but knowing you'll be there to help makes it easier."

"I'll see if I can befriend the girl," Benicio said. "I'm not above asking her for advice in dealing with them. It might make her feel important, and when you're the youngest in a large family like that, it's easy to feel unimportant. My younger brother certainly complained about it enough."

"That's very true," Alberto said. "I know I felt that way growing up."

That was the first Alberto had mentioned his family. "Do you have a lot of brothers and sisters?"

"Half brothers and sisters," Alberto said, "all a lot older than me. It was a second marriage for both of my parents, and I just sort of happened unexpectedly. The doctors had told my mother she couldn't have any more children after my youngest older brother was born. My next closest sibling is fifteen years older than me. I have nieces and nephews older than I am, actually. My oldest sister is a grandmother at this point."

Benicio blinked a couple of times as he did a bit of math. "Your parents must have started really young."

"My mother was sixteen when she had my oldest sister, and my father was twenty when his first son was born. They were both in their forties when I came along."

"Are either of them still alive?" Benicio asked.

"No, my mother died when I was eight and my father died about the time I started working as a guide," Alberto said. "It's just me now."

"I'm sorry," Benicio said. "That must be hard. You aren't close to your brothers and sisters?"

"No, they were all grown and gone and wrapped up in their own lives by the time I was born," Alberto said. "I have friends here in Cusco, and I have Señora Vargas."

"You should come home with me sometime," Benicio said on impulse. "My mother would love you."

"That's very kind of you," Alberto said.

Benicio scowled at him. "I mean it. Now that my father's gone, my mother is often at a loss for things to do. My younger brother just finished school and has moved to Calca to work. She loves having visitors, but they're few and far between. Everyone in the village is busy with the farms, and people outside the village don't come there often. I sometimes think her favorite time of year is when the missionaries come on their summer trips to help with the rebuilding after our summer rains, because then she has people to fuss over. It doesn't even matter that she can't talk to half of them because they don't speak Spanish or Quechua. She just wants to do for others."

Alberto relented. "We'll see what our schedule allows. How often do you go home?"

"Not very often," Benicio said. "It's a two-hour hike from Calca to the village plus the bus ride to Calca from Pisac. Not exactly conducive to a quick visit."

"Do you miss it?"

"The village?" Benicio asked. Alberto nodded. "Sometimes, especially when I've spent a lot of time in Cusco. It's so peaceful there. It's always noisy here. Even in Pisac, really, but especially here, and there's always too much light to really see the stars. I never feel like I know where I am if I can't see the stars in the sky at night. But I wouldn't have much of a life in Cancha Cancha. I'm not a farmer. My older brother loves it. You can see it in the smile on his face when he comes in at the end of the day. He's exhausted from the work, but he's happy. I wouldn't be. On the trail, though, I feel the same way he looks."

"It's important to like your job," Alberto agreed. "Can I be selfish and say I'm glad you chose the trail over the family farm?"

"Why is that selfish?" Benicio asked.

"Because if you'd chosen the farm, you wouldn't be here helping me now," Alberto replied.

Benicio's stomach lurched. He wanted those words to mean so much more than they really did. He was glad Alberto saw him as helpful, but he wanted it to be personal. "I'm glad I'm here too," he said in a strangled voice. Alberto looked at him oddly, but Benicio hid behind his beer and the moment passed.

NINE

ALBERTO LOOKED up as Benicio ducked into their tent, his long hair still damp from his shower. Alberto didn't know how Benicio stood the cold water, but they had more important things to discuss, like how they were going to survive the rest of trip with this group. Days like today made him wish Miguel were still guiding. Miguel always knew how to handle people.

"This group is going to give me ulcers," Alberto said when Benicio settled down next to him and started brushing his hair. Alberto followed the motion with his eyes, trying not to be too obvious about it. Benicio gave no sign of noticing, so he hoped he was succeeding.

"They're not as bad as all that," Benicio said. "I really enjoyed talking to Maria today, and you have to admit she got them moving when it really mattered."

"It shouldn't take a teenager to do our jobs for us," Alberto muttered.

"I'll go for taking whatever help I can get," Benicio replied. "I know you've got a certain amount of professional pride all wrapped up in this, but she's got fifteen years of dealing with them to give her an edge."

Alberto couldn't argue with that. "So how are we going to get through the next three days?"

"The same way we get through every day," Benicio said. "One step at a time. They don't seem to drive me quite as crazy as they do you, so if you need me to step in and give you a break at any point, just ask. If I take the lead, you can linger in the back and take a few minutes for yourself. You won't have any problem catching up with us. They don't hike that fast."

"I don't know why this is bothering me so much," Alberto admitted. "I mean, punctuality is something Miguel drills into all his employees because we don't ever want to make the tourists wait on us, but this isn't the first time I've had a group run late for a meeting or even for gathering the first morning to get on the bus. We pick them up very early so we can get to the checkpoint in time to make the day's full hike."

"They're very particular personalities," Benicio agreed. "Everything is a discussion, even when it isn't really open for discussion."

"But we can't just come out and say that because we don't want to be rude," Alberto finished.

"Exactly. So we go about it in other ways."

"Like what?" Alberto asked.

"Like starting the hike when it's time instead of waiting for them to all be ready. If Maria and her cousins start the hike, the aunts and uncles will hurry to catch up," Benicio suggested. "She did that a couple of times today, if you noticed. She'd start up the trail even a little ahead of us and call back that she was leaving and for them to come on."

"I did notice, actually," Alberto said. "I just didn't think to use that. Too frustrated, I guess."

"Don't let them get to you," Benicio said. "They're having a great time, even if you're not. Maria said she hadn't seen them enjoying themselves this much in a long time. Apparently storytelling is a large part of their culture too, so they really responded to our tale."

"That's good, at least," Alberto said. "It's almost dinnertime. We should start rounding everyone up."

"Let me do that," Benicio said. "Take another few minutes alone. It'll make dealing with them at dinner easier, because you know they'll want to talk about tomorrow, and that'll mean more discussion like last night. I'll nudge Maria to help when I can."

Alberto was pathetically grateful for the offer. "I'll be out in five minutes," he promised. "No matter how good Maria is, it'll take longer than that to round everyone up."

Benicio laughed. "Take your time. If everyone is ready before you've joined us, I'll come get you." He unzipped the tent and then turned back to Alberto. "We can do this. It'll just take a little more patience and planning than last time."

Alberto summoned a smile and pointedly didn't stare at Benicio's ass as he climbed out of the tent. When Benicio had zipped the tent flap closed, Alberto flopped back on his sleeping bag with a groan. He didn't know what was worse: the difficult tourists or his ever-increasing infatuation with Benicio. He knew his feelings were pointless, but that didn't seem to matter at the moment. Everything about Benicio appealed to him, from his looks to his passion for the Inca Trail to his perpetual good humor and determination to be helpful. Most of all, though, it was his belief in Alberto that had captured him. Benicio looked at Alberto the way Alberto had looked at Miguel the first year they worked together. He didn't deserve it, but he couldn't deny how good it made him feel. He wanted to be worthy of that regard.

ALBERTO BREATHED a sigh of relief as the last of the group reached the summit and the Sun Gate. He'd despaired of reaching it in time for sunrise, since they were the last group to leave Wiñay Wayna and make it through the checkpoint that morning. The sun was higher in the sky than it usually was when he arrived at Inti Punku, but it hadn't yet crested the mountain enough to bathe Machu Picchu in morning light. They would get at least some portion of the experience.

He settled against the boulder next to Benicio as he had done the last time and let the peace of the morning soak into him. Even after ten years, the sight of sunrise over Machu Picchu still moved him to the depths of his soul. All the tension of the past three days fled as he stood there and stared down at the wonder that was the Inca holy city. He had spent years studying it and talking about it, and the more he learned, the more amazed he was at the marvel his ancestors had created.

Turning his mind to business for a moment, he checked on his group, only to realize that for the first time since the meeting at the hotel four nights ago, his tourists were completely silent and still. No one was asking questions or debating anything. They were all standing along the edge of the trail staring at Machu Picchu with the same awestruck looks on their face that Alberto knew had been on his own the first time he'd stood there. They might have been garrulous in the extreme, but they weren't insensible to beauty when they saw it. The majesty of the mountains hadn't been enough to silence them, but Machu Picchu had done the trick.

Feeling more charitable, he took a deep breath and closed his eyes.

"Blessed silence?" Benicio murmured next to him.

"I didn't realize how much I needed it until I didn't get it," Alberto replied as softly. He knew the group didn't speak Spanish, but he didn't want to disturb anyone's silence with loud voices.

"You can tell me to be quiet if I'm ever the one interrupting your silence," Benicio said. "I know you can't say anything to the tourists, but don't let me deny you something you need."

"You aren't a disturbance," Alberto said honestly. He knew his attraction to Benicio was hopeless, but he wasn't going to pretend Benicio meant nothing to him either. "You're my partner, and this week, you've been what kept me from losing it with the tourists."

"Thanks," Benicio said. "That means a lot, but the offer still stands. I don't ever want to be part of the problem."

Benicio was all kinds of problem, but Alberto didn't want to get rid of the problems he caused. It was so easy to imagine the years ahead of them, perfecting their teamwork and deepening their friendship. Benicio could already read him almost as well as Joaquin, who he'd known for years. Benicio knew everything important about him with one exception, but Alberto had learned his lesson the last time he'd let a fellow guide know he was gay. That guide had refused to share a tent with him anymore and only worked with him twice more before he began finding excuses to take other jobs. Miguel had kindly not said "I told you so." Alberto would rather keep silent than see the same kind of revulsion cross Benicio's face.

He wanted to hike up to Cancha Cancha and meet Benicio's mother. He wanted to have a partner he could trust at his back on the trail for as long as his knees held out. He wanted to have someone who would share his passion for the Inca Trail so they could discuss all the new research that was going on about its history. He wanted everything a friendship with Benicio would mean, even if he couldn't have the return of the attraction he felt. He could live with that. He'd been doing it already. The important part was to keep all the things Benicio brought to his life that he hadn't had before.

The sun finished its ascent over the mountain behind them, bathing Machu Picchu in golden light, and the family began to talk again.

"That's our cue," Alberto said. "Let's get them through the city so we can go home. I need a drink after this week."

"I'm right there with you," Benicio said. "I'll bet you the first round of drinks all the evaluations are good ones despite how you're feeling right now."

"You're on," Alberto replied. He didn't actually expect there to be any bad evaluations, but if buying Benicio's drink meant he could keep Benicio at his side that much longer, he'd lose the bet gladly.

"SO WHO'S buying the first round of drinks?" Benicio asked as they sat together on the train back to Ollantaytambo. They'd have a bus ride after that, but the time would pass quickly enough with the two of them together. The time always flew when he was with Alberto.

Alberto opened the envelope with the evaluations and skimmed through them. Benicio tried his best to wait patiently and not snatch them out of Alberto's hands, but it was hard. He knew the evaluations were good. Maria had told him repeatedly how much her family was enjoying the trip. Benicio's impatience stemmed more from wanting Alberto to realize what kind of impression they'd made on the sometimes fractious group. It would hopefully restore his confidence. Benicio hated that this week had shaken it, but he'd watched helplessly as Alberto had gotten progressively harder on himself. He prayed next week would be easier, more like their first group, with only one or two problem tourists rather than a whole group that was hard to manage.

"I am," Alberto said after a few minutes. "You were right. They were very happy with the week, no matter how it felt to me."

"Can I say I told you so?" Benicio asked.

"You just did," Alberto replied, but he smiled, so Benicio figured he'd taken it the way Benicio intended. It was good to see him smiling again after a week of wrinkled brows and tension lines around his lips. Alberto's smile was too beautiful to be hidden by frowns.

They chatted all the way back to Cusco about the trip and what had worked with their story and what hadn't seemed to go over as well, about the porters, and everything else they could control on the trip.

"So, the same bar as last time?" Benicio asked when they got off the bus in Cusco.

"What time do you have to catch the bus to go back to Pisac?" Alberto asked. "If it's soon, then yes, but if not, I thought we could go by my place, clean up, and go to a bar near where I live. The one we went to before is fine, but I like the other one better, and we'll both enjoy it more if we don't reek of the trail."

It hadn't been hot enough that morning for Benicio to feel particularly grungy. He'd taken a shower at Wiñay Wayna while Alberto was taking the tourists to visit the ruins, but he wouldn't say no to seeing Alberto's apartment. It was such a silly thing, but it felt like a significant intimacy. Drinks were one thing. Inviting someone over, even just for long enough to get ready to go back out, was something else entirely.

"The last bus isn't until late," Benicio said. "We can go to the place near your apartment."

They caught the bus across town to Alberto's apartment. It was a simple studio, much like Benicio's place in Pisac. Alberto had a bamboo screen to create an illusion of privacy around his bed, but the rest of the space was open. The walls were decorated with brightly colored tapestries, the kind of weavings his mother made. The thick walls blocked out the noise from the street, leaving Benicio very aware of being alone with Alberto in a very intimate setting.

"Do you want the first shower?" Alberto offered. "I don't mind waiting."

"If you're sure," Benicio said. "It doesn't take me long,"

"There's no rush," Alberto replied. "Take your time and enjoy the hot water."

Benicio flushed and grabbed his bag to carry it with him into the bathroom so he'd have clean clothes to put on before he came back out. Alberto had seen him changing his shirt by flashlight in the tent, but he wasn't ready for Alberto to see him in just a towel in the full light of day. That crossed a line he wasn't willing to cross just yet. If Alberto were gay, if they were lovers, that would be different, but they weren't. They were professional partners and they were becoming friends, but that wasn't the same thing at all.

He showered as quickly as he could because the temptation to linger under the hot water and relieve a little of the tension that had sprung up in him when Alberto suggested coming here was strong, and he didn't want Alberto to wonder if he was doing exactly that. He dressed quickly and brushed his hair. It would leave a wet spot down his back, but it was better than being dirty. He'd taken a shower the day before, but it still felt good. He'd gotten spoiled living in Pisac. He could still take a cold shower on the trail, but the hot water was a luxury he wouldn't refuse.

When he came back out of the bathroom, Alberto was waiting for him, an open bag of chips on the table. "I was hungry and figured you might be too. Help yourself. I just opened the bag so they haven't had a chance to go stale while we were hiking. I'll just be a minute, but I've got to get the trail dust off."

"No rush," Benicio said. "I will have some chips. I hadn't realized I was hungry until you mentioned it."

Alberto flashed him a grin and disappeared into the bathroom, his clothes in hand. Benicio was glad for it. As appealing as it would be to watch Alberto walk out in a towel, Benicio knew it would be a bad idea. He'd give himself away if he did, and then he'd have to deal with Alberto's reaction. Benicio hadn't told many people he was gay, but he didn't need personal experience to tell him it was taboo. Maybe if he lived in Lima, things would be different, but here in Cusco and the highlands, attitudes hadn't even begun to change.

Benicio was so lost in his thoughts that he didn't hear Alberto come out the bathroom until Alberto spoke. "Are you all right? You have the strangest look on your face."

"I'm fine," Benicio lied. "Just tired. I'm still trying to get used to the hours we keep on the trail. It's hard to make myself get up that early on our days off so I haven't adjusted completely yet."

"You learn to cope with it," Alberto said, "but I'm not sure you ever get completely used to it, because you're right. We come off the trail tired, and so we sleep longer hours while we're home. I do the same thing, and Miguel told me he had the same problem when he was still working the trail. It's one of the downsides of the job."

"It's the only one I've found so far," Benicio said. "Are there really others?"

"Wait until you're out on the trail when a storm comes up and see how you feel then. You know how fast the weather can change in the mountains."

Benicio had gotten drenched more than once walking home from school. That had been bad enough, with a warm, dry house at the other end. On the trail, he'd only have a tent that would hopefully be waterproof. "Okay, I can see that being unpleasant."

"If you don't have a cover for your backpack, you should get one. Any store that sells camping gear will have one. They aren't very expensive, and they're worth their weight in gold when you have dry clothes at the end of a rainy day," Alberto said.

"I'll have to get one," Benicio said. "I didn't really think about it with it being the dry season."

"There's a store near the hotel that gives discounts to guides," Alberto said. "I'll meet you early before our next informational meeting and show you where it is. For now, though, I owe you a drink. Shall we go?"

"Sure."

The bar was just down the street. Alberto greeted the bartender by name when they walked in. Benicio wished he had Alberto's knack for carving a niche for himself. He hardly knew anyone in Pisac. He recognized his neighbors, but he didn't have a restaurant or a bar where he was known by name. He lived there, but he wasn't part of the community the way Alberto seemed to be part of the fabric of life in his corner of Cusco.

"What are you having?" Alberto asked Benicio.

"Um, just a beer," Benicio said. "I'm not picky."

"Local or imported?" the bartender asked.

"Which is better?" Benicio asked.

"Imported beers are stronger," the bartender said. "It depends on what you like."

"Get a Cusqueña," Alberto advised. "You can always get something else later if you want something stronger."

"Okay." The bar probably didn't have chicha, and even if it did, everyone had their own recipe for the corn-based beer, and Benicio hadn't found any he liked as well as his brother's. A regular beer was less likely to be a disappointment in comparison.

The bartender brought them two beers, and Alberto paid, as agreed. He took a long swig of the beer and let out such a long, deep sigh that Benicio wondered how he'd breathed in that much air.

"I've never been so glad for a four-day break as I am today," he said. "I know we have to meet with Miguel tomorrow, but then it's nothing but football and beer until it's time to meet the next group. They *have* to be easier than this one."

"You realize that's tempting fate, right?" Benicio said. "Yes, it was a little like chasing after guinea pigs, but they weren't unpleasant or unappreciative of our efforts. It could have been a lot worse."

"I know," Alberto said, "but unpleasant and unappreciative doesn't happen very often. People don't pay that kind of money to come hike the trail if they don't want to be there. It could be worse, but it so rarely is that I can't remember the last time I had a group like that, or even a person like that, actually."

"That's good to hear," Benicio said. "If this group really is as bad as it gets, that's not bad at all."

"No, I guess it's not," Alberto said. "It's all a matter of perspective."

"And you're judging based on ten years of good experiences, and I'm judging based on my experience with people in general rather than people on the trail," Benicio agreed.

"Has your experience with people in general been so bad?" Alberto asked.

"Not really. I've just seen people being rude or judgmental or otherwise difficult to get along with. It's nice to know people like that tend not to come on the trail. It would ruin the experience for me, I know, and possibly taint the way I see the trail overall."

"Don't ever let it do that," Alberto said. "Your passion for the trail is one of your best traits. Don't let anyone take that from you."

"I'll try." Benicio's pulse picked up in pleasure at the compliment. Alberto kept saying those kinds of things to him, and Benicio didn't know what to make of it. It couldn't mean what Benicio wanted it to mean, which meant it had to just be Alberto's way of reassuring him as his mentor. If only he could react to it as praise from a mentor.

TEN

"WE AREN'T expected to speak Norwegian, are we?" Benicio asked two weeks later as they sat at Señora Vargas's café and looked over the packets Miguel had given them that morning.

"No, of course not," Alberto said. "See, Miguel gives them the choice of English, Spanish, French, or Portuguese. He has guides who speak those languages. If they can't pick one of them, he has a list of agencies that specialize in less common languages, and he'll refer them there. They picked English, so it'll be very much like the last few trips, only instead of English being our tourists' native language, it'll be a second language for them as well."

"Does that make it easier or harder?" Benicio asked.

"It depends on how well they speak English," Alberto said, "but usually there's at least one person in the group willing to play translator for anyone whose English isn't up to understanding our presentations. I've never had a group that picked English and then had no one I could communicate with."

"Have you had it in Spanish?" Benicio asked.

"No, of course not," Alberto said, "but they don't pick Spanish usually unless that's their native language. English is the default if they're going with a second language."

Alberto's phone buzzed, interrupting their conversation. "Hold on just a minute."

Benicio finished the last bite of his lunch while Alberto read the text on his phone.

"Do you play football?" Alberto asked, looking up.

"That depends on how you define playing," Benicio said. "I've played with other kids in the village, but never really on any kind of team or anything. Why?"

"There's a group that gets together sometimes when there are enough of us," Alberto said. "We'd planned to get together today, but a couple of people canceled. We need at least one more player to have a game. It's nothing formal, just a bunch of friends, like you and the kids in the village. Do you want to join us?"

"If you're sure you don't mind me tagging along," Benicio said, "although I don't have anything to wear. I didn't come to Cusco planning on playing football."

"The shoes you're wearing are fine, and you can borrow a pair of shorts and a T-shirt from me," Alberto said. "It's not a formal thing, no jerseys or anything. We're close enough to the same size that my things should fit you."

"As long as you're sure," Benicio said. He knew he was repeating himself, but he didn't want to take undue advantage of Alberto's kind nature. They'd been getting along so well and Alberto had taken to including Benicio in things, which he appreciated, but he didn't want to be a burden.

"Of course I'm sure. I wouldn't have invited you otherwise," Alberto retorted. "Let me tell the guys we're still on for this afternoon, and then we can finish up here and go back to my place to change."

Alberto texted his friends while Benicio read through the rest of the packet from Miguel.

"Okay, that's done. Anything else in there that we need to know about?"

"An allergy to shellfish," Benicio said, "but we don't usually have shellfish on the trail anyway. Trout, sometimes, but I don't think that counts."

"We'll still let Luis know," Alberto said, "although Miguel has probably already done so. We don't want there to be any problems out on the trail. We should ask the person with the allergy what happens if they're exposed to it and how to deal with it, just in case."

Alberto grabbed his phone and sent another text. His phone buzzed back almost immediately.

"Luis knew about the allergy. He said he's already planned on substituting something for the rainbow trout just to be safe," Alberto said. "If there's no seafood of any kind on the menu, we don't have to worry."

"That's all I see," Benicio said.

"Then let me say good-bye to Señora Vargas and we can go."

Saying good-bye meant paying for both their lunches, but Benicio had stopped arguing with Alberto over it. He insisted all he did was hug the restaurant owner, but Benicio had seen him slipping soles into her apron pocket on more than one occasion. Far be it from him to tell them how to manage their relationship.

They left the café and went back to Alberto's apartment. Alberto disappeared behind the bamboo screen and came back out with clothes that he tossed to Benicio.

As Benicio changed in the bathroom, he couldn't stop the helpless thought that wearing Alberto's clothes was probably the closest he'd ever get to touching Alberto's bare skin. Ordering himself to stop moping, he finished changing and rejoined Alberto in the living room. "So who do you play football with?"

"A group of guys I've met over the years," Alberto said. "And anyone they bring with them. Sometimes those people will become regulars, sometimes they'll just play that day, but there's a core group of about ten of us. We try to play at least once a week, although I miss some games because I'm on the trail. The others have jobs here in town and more regular schedules."

"What do they do when you're gone?" Benicio asked.

"Someone else brings a friend, just like I'm doing with you today," Alberto replied. "I promise, no one will mind that you're coming with me. They'll just be happy for the chance to play instead of having the game canceled. You ready to go?"

They took the bus across town to the football field on the edge of the city. Benicio could see a group of guys already kicking around a ball, so he figured those were Alberto's friends. The introductions passed in a blur of faces and names that Benicio wouldn't retain, but if they invited him back, he'd learn a few more, and he knew it would get better each time.

One man stuck in Benicio's memory, though. Joaquin, Alberto's best friend—a position Benicio wanted for himself if he couldn't have the position he really wanted—was friendly, but Benicio couldn't help feeling jealous at the easy way they touched, like they knew everything there was to know about each other and had no personal space left to preserve between them.

He wanted to bat Joaquin's hands away from Alberto, but he didn't have that right when Alberto seemed perfectly comfortable with it, and none of the others seemed bothered or even surprised by it.

"Are we going to stand around all day or are we going to play?" one of Alberto's friends razzed.

The group broke naturally into two teams. Benicio made sure to stay close to Alberto so he would be on a team with the one person he knew. To his surprise, Joaquin moved to the opposing team. Maybe this wouldn't be an exercise in torture after all.

"GOOD GAME," Leonardo said as they all walked off the field. "Are you going to join us for drinks, Benicio?"

Benicio glanced at Alberto, who shrugged. "You're the one who has to catch a bus back to Pisac, not me."

"I can stay for a while," Benicio said.

"Good. You're in for a treat," Leonardo said. "We've found the best chicheria in Cusco. You do like chicha, right?"

"Of course," Benicio said. "What highlander doesn't?"

"That's the spirit," Leonardo said with a grin. "We highlanders have to stick together against these lowland boys."

"Lowland?" Joaquin protested. "Since when is three thousand meters lowland?"

"Since Cancha Cancha is above four thousand meters," Benicio retorted.

"And you know I grew up in the mountains too," Leonardo added. "Maybe not quite that high, but certainly higher than here. Cusco might not be lowlands compared to Lima, but it's nothing like growing up in the mountains."

Benicio nodded in agreement. The natives of Cusco or even Pisac had grown up with advantages Benicio couldn't have imagined as a child. "They have real chicha?" he asked Leonardo before Joaquin could continue the mock argument.

"The best I've found anywhere outside of home," Leonardo said. "You know how that goes. Nothing will ever compare to the homemade chicha you grew up with."

"So true," Benicio said, "although there's a woman in Wayllabamba who makes a pretty good brew. It's not my brother's recipe, but it's the best I've tasted since I left home."

"You'll have to bring me some," Leonardo said. "I'd have to pay to hike up there, if they'd even let me go just that far, what with all the restrictions."

"I can carry an extra bottle and fill it for you. It'll be a couple of days old, so it won't be quite as good as when it's fresh."

"Thanks."

They arrived at the chicheria and headed inside. Benicio took a moment to simply enjoy the smell. So many things in his new life were strange and foreign, but this was familiar. The brew might not be exactly the same as what his brother made, but it would still be a taste of home.

The woman behind the counter served them with a toothless grin, proof, as far as Benicio was concerned, that she was a true highlander. Her lined face spoke of age and experience, but her dark eyes sparkled with life as she greeted everyone, including Benicio in her warmth. She could have been his mother, his grandmother, any of his aunts, or the other women of the village, and he responded to her without thinking, greeting her in Quechua as he would a most respected elder.

"Oh, you've brought me a good boy this time," she said to Leonardo. "Someone who will appreciate my chicha."

"We all appreciate your chicha, *abuela*," Joaquin protested. "Best in the city."

"Best in the Andes," she corrected.

"Of course, señora," Alberto said. "This is Benicio, and yes, he's a highlander. He's from Cancha Cancha."

"A good boy," she repeated. She poured glasses of chicha and handed them around to everyone. When she got to Benicio, she patted him on the cheek. "Anytime you need a taste of home, you come see me. It's hard being a highlander in the city."

She spoke in Quechua and softly enough that Benicio doubted anyone else heard or understood her, but he glanced around anyway. No one seemed to be paying them any attention, so he relaxed and took a sip of the chicha. He closed his eyes in delight as the flavor exploded on his tongue.

"Don't tell my brother I said this or he'll disown me, but you're right. Best chicha in the Andes."

She cackled, a warm, wondrous sound that filled the small, dim room. Benicio swore the space brightened just from the sound. "Don't be a stranger," she ordered.

"I'll come when I'm in town," Benicio promised. "I live in Pisac and work on the Inca Trail, so I'm not always here, but if I am, I'll come see you. We'll drink chicha and talk of home."

"Go talk with your friends now," she said. "You've spent enough time on an old woman like me."

"There's no such thing, señora," Benicio corrected, but he did as she said and rejoined the others.

"You made her very happy," Alberto murmured when Benicio took a seat at his side. "Most of us don't speak enough Quechua to really talk with her. She speaks Spanish, of course, but it's not the same for her, even if it gets us what we came for."

"No, it wouldn't be the same," Benicio agreed. He felt the same when he spoke with the porters in Quechua. It soothed something in his soul that nothing else could. "I had a really good time this afternoon. Thank you for inviting me."

"Of course," Alberto said. "You're welcome to come play anytime."

"You'll have to tell me when the games are so I can plan to be in town," Benicio said. "Unless we're on the trail, of course."

"Every Saturday and Sunday afternoon," Alberto said. "Assuming we have enough guys to play, but being able to count on you when we're not on the trail will make it that much more likely we'll have enough."

"As long as nobody else minds me being here."

"Do they look like they mind?" Alberto tipped his head toward the rest of his friends to prove his point.

"No, I guess not," Benicio said.

Alberto shook his head. "We've got to work on this confidence problem of yours. Miguel wouldn't have hired you if you didn't have what it took to be a guide. I wouldn't have invited you to play if we hadn't wanted you here. The guys wouldn't joke with you if they didn't like you."

"Sorry, it's a bad habit. It comes from being the kid who never fit in at home," Benicio replied. "I was never as interested in the farm as I was in my books. Definitely not the typical Quechua kid."

"It's a habit we're going to break, because you do fit in here," Alberto said firmly. "Your glass is empty. You want another?"

Benicio knew it was a bad idea, but it was a taste of home and he was with a group of guys who had the potential to become new friends and saying no seemed rude. "Sure, but you bought the round earlier this week. It's my turn."

"WHAT TIME is it?" Benicio asked. He had no idea how many glasses of chicha he'd drunk, but he was feeling them all of a sudden. "I don't want to miss my bus."

"Too late," Alberto said after glancing at his watch. "The last bus left an hour ago."

"Shit, that means I'll wake my cousin up if I call him," Benicio said, "and I didn't bring enough money with me for a hotel. I wasn't planning on staying tonight."

"You can sleep at my place," Alberto said. "It's the least I can do since I made you miss your bus."

Benicio flushed at the thought of sleeping at Alberto's apartment. He'd gotten used to dropping by there after they hiked so they could clean up before going somewhere to discuss how things had gone, but those were always short intervals, just long enough for quick showers and a change of clothes. Sleeping there was intimacy of a different order entirely.

"Are you sure? I don't want to impose."

"Benicio, we spend three nights a week sleeping less than a foot apart. I think I can deal with you sleeping in my apartment. The couch is farther from my bed than our sleeping mats are in the tent. It'll be fine," Alberto said.

Fortunately the chicheria was closer to Alberto's apartment than Benicio realized, because the city buses had also stopped running, and Benicio doubted they'd have any luck finding a taxi at that hour of night. They made their way back to Alberto's apartment in a mostly straight line, laughing and stumbling a little on the uneven sidewalks.

"We're a pair, aren't we?" Benicio said as they reached Alberto's apartment.

"Yes, but a pair of what?" Alberto laughed as he spoke, nearly obscuring his words.

"A pair of drunken fools?" Benicio proposed, laughing in turn.

"Drunk, no doubt, but not fools," Alberto slurred.

Benicio thought he was pretty damn foolish for agreeing to sleep on Alberto's couch. In his current state, who knew what would come out of his mouth? He'd end up blabbering about his attraction to Alberto and ruin everything if he wasn't careful.

They staggered up the stairs and through the door, still laughing like loons. "I'm so drunk I think I could sleep on the floor and not notice it," Benicio admitted.

"How many chichas did you drink?" Alberto asked.

"I don't know. People kept giving them to me, and Señora Yupanqui wouldn't let me pay for anything at the end of the night. Something about welcoming a highland boy to town. Some welcome. I'm going to be so hungover tomorrow."

Alberto chuckled. "There's a reason it's the best chicha in town. It's the strongest."

That wasn't what made it the best, but Benicio was in no state to debate the merits of various recipes for brewing chicha. That was a conversation more suited to his brother anyway. "You can argue with my brother about that when we go to Cancha Cancha. Just don't tell him I said Señora Yupanqui's was better than his or he'll disown me."

"Wouldn't dream of it," Alberto said sleepily. "Bed's through there. I'll take the couch."

Benicio froze. He'd dreamed of being in Alberto's bed, but in his dreams, it hadn't been because he'd missed his bus, and he hadn't been alone. He couldn't just walk in there and climb between Alberto's sheets and fall asleep like it meant nothing. He swallowed hard. "No, I can't take your bed. The couch will be fine for me. Really."

"Please, I insist," Alberto said. "You're a guest."

"I'm an idiot who lost track of time," Benicio retorted.

"You're a guest," Alberto repeated. "And guests don't sleep on the couch."

Benicio had heard that often enough growing up. They didn't have many guests since all their family lived in the village, usually just the missionaries who came to help in the village, but when they did have guests, his mother had always insisted on giving them the beds and putting the children, and sometimes even herself and his father, on mats on the floor. This wasn't the village, though, and he wasn't a random stranger being offered Andean hospitality.

He wasn't going to win this one, he feared, but he had to try.

"Don't be ridiculous. You don't need to impress me with your good manners. I'll be fine on the couch. Just wake me in the morning when you're ready for breakfast."

"I'm not the one being ridiculous," Alberto said. "I'll get you something to sleep in, and then we'll share the bed because I refuse to let you sleep on the couch."

"I can't sleep with you!" Benicio protested. He'd never manage to hide his reaction to Alberto if they shared a bed like that.

"What? You think I'm going to take advantage of you while you sleep?" Alberto demanded.

"No, of course not," Benicio replied quickly, not adding that Alberto could take advantage of Benicio all he wanted. That was the problem. Benicio wanted it to be more than it was. If Alberto loved him, even if Alberto just wanted him as a lover, the invitation would be completely different, but to be offered everything he desired and have it mean nothing was more than he could stand.

"Don't tell me you've never shared a bed before. I've been in villages like yours. Everyone shares with someone at one time or another."

Not since he was old enough to realize he was more interested in boys than girls. He'd chosen the mat over sharing a bed with any of his cousins. His mother had praised him for being a good host, never realizing his ulterior motives.

"That doesn't mean I'm comfortable doing it now," Benicio said.

Alberto muttered something under his breath. Benicio suspected he didn't want to know what it was. He worried this would mess up their working relationship and even their friendship, but it wouldn't be as bad as Alberto finding out he was gay because he woke up with a hard-on in the morning.

"Fine, do what you want, but don't blame me in the morning when your back hurts." Alberto stalked behind the bamboo screen and returned a moment later with clean clothes. He threw them in Benicio's general direction and went into the bathroom. Benicio winced when the door slammed shut between them.

Alberto stomped back out a minute later and threw a blanket on the couch. "Sleep well."

Benicio flinched at Alberto's tone. He might have said the right thing, but only because his mother raised him right. His biting tone made it clear he'd rather have told Benicio to fuck off.

Benicio unfolded the blanket and arranged it on the couch, wondering exactly how everything had gone sideways so quickly. The evening had been going so well. He'd gotten what he wanted—to sleep on Alberto's couch instead of in his bed—so why did it feel all wrong? He listened to Alberto moving around behind the screen and bit back the urge to apologize and agree to sleep in the bed if it would get rid of this awful tension between them. He'd regret it in the morning, though. Of course, he'd regret their argument in the morning too, especially if they couldn't find their way back to even footing. His job was predicated on his ability to work with Alberto. If they couldn't work together, Benicio didn't know what Miguel would do. Pair him with another guide if he was lucky, but he'd be just as likely to fire him for being difficult to work with. Benicio could probably find a job with another agency, but it would be a step down, going from the best agency in Cusco to a lesser one. If Miguel wouldn't give him a reference, he could end up stuck working as a porter. He'd do it if he had to. It would be worth being able to stay on the trail, but it wouldn't be nearly as much fun.

As the night wore on, Benicio began to see why Alberto didn't want him to sleep on the couch. It was fine for sitting, but it was a bit too short for him to stretch out all the way and the cushions weren't even, creating a lumpy surface. He tossed and turned, trying to get comfortable. To make matters worse, the sound of Alberto's breathing drifted out from behind the screen that separated them. It shouldn't have been any different than sleeping in the tent on the trail, but then they were working and Benicio was too tired to do anything but fall asleep the minute he lay down. Now Benicio was awake, the chicha was wearing off, and he was keenly aware of their fight. He hated fighting with people, especially with people who mattered to him. He'd have to find a way to apologize and explain in the morning without giving himself away. He didn't know how that would work, but he'd have to figure something out, because he valued their friendship too much to let this ruin it.

He pulled the blanket up over his shoulders, trying to get comfortable. The scent of Alberto's aftershave wafted around him, triggering an instant response. He was lying on Alberto's couch, wearing Alberto's clothes, under Alberto's blanket, and his body responded without his conscious volition. He stifled a groan and tried to figure out if he could get away with taking care of his desire under the cover of darkness.

He'd just slid his hand into his shorts when he heard Alberto roll over in bed and mumble something. Benicio froze, not sure if Alberto was talking in his sleep or if he was awake for some reason. Either way, he couldn't do this. He'd just have to will away his erection and take a cold shower in the morning to make sure it stayed away until he was safely back in his own apartment with no one to see or hear as he fantasized about what he could never have.

THE SUN coming in the window woke Alberto the next morning. His head pounded as he opened his eyes, and he turned to bury his face in his pillow with a groan. What the fuck had he been thinking, drinking like that last night? He knew better than to let the guys distract him while they were drinking, but he hadn't counted on the effect Benicio's presence would have on him. He'd lost track of time and of the amount of chicha he drank. As long as there was a glass in front of him, he hadn't questioned if it was the same one as before or a fresh one. Señora Yupanqui had ended up pouring them pitchers of chicha, so no one's glass had ever gotten completely empty before someone refilled it. Alberto had a vague memory of Leonardo going to refill the pitchers at one point, but for all he knew, that could have been the fifth time he'd done so instead of the only time.

The sound of soft snoring from the other room dragged up the memory of the rest of the evening, the part he wished he could undo. A hangover was a pain, but a few aspirin and some coffee would take care of that. He didn't know how he was going to take care of all the awful things he'd said to Benicio the night before. Yes, it had hurt, thinking Benicio didn't trust him enough to sleep next to him, but that didn't give him the right to be nasty about it. He knew Benicio wasn't interested in him, and he wouldn't have done anything but sleep. Even drunk, he had that much control of himself. He just wanted the memory of Benicio in bed next to him to keep him warm on the cold winter nights ahead. It wouldn't mean to Benicio what it would have meant to him, but it would have been a good memory. Instead he had a fight to remember and make up for. He could practically hear Joaquin laughing at him for moping around after a straight guy, but Alberto couldn't seem to stop.

He took a deep breath to brace himself for facing Benicio and crawled out of bed, shivering a little as the cold air hit his skin. He pulled on jeans and a sweater along with a thick pair of socks. It would warm up later in the day, but for now, even the thick walls of the apartment building couldn't keep the cold at bay. Almost as an afterthought, he grabbed a sweater for Benicio as well.

Benicio was still sound asleep on the couch, so Alberto set the sweater on the back of the sofa and went into the bathroom to find some aspirin. He stared at himself in the mirror for a moment. His eyes were rimmed in red and he had dark circles under his eyes. He downed two aspirin, washed his face, and brushed his teeth. It wouldn't do anything for his appearance, but it made him feel a little more alert. He'd take what he could get because when Benicio woke up, he had some explaining to do. He only hoped he could make it sound plausible without giving away more than he was willing to say.

Benicio hadn't moved, so Alberto set water to boil on the stove so he could make coffee. He didn't know what Benicio would want when he woke up—he drank coca tea on the trail, but that didn't make it his usual drink when he wasn't working—but at least the water would be hot for whatever he wanted.

The whistle on the kettle startled Alberto. He cursed under his breath as he moved it off the heat. He'd meant to catch it before it whistled so it wouldn't disturb Benicio, but his thoughts had drifted and he'd been too slow. Across the room, Benicio opened his eyes and flinched.

"There's aspirin in the bathroom if you want some," Alberto said, "and there's hot water for coffee or tea. Just tell me what you want."

"Coffee." Benicio's voice was rough, from lack of sleep or his hangover or both. The sound rubbed along Alberto's spine, making him wonder if Benicio sounded the same way when he was wrung out from passion. By all the gods, he'd give anything to be allowed to find out, but that wasn't to be, and he had to accept that and move on. He couldn't let his unrequited lust keep interfering in their relationship.

He made a cup and handed it to Benicio in silence. Benicio sat up and took a sip. The blanket fell around his waist, leaving his arms bare to the cool air, and Alberto watched as the skin puckered up. "There's a sweater behind you if you're cold."

"This isn't cold," Benicio said. "Try waking up with snow on the ground and the fire out. That's cold."

Alberto shivered at the mere thought. "No, thank you. This is quite cold enough for me."

"Then bring a coat when we go to Cancha Cancha. Mama does her best to keep the fire stoked for the night, but sometimes it goes out."

Alberto felt something inside him unclench. If Benicio was still talking about taking him to Cancha Cancha, he hadn't screwed up entirely. "I'll keep that in mind," he said. "Look, about last night, I was out of line. I'm sorry. I was drunk and said some things I shouldn't have said. Can we pretend it never happened?"

"If that's what you want," Benicio replied. It wasn't quite the enthusiastic agreement Alberto had hoped for, but Benicio had only just woken up and was still clearly in the clutches of his hangover, so Alberto would accept it at face value and be grateful.

"It is. I'd hate to lose you as a friend because I was drunk and stupid."

The way Benicio perked up at hearing Alberto call him a friend was almost worth the hangover and the idiocy. Almost, because he could have found a better way to go about it.

ELEVEN

"YOU'RE KIDDING," Alberto said when Miguel handed them their folders a little over a month later. They'd found their balance again after their argument. Benicio had played football with them every Saturday and Sunday they were in town and had even continued to go to the chicheria with them, but he was always careful to leave in time to catch the last bus home. Alberto wasn't sure if that was to avoid another fight or so he wouldn't have to sleep on Alberto's couch again, but either way, they'd gone back to bumping along. Now, though….

"What?" Benicio asked. "Why is this group different?"

"Because this is the second time this group has hiked the Inca Trail," Miguel said. "They met by chance ten years ago, the first time they hiked the trail, and they've kept in touch. This year they decided to come back to celebrate."

"Has it really been ten years?" Alberto asked.

"Yes, it's their tenth anniversary."

"Whose?" Benicio asked.

"Shaun and Don," Miguel replied with such ease that Alberto blinked twice. It had been such a source of unease the first time around, but it seemed ten years of being Alberto's friend and mentor had blunted some of Miguel's initial reaction to the flamboyant, enthusiastic gay couple. "They hiked the Inca Trail on their honeymoon, and the people who hiked with them were so taken with them that they're all coming back to celebrate their anniversary too. They specifically asked for Alberto as their guide, since I'm not working the trail anymore."

"Shaun and… Don?" Benicio repeated. "I know my English isn't great, but I thought those were both men's names."

"They are." Alberto braced for Benicio's reaction. "Is that going to be a problem? Because if it is, you need to tell me now so I can find someone else to work with on this trip. They're good men, and they're here to celebrate. They don't deserve to put up with any homophobic crap on their anniversary trip."

"Of course not!" Benicio exclaimed. "I would never…. People love who they love. I just wanted to make sure I understood."

"That's a very cosmopolitan attitude," Miguel said. "I'm glad to see you aren't as hidebound as some people from the highlands."

Benicio flushed beneath his tan, his skin darkening enough that Alberto could see the change. It made him wonder—maybe even hope a little—what Benicio was hiding. "It's not my job to judge the people who hire us to guide them, just to make sure they have the best experience possible, right?"

"That is right," Miguel agreed, "but that's not what you said. Don't feel bad about it. I'm glad to hear it. I was just surprised."

Alberto glared at Miguel for a moment. Just because Benicio wasn't completely homophobic where the tourists were concerned, that didn't mean Benicio would want to share a tent with him if he knew about Alberto's own preferences. Nor did it mean Benicio himself was gay and interested in Alberto the way Miguel's gleeful look seemed to imply. He wouldn't bring it up now, though, because that would out him for sure.

"Do we want to do anything special for them besides make them a cake on their anniversary?" Alberto asked, determined to get the conversation back on a professional track and away from the morass of his personal life.

"They didn't make any special requests beyond wanting you as their guide, if that's what you're asking," Miguel said, "but I'm open to suggestions if you have any. I have fond memories of them, as they obviously do of us to want to come back and repeat the trip."

"My thought was to throw them a real party," Alberto said. "With chicha and beer for the less adventurous and music. The way we'd throw a party for someone celebrating an anniversary here."

"And when would you do that?" Miguel asked. "We can't legally ask the porters to carry any more than they already do, even if I felt comfortable doing it. We could hire an extra porter or two for the trip, if we can get the numbers approved above our usual, but that also compounds the equipment and food the men have to carry."

"Actually, I was thinking about doing it here in Cusco," Alberto said. "They're coming in a few days before the hike starts, right? So one night, instead of leaving everyone on their own for dinner, we plan something and take them to the party."

"I don't know them, so I don't know how they would react to it, but what about the chicheria?" Benicio proposed. "If we want a real Peruvian party, that would be the perfect place."

"How would Señora Yupanqui react to celebrating the wedding anniversary of a gay couple?" Alberto asked. He liked the idea, but not if it meant exposing Shaun and Don to some of the more provincial attitudes that still prevailed in the highlands.

"I don't know, but if we're paying her for the space and the chicha and maybe even to help us with the food and everything, she might go along for the money," Benicio said. "She's making ends meet, but she's not well off. A little extra to help out wouldn't go amiss. She was telling me last week that her grandson needs new clothes for school, and she doesn't know how her daughter is going to pay for them. The way she talks about the kid, I know he's brilliant, but if he doesn't have clothes to wear, he can't go to school, and without an education, he'll end up with no future. If we offer her enough beyond what she would take in normally in an evening that she can buy him clothes, I think she'll agree regardless of what we want to celebrate."

Alberto shook his head in amazement. "How do you know that? I've been going there for eight years and I didn't even know she had a daughter, much less that she had grandkids."

Benicio shrugged. "It's just talking to people and listening to what they have to say. You're there with your friends after a football game. You're focused on them. That's perfectly normal, but I barely knew any of them the first time we went in, and the señora was so much like my grandmother that I talked to her. Now I take a few minutes and talk to her every time we go in. I think not a lot of people do."

It was the sad truth, Alberto realized. Everyone greeted her as they came in. They'd been raised to be polite, after all, but once they had said hello and gotten their drinks, their attention turned away from her and back to whomever they had arrived with. They paid her at the end of the evening and said their good-byes as their mamas had taught them, but they never asked after her family, her cares, her worries. She was a means to an end for them, but not for Benicio.

"So what do you have in mind?" Miguel asked. "We only have a week to get it together."

They spent the next hour making plans, dependent on the venue. When they had everything in place, Miguel sent them to talk to Señora Yupanqui. "If she agrees, call me so I can get the rest of the plans moving. We don't have long to make the arrangements."

"I will," Alberto said as they left. They caught the bus to the other side of town and let the ride pass in silence.

"Do you really think she'll agree?" Alberto asked after they got off the bus.

"I think it will depend on how we approach her, but I do think we can convince her," Benicio said. "Do you trust me to lead the conversation?"

"Of course," Alberto said. "You've already proven better at talking to her than I am."

They went inside, and Alberto sat back to watch Benicio work his magic. Señora Yupanqui came out from the back room as soon as they walked in and set off the chimes above the door.

"Benicio, what are you doing here?" she asked. "It's not the weekend."

"No, it's not, señora," he agreed. "How are you today?"

"Oh, I'm well enough," she replied with typical Andean diffidence. She could be on her deathbed and she'd give the same answer.

"That's good. How's that boy of yours? Still enjoying school?"

"Oh, he's a marvel, but I still don't know how we're going to keep sending him," she said. Alberto could see the disappointment and frustration on her face.

"We might have a solution to that," Benicio said.

"I don't want charity," she protested.

"Not charity," Benicio promised. "We have a special group coming to hike the trail, and we want to give them a real highland celebration for the anniversary of one of the couples. We'll make them a cake on the trail the day of their anniversary, of course, but it's not the same thing."

"No, it wouldn't be," she agreed sagely. "What did you have in mind?"

"Everything," Benicio said. "Music, dancing, chicha, beer for the gringos who might not like chicha, food to nibble on. We'd pay for all of it. All you'd have to do is let us use the bar for the night and keep track of what people drink so we can pay you for that as well."

Señora Yupanqui studied Benicio's face for a minute and then turned to Alberto. "You don't think I'll say yes. Everything Benicio has said sounds good to me, so why would I say no?"

"Because the couple we're celebrating with is different," Alberto said. "Not many people I know would be willing to celebrate with them."

"Do you know how hard it is to be a woman alone in the Andes?" Señora Yupanqui asked. "Do you know how hard it is to run a business and raise a family and provide for everyone when you don't have a husband to help or the support of the community? They all said I should find another man to marry as fast as I could, but I loved my husband. I still love him even after he's been gone for twenty years. I know what it's like to be different, and I know what it means to go on despite it. So you tell me how they're different, and I'll tell you it doesn't matter and that I'll host their party with even more joy because of it."

Alberto wanted to believe the conviction in her voice. He had yearned for approval of his sexuality since he was old enough to understand, but everyone who'd found out had reacted badly, although Miguel had come around with time.

Benicio said something in Quechua Alberto didn't understand.

Señora Yupanqui frowned and turned back to Alberto. "You accept them or you wouldn't be here trying to arrange a party on their behalf. Why are you so sure I would be any different?"

"Because too many people are," Alberto replied honestly. "They're my friends. They came to Peru to hike the trail when they got married. Now they're coming back to celebrate ten years together. I don't want anything to mar that."

"I won't allow that to happen here," she said. "The rest is up to you."

Alberto nearly sagged in relief as all the tension that had been building up fled. "Thank you, señora."

"Hmph. The day someone has to thank me for being a decent person is a sad day indeed," she replied.

"Not *has* to thank you," Alberto said. "Chooses to thank you for showing a respect too few people do."

He'd said too much already, judging by the speculative look on both Señora Yupanqui's and Benicio's faces, but he couldn't bring himself to regret it. Benicio was helping him organize a party for the two men, so he couldn't be too disturbed by their relationship. He might finally have found a partner who wouldn't be afraid to share a tent with him, even if he knew.

Señora Yupanqui humphed again, but instead of continuing to scold him, she asked, "When do you want to have this party? I'll need time to plan and make sure I have plenty of chicha. How many people will there be?"

"Next Friday," Alberto said, "and fifteen to twenty at the most. There are twelve in the group, including Shaun and Don, plus Benicio, Miguel, and me, and maybe Miguel's family. I'm not sure if he'll include them, since Shaun and Don didn't meet them the last time they were here."

"That's not too many, then. I'll make an extra batch of chicha for the night just to be safe, but that should be enough. I don't have a good kitchen here to cook, but I could make dishes at home and bring them," she said.

"Whatever you think is best," Alberto said. "When they were here the last time, they all tried everything we offered, from the cuy and alpaca to the chicha, so I think a traditional spread of light foods, easy to eat with fingers or on a small plate, would be fine. Or we can find someone else to do the food if that's too much work for you. We don't want to overtax you."

That earned him a glare that would have made any Andean mother or grandmother proud. "You live my life for a month, then you can talk about overtaxing me."

Benicio intervened in Quechua again, making Alberto wish he understood more of the language beyond the things he'd learned working with the porters on the trail. He'd have to get Benicio to teach him if they survived the next two weeks as friends. Shaun and Don knew about him. If he had the chance to speak with them privately, he'd ask them not to say anything in front of Benicio, but he didn't really expect to get through the hike without someone giving him away.

Whatever Benicio said appeased Señora Yupanqui, because her glare softened. "You worry about the music and the decorations, if you want any. Leave the food and drink to me," she told Alberto. "Your friends will have a party they'll never forget."

"Thank you, señora."

BENICIO KEPT turning the day's conversations over in his head after they left the chicheria. Alberto called Miguel to report in on the arrangements they'd made, and Benicio stood there and stared at him, trying to weigh Alberto's various comments. The two men who were coming clearly meant a lot to him, and Benicio admired him all the more for it, but the tenor of some of the comments went deeper than defending his friends, or so it seemed to Benicio. It would be so easy to read too much into them, though, and Benicio didn't want to rock the boat again after they'd finally gotten back on an even footing.

On the other hand, if he was right, Alberto could be a resource to him, helping him find places where he could be himself instead of having to hide his preferences. Benicio didn't delude himself by thinking that Alberto could ever be attracted to him, no matter how much he wanted that, but having a gay friend would be better than nothing.

Alberto's hand on his shoulder startled him out of his thoughts.

"Are you all right?" Alberto asked. "I called your name three times and you didn't seem to hear me."

"Sorry, I was just thinking," Benicio said.

"Those must have been some deep thoughts," Alberto teased.

"They were, actually," Benicio said. "I wanted to talk to you about something, but I'm not sure how to start."

"Just tell me," Alberto replied. "Unless you're telling me you've changed your mind about leading the hike with me when Shaun and Don are here."

"No, of course not," Benicio said. "I'd never do that."

"Relax, I was joking. Apparently it was a bad one."

An absolutely terrible one, since Alberto could well be the one refusing to hike with Benicio if this conversation went the wrong way. He could brush it off, forget he'd ever entertained the thought, and everything could stay the way it was. He could do it easily. Alberto wouldn't push if Benicio said he didn't want to talk about it. If he did that, though, he'd miss the opportunity, because he doubted it would come up again. It was now or never, and he needed to do this. He needed to stop feeling like he was torn between living a lie and being outcast. Even if he was wrong about Alberto being gay, he hoped Alberto wouldn't mind that he was, given how he had defended his friends.

"Could we go back to your apartment? I don't want to have this conversation on the street or even at Señora Vargas's café."

Alberto sobered. "This is something serious, isn't it?"

Benicio nodded, unable to put words to the turmoil of his emotions at the moment.

"Let's go, then," Alberto said.

By the time they reached Alberto's apartment, Benicio's stomach had tied itself into knots so tight he thought he might throw up before he said the first word, but Alberto waited him out, taking a seat on the couch and letting Benicio gather his thoughts.

"Are you gay?" Benicio finally blurted out.

The look that crossed Alberto's face at the question was nearly enough to make Benicio run, but after a moment, Alberto nodded.

"Is that going to be a problem?"

"No," Benicio said, leaning forward to convey his sincerity. "No, not at all. I don't care. Or rather, I care, but not for the reasons you're thinking."

"What other reasons are there?" Alberto asked in a voice so bitter Benicio wanted to hug him right then, but he couldn't yet. He still had more to say.

"Because I am too," Benicio said. He felt lighter the minute the words were out of his mouth. If this was what telling people felt like, he'd tell the whole world, except he knew the reaction wouldn't be the same from everyone else as the slow smile spreading across Alberto's face.

"That certainly changes things," Alberto said after a moment. "Does Miguel know?"

"You're the first person I've told," Benicio replied. "I was afraid to say anything to anyone else. You said it yourself. Highlanders aren't known for being accepting of it."

"I won't say anything, but you can tell Miguel if you want. He knows about me, and he's come a long way from his initial reaction to finding out."

"How did he find out?" Benicio asked curiously.

"Shaun and Don," Alberto said with a laugh. "You'll see when you meet them. They're a force of nature when they put their mind to something. I don't know what gave me away—I never asked—but they pegged me the first day, and when I said I didn't have a girlfriend, they asked me if I had a boyfriend. I was so flustered that I don't even know what I said, but they took it as 'not now, but not because I'm not looking' and spent the rest of the trip giving me advice on finding the right man."

"You don't seem to have taken their advice," Benicio said. "Or is there someone you never talk about?"

"No, there isn't anyone," Alberto said. "But not for lack of taking their advice. In fact it's probably because of their advice. They made me really think about what I wanted and told me never to settle for anything less. Until I find that, I'm happier living alone."

Benicio wanted to ask what he was looking for, but that was more personal than he was comfortable with. Asking if Alberto was gay had been hard enough. "That sounds like good advice."

"Wait until you meet them," Alberto said. "They're living a dream. They're from California, so their marriage is actually legal, not just their promises to each other. Their families and friends all know. They don't have to hide or be afraid of people knowing about them."

"That would never happen here," Benicio said sadly.

"Maybe in Lima, but not in Cusco anytime soon," Alberto said. "That doesn't mean I can't dream of meeting the right man someday, though. We'd just have to find a way to live our lives discreetly."

Benicio considered that—all the ways he would have to spin stories to play down the depth of their attachment, the reasons for their cohabitation, the touches they could never share in public. It would be a restrictive life, but it might be worth it if he had someone special to come home to at the end of the day, if he had a lover to fall asleep next to at night. It wasn't ideal, but just the thought of it being possible made his heart lighter. He could follow the same advice Alberto's friends had given him and look for the right person. "You'll have to show me around places where I might meet the right man. I don't even know where to start looking."

"Not in Pisac, that's for sure," Alberto said. "But if that's what you want, I can take you to a club or something after we get back from the next hike. I don't think we'll really have time before we leave on this one."

"I wouldn't get in your way," Benicio promised when he heard the reticence in Alberto's voice. "You don't have to admit to knowing me, even, if you're worried about being seen with someone like me. Just tell me where to go. I can even go on a different night than you do."

"No, that's not what I meant at all," Alberto said. "Just… clubs aren't really the best place to start a meaningful relationship. Most of the guys who hang out there are looking for someone to pass the time with, not someone to settle down with."

"That's not what you're looking for," Benicio said. "At least, that's not what you said."

"It's not what I'm looking for," Alberto agreed, "but it's all I've ever managed to find, no matter what I'm looking for. It's okay for blowing off a little steam, but not for settling down."

The image of Alberto entwined with a faceless lover floated before Benicio's eyes and wrenched at his heart. He'd thought he could go to a club with Alberto and pretend not to notice if Alberto met someone, but now he wasn't so sure. "So where do you meet someone for settling down?"

"I wish I knew," Alberto replied. "I haven't found it yet."

TWELVE

ALBERTO WAS all but bouncing on the balls of his feet as he and Benicio stood near the baggage claim area of Cusco's airport. The morning flight from Lima had landed, which meant everyone would be there in a matter of minutes. He and Miguel had talked extensively about the first two days of the trip, time usually spent going on a tour of Cusco and then of the Sacred Valley. This group had already done that, though, so they had brainstormed a list of other options for the group to choose from. Benicio had even proposed taking them up to Cancha Cancha if they wanted a glimpse of rural life in Peru at its purest. Best of all, Miguel had agreed to let Alberto be their guide for whatever they decided, as well as for the Inca Trail.

"Alberto!"

Alberto looked around at the sound of his name and just had time to brace himself before he was enfolded in an all-encompassing hug from three sides. Holly, Nancy, and Julianne had found him. Now he just needed their spouses and the other three couples.

"You haven't changed at all!" Julianne said as the three women stepped back a little. "Just as dashing as ever. Are you still breaking hearts left and right?"

"I try never to break hearts," Alberto replied. "Is bad… karma? Is that the word?"

"Yes, that's the word," Holly said. "And yes, it is bad karma, but you didn't answer Julianne's question. Do you have someone special to introduce us to after all this time?"

Alberto glanced at Benicio, who stood a few steps away, and wished he could say yes and draw Benicio into the conversation, but despite the somewhat awkward coming out to each other, Alberto hadn't found the right way to broach his attraction to Benicio, particularly since he'd had no sure sign that Benicio returned his interest. "Just my new partner for the trail. Benicio, come meet everyone."

As he started the introductions, Mike, Ed, and Gerald joined them. Alberto offered his hand for them to shake, laughing when they pulled him into hugs as well. "It's so good to see you all," he said, "but where are Shaun, Don, Connie, Bobby, Jess, and Keith? They didn't miss the plane, did they?"

"No, they're here," Ed said. "We were all seated together from Miami to Lima, but they were in the very back of the plane from Lima here. We tried to switch seats around, but there were several families with young kids and we couldn't ask them to sit apart from each other. It was only an hour anyway. They'll be here any minute."

Alberto heard Shaun and Don before he saw them, their joyous, boisterous laughter ringing down the corridor to announce their arrival.

"There they are," Mike said. "So what's the plan? Miguel's itinerary was less detailed this time around."

"That's because the plan depends on you," Alberto said. "Benicio and I are at your service for the entire time you're here."

"Now that sounds kinky," Shaun said, elbowing his way into the group so he could grab Alberto in a huge hug. To Alberto's surprise, Shaun lifted him off the ground and swung him in a circle. "I'm so glad you could be our guide again."

"Hey, no hogging Alberto," Don scolded from behind him. "I want my turn."

Alberto braced himself for Don's hug. He'd learned the first time around that the two men were incredibly competitive in everything they did. Between them, it was all in good fun, but Alberto pitied anyone they competed with professionally. They'd never stand a chance. True to form, Don repeated Shaun's hug, spinning Alberto around, but when he set him down, he planted a loud, smacking kiss right on Alberto's mouth.

Everyone laughed, and a furtive glance around the terminal didn't reveal anyone outside their group paying them any attention, so Alberto relaxed. "Are you sure you should be kissing other men with your husband standing right there?"

"He doesn't mind as long as I stop at kissing," Don said with a wink for Shaun. Alberto laughed and shook his head. He would never understand those two. If he had someone for his own, he wouldn't even want to share his kisses—not that Don's kiss had been anything other than an overly enthusiastic greeting, but that didn't change Alberto's reaction to the thought. He was just glad Shaun was more understanding.

"Shaun, Don, this is Benicio," Alberto said, tugging Benicio forward. "He's the other guide who'll be with us this time around. Please don't scare him off before we even get out on the trail. I need him."

"Now we just need Connie, Bobby, Jess, and Keith, and we can go," Gerald said. "Are we staying at the same place as before?"

"Yes," Alberto said. "We kept as much as we could the same as last time, but a few things will be different. Miguel will join us for some things, but he won't be on the trail with us, and since you've already been to the Sacred Valley, we thought you might enjoy something a little different this time."

"Different is good," Shaun said. "We like different."

The other two couples joined them, Alberto finished the introductions and sent them to get their luggage, and then they all piled into the bus that would take them to the hotel.

They got to the hotel, got everyone checked in and settled, and then gathered in the fourth-floor breakfast area. "Welcome back to Peru," Alberto said when everyone was settled. "I know I said hello at the airport, but it's more than just hello. It's so wonderful to have you all here again."

"I think I speak for everyone when I say it's good to be back," Keith said. The oldest of the group and a former Marine—he'd been on leave from the USMC when they'd first come to Peru—he often took charge and spoke for the group, not that any of them was shy about sharing opinions.

"You mentioned something different this time," Connie said. "What did you have in mind? I thought the route on the Inca Trail was pretty much set in stone."

Alberto chuckled. "It is set in stone, the paving stones the Inca people used to build it centuries ago. We were thinking more of today and tomorrow. Usually we'd offer our guests the city tour of Cusco today and a tour of the Sacred Valley tomorrow, and if you want to revisit those places, we can certainly do that, but we thought you might like to see a different side of Peru, the side we see as we live here rather than what the tourists see when they come."

"Like what?" Holly asked.

"Like the market where I shop instead of the one aimed at tourists," Alberto said. "Like the village where Benicio grew up, if you're willing to add another day's hike to the four days on the trail. Or villages like it if you don't want a two-hour climb into the mountains. The real Peru, not the cleaned-up version we usually show our guests."

"If we're going to hike, can we do it today so we have a day to rest before we go on the Inca Trail?" Bobby asked. "My knees aren't as young as they used to be."

"Today would be better," Alberto said. "We have something special planned for dinner tomorrow night, so we don't want to be exhausted or late. If we're going to Cancha Cancha, we'll have to hurry. It's almost a two-hour drive to Calca, and then it's a two-hour hike up the mountain to Cancha Cancha. We can drive back in the dark, but we don't want to be hiking down the mountain in the dark."

"Unless we stay the night," Benicio proposed from beside him. "Is not hotel, but is real Peru."

"Your relatives won't mind?" Alberto asked, switching to Spanish. "They don't even know we're coming, much less that we're coming to stay."

"They won't mind," Benicio said. "My mother loves guests. Even unexpected ones."

"Will she let Miguel pay her for the food?" Alberto asked.

"Probably not, but if we put the money on the table before we leave, she won't have any way to give it back to us."

"Sneaky. I like that in a man." Benicio's smile was so bright that Alberto's gut clenched in response. Deciding it was safer to talk to their guests at the moment, Alberto turned back to the others. "So what do you think?"

"Will it be a hardship for the village if we stay the night?" Nancy asked. "We'd like to do it. It's one of those opportunities that doesn't come around twice, but we don't want to put anyone out or deprive anyone because we're there."

"We'll make sure everyone is paid for the food and lodging they provide," Alberto assured them.

"But no say anything about it," Benicio added. "Highland people are proud. They see you as guests, they treat you as guests, not customers."

"Then we're in," Shaun said. "What do we need to take with us?"

"Water, warm clothes, and a hostess gift, if you have anything you can give the family you're staying with. Even snacks from the US would be something special for them," Alberto said. "If you don't have anything, let me know, and we'll stop somewhere and get something you can carry with you. It's not polite to arrive at someone's house empty-handed."

"Give us half an hour," Don said, "and we'll be ready to go."

"I'll let Miguel know what we're planning," Alberto said, "and we'll meet in the lobby in thirty minutes."

BENICIO WAS glad he'd decided to stay in Cusco the next few days before they went on the trail, because he had brought his gear with him for the trip as well as clothes for the next few days. He hurried back to his cousin's house to get his pack, a change of clothes, and his hiking boots. He hadn't really expected the group to agree to the suggestion of going to Cancha Cancha, much less today. By the time he returned to the hotel, the full thirty minutes had passed and he was breathless from the rush.

"Ready?" Alberto asked with the same broad grin that hadn't left his face all morning. Benicio wanted to resent that someone other than him had put that smile on Alberto's face, but it was too contagious an expression for him to stay annoyed long.

"As I'll ever be," Benicio said. "Are they ready?"

"They arrived ready," Alberto replied. "Unlike most of our groups, they know exactly what to expect. They've been outside to buy their coca leaves, they've had coca tea, and they're ready to go."

"I hope they aren't disappointed by Cancha Cancha," Benicio said. "It's not a place tourists usually go."

"I wouldn't have agreed to you suggesting it if I didn't think they'd appreciate it for what it is," Alberto assured him. "They aren't here to judge. They're here to experience everything they can."

"I'll just have to keep reminding myself of that," Benicio said. He only hoped Alberto would be as generous in his assessment of Benicio's village as he said the tourists would be. He didn't know what he'd do if Alberto sneered at his childhood home the way some of the other guides on the trail had done. Alberto hadn't done so in hearing about Cancha Cancha, but seeing it was an entirely different matter.

They boarded the bus and headed for Calca. Always before, Alberto had sat in the front of the bus with Benicio when they were traveling with a group of tourists, but this time, he sat farther back, chatting with this group like old friends. Benicio tried to match faces to the names he'd studied in the packet, but he only succeeded in confusing himself more. Shaun and Don were easiest to pick out because they sat snuggled up together, making it rather obvious who they were. The others, though, were harder to distinguish. Three of the women had red hair of varying shades and lengths, and none of them wore glasses or had other obviously distinguishing features. He'd have to ask Alberto to go over the names with him again, more slowly this time, so he could introduce everyone to his mother. She'd have his hide if he brought guests and couldn't even introduce them properly.

He could admit to a little bit of jealousy at how easy Shaun and Don were in their affection for each other. Even if Benicio had someone to love like that, he wouldn't be able to show it so freely. Watching them with Alberto was even worse. They touched him so freely. It was just friendly—he could see how devoted they were to each other—but they were at ease with themselves and their sexuality in a way Benicio wasn't. He could say he was gay, had finally admitted to someone other than himself, but it was still primarily an academic exercise. He'd never had the chance to act on those feelings outside his own fantasies. At the rate he was going, he probably never would.

Laughter from the back of the bus drew his attention, and he turned to see Shaun striking a pose in the aisle between the seats. Benicio had no idea who he was imitating, but the others obviously did from their catcalls and laughter. He had to find a way to join the group or the next week would be miserable indeed. He took a deep breath to steel his resolve and stood up to join Alberto with the others. If Alberto didn't feel the need to maintain a professional distance from this group, then Benicio didn't need to do it either.

THE BUS dropped them off at the base of the trail leading up to Cancha Cancha, and Alberto verified with the driver that they would meet back at the same spot at noon the next day. That would give them time to get up and eat a leisurely breakfast before hiking back down the mountain. It would be the only leisurely morning of the trip, but everyone knew that already, so Benicio didn't dwell on it. Instead he focused on the trail ahead of him. He would have to lead this part of the hike, since he was the only one familiar with the way, and unlike the Inca Trail, this one wasn't paved in stone. In places, it was little more than a thin dirt track along the edge of the mountain.

No one commented on it as they began the hike. Instead they asked about everything from the vegetation to the likely weather at the top, and Benicio slowly relaxed. Alberto might be acting much more relaxed than usual, but this was still a group of tourists here to discover Peru, and in a way, they were even more willing to be pleased with the experience because they knew what to expect and what not to expect. They had come planning on camping in tents for three nights. A night in a mud-brick house in Cancha Cancha would still be a step up from that. Alberto had said they embraced the native foods when they were here before, so if his mother served cuy, they wouldn't freak out on him. He didn't actually think she'd serve cuy. Chicken was far more likely for a group this size, but he couldn't always predict what she would do.

"You're a lot quieter than Alberto is," one of the redheads said as she walked up beside him. "Have we frightened you off?"

"No, is not that," Benicio said. "My English no is good. Is hard with lot of people and fast talking."

"Which means you probably didn't catch all our names, even," she said. "I'm Jess. My husband Keith and I are from Virginia. He was in the military, and when he got out, we stayed."

"Keith is which one?" Benicio asked.

"The one with the black backpack and the military haircut," Jess said. "He got rid of the job but kept the hair."

Benicio looked back and found the man in question, repeating their names over in his head until he thought he could remember them.

"Is nice in Virginia?"

"Yes, but not like this," Jess said. "I mean, look around you. I know you grew up here, so maybe you don't see it, but my God, these mountains are incredible. We don't have anything like this at home. The closest thing would be the Rockies in the western part of the country, but even they aren't like this. There might be a few mountains whose highest elevation comes close to what you have here, but that's the summit, not the elevation where people live. And because it's equatorial, there are such interesting climate zones. We don't have cloud forests in our mountains, that's for sure."

Benicio took a minute to look around and consider Jess's words. He had grown up in the mountains, and his father had taught him to appreciate their beauty, but he had also grown up aware of the power and danger of them. At more than four thousand meters, Cancha Cancha wasn't in danger of flooding like Calca and the other towns of the Sacred Valley, but the earthquakes that racked the mountains on a regular basis had given him a healthy respect for the power of Pachamama—the earth goddess.

"Thank you for the reminder," he said. "Is easy to look but not see when is home."

"That's what you have us for," Jess said. "Well, us and all the other tourists you take on trips. Alberto didn't say. How long have you been working together?"

"Few months now. I start in May and is August now, so makes three months," Benicio replied. "He is good teacher."

"I bet he is," Jess said. "He was a great guide ten years ago when he was relatively new. I'm sure he's only gotten better with time."

"Are you hogging our guide?" Shaun asked, coming up beside Jess and Benicio. He slung an arm over her shoulder and winked at Benicio. Benicio couldn't help but grin in reply.

"No, she asks questions," Benicio said. "Good questions. Makes me think."

"That's our Jess," Shaun said. "Always keeping people on their toes."

"¡*Feliz Aniversario*!" he added. "Is first time I have to say to you."

"Thank you," Shaun replied. "Don and I are touched that everyone would come back to celebrate with us again. And, of course, to have new friends to celebrate with too."

"Ten years is worth celebration," Benicio said.

"And we wouldn't have missed it for anything," Jess added. "E-mails and Facebook posts are no replacement for being together."

"You have to come all the way to Peru to be together?" Benicio asked. "Is no closer place?"

"I'm sure there is," Shaun said, "but Peru is special. We celebrated our honeymoon here. We wanted to come back for our anniversary."

"*Sí*, I understand, but between? To no wait ten years?"

"It wouldn't be the same," Shaun said. "I'm sure we'll go to that at some point when we're all too old to hike the trail, but until then, we'll plan our reunions here."

"Even then, we'll still come," Jess said. "We'll just take the train to Machu Picchu instead of hiking the trail. It won't be quite the same, but it'll still be Peru."

Benicio couldn't help but be amazed at the devotion they showed to coming here. Peru was his home and he loved it, but while he'd seen plenty of groups of tourists enjoy their trip, he'd never had one so determined to come back repeatedly.

"Why is so special?" he asked. "For me, is just home, but for you, why here?"

"Don't get them started," Jess said with a laugh. "When he and Don get started, they could write a book on how much they love Peru."

"We probably could," Shaun agreed, "but it boils down to two things: the people and the history. We were welcomed warmly despite all the warnings we got to be discreet while we were here, and we're both fascinated by the Inca Empire as well as by Andean culture as a whole. We actually met at an exhibit of Andean textiles at the Museum of Folk Art in Santa Fe fifteen years ago."

"Where is Santa Fe?" Benicio asked, curious about Shaun and Don's home, as he had been about all the other tourists' places of origin.

"In New Mexico, but we don't live there now. We moved to San Francisco a couple years after we met. It's easier to be gay in a large city than in a small town, but I don't have to tell you that, do I?"

"Shaun," Jess scolded. "Not everyone is gay just because you want them to be."

"I know that, but I'm not wrong either."

"No," Benicio said, "you no are wrong, but Pisac is still small town. Even Cusco no is big city like you mean."

"Cusco has a few places for gays," Shaun said. "I know because we went dancing at one of them. It's not San Francisco, but it's not the middle of nowhere either."

Benicio shrugged. "Only Alberto knows about me. *Por favor*, no tell my mother. She is…."

"Conservative?" Shaun supplied when Benicio's English failed him. "I won't say anything, and I'll tell Don not to say anything either."

"*Gracias*. My life is in Pisac and Cusco now, no in Cancha Cancha. Is no reason to upset my mother."

"So you and Alberto?" Shaun prompted.

Benicio shrugged again. "We work together."

"Shaun!"

"Go away, Jess. This is boy talk."

She rolled her eyes but fell back to hike with the others.

"He knows you're gay. Does he know you're crazy about him?" Shaun pressed.

Benicio's cheeks grew hot. "I no am—"

"Don't tell me you aren't interested in him," Shaun interrupted. "I've seen the way you watch him, and I know he's still single. Why aren't you together?"

"I no am what he wants," Benicio replied. "Why is so important to you?"

"Really? What does he want?" Shaun asked.

Benicio almost demanded an answer to his question that Shaun had completely ignored, but instead he sighed and answered, "No me."

"I think you're wrong," Shaun said, "but I'll give you the benefit of the doubt for the moment. We're going to talk about this again before the week is over, though."

"Why is so important to you?" Benicio repeated. "Is my life."

"Because I consider Alberto a friend," Shaun said, "and I've seen the way he looks at you too. I know what it's like to feel like you can't tell anyone about yourself, and I know what it's like to almost miss the best thing to ever happen to you because of that fear. I don't want to see someone else make the same mistakes."

Benicio still didn't think Shaun was right or that it was his business, but he let it go for now since Shaun seemed content to do the same. They talked about San Francisco for the rest of the hike to Cancha Cancha.

THIRTEEN

CANCHA CANCHA reminded Alberto of the village of Wayllabamba, where some of the hiking groups camped the first night, only without all the stalls where the locals sold items to the tourists. The houses were made with the typical mud-brick construction prevalent in the highlands, and the surrounding land was dry with winter drought, but the villagers were decked out in bright colors and had smiles, albeit bemused ones, on their faces as Benicio led the group into their midst.

The flurry of Quechua that passed between them went straight over Alberto's head, but he heard his name and stepped forward to greet Benicio's older brother and mother. Alberto shook hands with them both and then listened as Benicio's mother fussed at him in Quechua some more. He only caught a few words, but they centered around him not coming home often enough, from what Alberto could understand, rather than around him arriving with thirteen extra people in tow.

"Mama," Benicio finally interrupted in Spanish, "we've talked about this. I can't come home more often than I do because I'm out on the trail so much. Now, my friends have hiked all this way. I'm sure they're tired and thirsty, maybe even hungry. Can we get them settled somewhere?"

"Cheeky boy," Señora Quispe replied in Spanish as well. "How many beds do they need?"

"Six," Benicio said, "plus somewhere for Alberto to sleep."

"A mat is fine with me," Alberto interjected. "I don't need a bed. I don't want to put anyone out."

"Nonsense," Señora Quispe said. "You'll take Benicio's bed. He can sleep on the mat."

Alberto smirked at Benicio. "Should I tell her you wouldn't take the bed at my house and insisted on sleeping on the couch?" he asked softly in English. He saw the confusion on Señora Quispe's face but left it to Benicio to explain if he wanted to.

Benicio glared at him for a moment before asking his mother, "Where should I send everyone else?"

"Two couples with us, one with your brother, one with your aunt. I'll have to find somewhere for the others. For now, they can all come home to sit and have something to drink. Do they like chicha? Your brother made a fresh batch last night."

"Several of them developed quite a taste for it the last time they were here," Alberto said. "I'm sure they'd appreciate a glass. Benicio has told me how good his brother's chicha is."

Señora Quispe preened under the praise. "His father, rest his soul, taught him."

Alberto crossed himself automatically at the reference to Benicio's deceased father. He wasn't the most pious of men, but his mother had driven a respect for the dead into him from an early age.

"Tell them to come along," she said. "I don't suppose they speak Spanish."

"A few of them do, señora," Alberto said. "Holly and Mike speak it the best, although Shaun, Jess, and Ed aren't bad at it either."

"Then I'll put them with other families since they won't have you and Benicio to smooth communication," she decided.

"I don't mind going to another family too, if that would help," Alberto offered. He could honestly do without sleeping in Benicio's bed. The fantasies that would inspire would not be conducive to restful sleep.

"Nonsense," she said. "You're Benicio's guest. You'll stay in Benicio's room."

Alberto gave in, because what else could he do, but he fully intended to remind Benicio of the reverse of this conversation the night Benicio stayed at Alberto's apartment. Alberto would take the mat on the floor, and Benicio could explain to his mother in the morning why he hadn't taken Alberto's bed when it was offered and so why Alberto had taken the mat. Or else they'd keep another couple at her house to have Benicio's bed and both he and Benicio could take mats.

That was probably the best solution. He'd have to find a moment to talk to Benicio and explain the situation. Benicio would know best how to convince his mother to relegate them both to the floor in favor of the real guests.

Benicio had already gathered the group and was leading them toward a house at the end of the village, so Alberto followed along in time to hear everyone exclaiming over the houses and the quality of the cloth the villagers were wearing. Alberto hoped some of the villagers had pieces ready to sell, because this group would pay well for them, and by selling directly, they wouldn't lose anything to a middleman.

The interior of the small house was cool and dark, much like the house Alberto had grown up in, with guinea pigs in a hutch in the corner and some kind of stew simmering on the stove. The tourists were making a fuss over Señora Quispe, thanking her for her hospitality and complimenting her on everything from her house to her son, with Holly and Mike acting as translators, so Alberto drew Benicio aside.

"Convince your mother to keep a third couple here tonight," he said in English. "Unless you want to explain to her why I won't take your bed."

"Why you no take my bed?" Benicio asked, and Alberto could almost have imagined Benicio was flirting with him, except that kind of wishful thinking wouldn't lead anywhere except disappointment.

"Because you didn't take mine when you slept at my apartment," Alberto answered.

Benicio rolled his eyes, but when he stepped away from Alberto, he went to talk to his mother. That was good enough as far as Alberto was concerned.

"Don't watch him quite so intently if you don't want his mother figuring out you have designs on her son."

Alberto startled at the unexpected voice. He turned quickly to see Don standing next to him. "I don't know what you're talking about."

"Of course you do," Don said. "You can pretend you don't, but we both know that isn't the truth."

"This isn't the time or the place to discuss it," Alberto insisted.

"She can't understand us, can she?"

"No, but he can if he hears you," Alberto replied.

"Would that be such a terrible thing? He watches you too, you know, when he thinks you aren't looking. If you haven't caught him yet, it's just poor timing, not lack of interest on his part."

"Of course he watches me," Alberto said. "I'm teaching him how to be a guide."

"That's not why he watches you," Don said. "Trust me. I recognize the look on his face. It's the one I see in the mirror every time I think about Shaun."

"Even if you're right—and I'm not saying you are—but even if you're right, look around you, Don. This is his home, a home he was comfortable enough to bring us to without telling his family first, and they didn't blink an eye when he did it. I can't take that away from him," Alberto said. "Family like that is too important to let go."

"It is," Don agreed, "but you're assuming he'd lose them."

"This isn't America. Couples like you and Shaun aren't accepted here," Alberto said.

"I know that," Don assured him, "but there were gay couples at home long before they were accepted. They were confirmed bachelors who shared living space to save money, or they maintained separate residences for appearances but spent all the time they could together. They were partners of one kind or another so they could spend long hours 'working.' I wouldn't want to live that way if I had the choice, but if it was that or give Shaun up, I'd do it in a heartbeat. You never know. Maybe he would too."

"He'd have to feel the same way."

"Yes, he would," Don said, "but he's not going to bring it up. Look around you. You're seeing his family and his ties to them, but if this is where he grew up, how much experience do you think he really has with being gay? He's not going to say anything if you don't, because he won't even know where to begin."

"Now you're the one underestimating him," Alberto said. "I know about him because he brought the matter up, not the other way around."

"I'm impressed." Alberto shot him a disbelieving look. "No, I am. That took a lot of courage, but it doesn't change my point. How many other gay men do you think he's met? How many chances do you think he's had to see relationships start, even straight ones, in a village this size? He's got the courage, but he doesn't have the frame of reference to know where to start, and the only person he has to ask is the person he's interested in."

Alberto agreed with him up until the last statement. "I wish he were interested in me."

Don sighed. "Then do something about it. Take him out. Make it clear what you're offering—all of what you're offering, not just sex. Let him know it's a possibility and see what happens. Maybe I'm wrong and he isn't interested. So you're a little embarrassed. But I'm not wrong."

"You only met him a few hours ago. How can you be so sure?"

"Because I have eyes," Don said. "If you don't believe me, ask any of the others. They've all seen it too. They just left it to me to say something, gay man to gay man."

"I can't say anything while we're here. That would put Benicio on the spot with his family around, and I can't focus on anything but the trail when we're out there. It could be dangerous if I was distracted. I'll think about it, and I'll look for what you say you see, and when we get back, I'll decide what to do."

"What you do is take the boy home, take him to bed, and never let him go," Don said. "There, problem solved. Is that chicha Benicio's mother is serving? I haven't had chicha since the last time we were here."

Alberto blinked at the sudden change of subject. Before he could decide how to answer, Don had already crossed the room and charmed a glass of chicha out of Benicio's mother. Alberto watched the scene for a moment longer before Julianne called for him to join them. He put on a smile and went to take his own glass of chicha from their hostess.

ALBERTO LOOKED around Señora Yupanqui's chicheria with a satisfied smile. His friends were having a great time. The band Miguel had hired played a mix of folk and dance music that seemed to be universally appreciated, although no one had gotten quite drunk enough to start the dancing yet. Looking at Shaun and Don snuggled up together at one of the tables, Alberto didn't think it would be long, though. Neither was the type to sit still for long, and the music was a temptation they wouldn't ignore forever.

"We did well," Benicio said as he came up to stand next to Alberto. "Shaun and Don were surprised and touched."

"They're that kind of men," Alberto replied. "They take the small gestures to heart."

"All the more reason to make them, because not everyone thinks to."

"Especially not for people like them."

"Like us, you mean?" Benicio said.

Alberto nodded sharply, trying not to think about the former friends who now avoided him because they'd seen him coming out of Cusco's gay club one night. Fortunately not all his friends had reacted that way, but enough had to leave a sour taste in Alberto's mouth.

"Not everyone is like whoever put that scowl on your face," Benicio reminded him. "Even here in Peru. Señora Yupanqui doesn't care."

"We're paying her not to care," Alberto said.

"It goes beyond that and you know it," Benicio snapped. "Why are you in such a bad mood tonight? We're supposed to be celebrating."

"Sorry," Alberto muttered. "It's hot in here and I have a headache. I'm going to step outside for a minute. I don't want to ruin the party for anyone else."

The icy breeze off the mountains burned his skin, a welcome change after the heat of the bar and the scent of the chicha brewing in the back room. The smell didn't usually bother him, but tonight, like everything else, it grated on his nerves. "What is wrong with me tonight?" he muttered. "I've been looking forward to this all week."

However unflattering it was, the answer stared him in the face. He was jealous. Horribly, miserably green with envy at the life Shaun and Don had built together, at the freedom to be themselves and the security to share that with those around them. Even if he got lucky one day and found a man to spend his life with, he wouldn't have that freedom. They'd have to live hidden in plain sight, if not hidden entirely. They'd never have rings on their fingers to show what they meant to each other. They'd never be able to walk down the street holding hands. They could never give any outward sign of their relationship anywhere but a few select safe places.

"Alberto?"

Alberto pushed off from the wall where he had been leaning when he heard Connie calling his name. "I'm here, Connie. I just needed some fresh air. I was getting a headache."

"The party was a wonderful gift for Shaun and Don. They're having a great time."

"I'm glad," Alberto said, and he was. He wanted them to have a good time and enjoy themselves. His own ugly emotions were his problem, not theirs.

"I look at them and see Matt," she said. It took Alberto a minute to make the connection.

"Your son?"

"Yes. He's sixteen. He came out about a year ago. I don't know if you saw me talking about it on Facebook or not."

"Not in any detail," Alberto said. Now that she mentioned it, he had seen passing references to it, but he didn't know the story behind them.

"It's hard being gay in Idaho. It's not like San Francisco. Bobby and I won't ever turn him away, of course, but he hasn't been as lucky with his friends. Some of them have stood by him, but a lot of them turned on him," she said. "It makes Shaun and Don's story all the more powerful, knowing what Matt will face as he continues in school. It gives me hope, though. If they can find their happiness, I have to believe Matt will too."

"Can he find it in Idaho?" Alberto asked.

"That's the thing about happiness," Connie said. "It comes in as many shapes and sizes as people do. When we first moved to Idaho, I expected to hate it, and there are things I still don't like. It's a lot more conservative than I'm comfortable with most of the time, but it's amazing in other ways. The scenery is fantastic. Maybe not quite as impressive as the Andes, but beautiful in its own right. The people are the salt of the earth. They take care of their neighbors. They help out when there's an emergency."

"You just said some of them turned on Matt. How is that taking care of him?" Alberto asked.

"There are bad apples in every bunch," Connie said. "Even in San Francisco, there are people who hate gays. They're just in the minority. And the ones who stood by Matt have been stalwart in their defense of him. Matt loves Idaho despite the reaction of some of his friends. I think he figures he'll change their minds one person at a time until he's carved out a life for himself. Everyone's in an uproar right now, but he just goes about his day like it doesn't matter. He told me they'd forget about it when the next big scandal came along that didn't involve him. His money's on the high school quarterback getting the head cheerleader pregnant before the end of football season. That'll be far worse than him liking boys instead of girls."

"Really?" Alberto asked. "I'd think that was at least 'natural.'"

"Ah, but they're actually fornicating. He's just looking," Connie explained. "There's a difference."

Alberto laughed despite himself. "When you put it that way, I suppose there is. What does Bobby think of all of this?"

"That if Matt is old enough to make the decision to tell his friends, then he's old enough to bear the consequences," Connie said. "We're supporting him in every way we can, but he's not a child anymore. He's picked a hard road to walk, coming out in our small town the way he did. Not to us. We would never judge him, but to the town. If he wants to stay in Idaho and still be who he is, he's going to have to figure out how to walk that road."

"Is that even possible?"

"Not if he wants a life like Shaun and Don have," Connie said. "At least not the way things stand now. He'll have to weigh all the different things he wants and decide what's most important. I can promise you there are gay couples living in Idaho. They're just doing so discreetly, and there's nothing wrong with that. They've made a choice to live where they live for whatever reason, and those choices have shaped what their lives look like. Shaun and Don made different choices, and their lives look a little different. That doesn't mean they're happier. Would you really be happy in Lima, for example?"

Alberto shuddered. "No, I've been there a few times, and it was nice to visit, but I need my mountains."

"Even though you'd have an easier time being gay in Lima?" Connie pressed.

"My life is here," Alberto said.

"Exactly. Matt feels the same way about Idaho, and as long as that's true, he'll find a way to live there because he'd be miserable elsewhere, even if it means compromising on other things," Connie said.

"So you're saying I shouldn't be jealous of Shaun and Don?" Alberto asked.

"No," Connie said. "I'm terribly jealous of them on Matt's behalf. I want him to be able to have their life and still live where he wants to, but I'm realistic enough to know that isn't possible right now. Until it is, I have to let him decide where his priorities lie and help him carve out the best life he can have while staying true to them. Things are changing. I'm holding on to hope that in his lifetime, even if not in mine, he won't have to make those choices anymore, and I believe he'll be part of making that change come to fruition. It's easy to be prejudiced when you don't know anyone who falls in the group you're prejudiced against. It's a lot harder when you know the person."

Alberto nodded slowly, trying to take in everything she'd said and apply it to his own life. He didn't see things changing as quickly in Peru as they were in America, but that didn't mean they couldn't change at all. Change would come more quickly in Lima, but Cusco was home. Alberto could make the best of it or be miserable. He took a deep breath. "We should go back inside. We have friends to celebrate with."

"Yes, we do," Connie said, "and they've come a long way to see you. We don't want to disappoint them."

"Think they'd like to learn to salsa?" Alberto asked. "The music's just right for a little dancing."

"Just don't shock our hostess. The chicha is too good for that."

"No shocking, I promise." He grabbed her hand and tugged her back inside and into the clear area between tables. "Have you ever done this before?"

"Never, but I'm a quick study, and we're among friends. Do your worst."

Alberto shook his head. "No, I'll do my best."

FOURTEEN

"CONNIE SAYS she doesn't know how to salsa," Alberto informed the room. "She can't be an honorary Peruvian if she can't salsa!"

"Does that apply to the rest of us?" Don asked from his seat on Shaun's lap. He must have moved when Alberto was outside talking with Connie, but where before, the sight would have bothered Alberto, now he simply smiled. Yes, he was still jealous, but he wouldn't let it spoil the evening. No one seemed bothered by the display of affection. Even Señora Yupanqui was sending indulgent smiles in their direction.

"*Sí*, come dance," Alberto insisted.

"We already know how to salsa a little," Holly said. "Mike and I took lessons in Miami last year on vacation."

"Good. You can help me teach everyone else."

No one else knew even the basics. "Benicio," he called. "Come help me."

"I don't know any more than they do," Benicio replied in Spanish.

"Come learn, then," Alberto replied in kind. "It's fun."

Benicio hesitated just long enough for Alberto to wonder if he'd refuse, but then he got up and joined the rest of them. Alberto had never taught anyone to dance before, but he figured showing them the steps was a good place to start. "Like this," he said and began the basic salsa step, not bothering yet with the rhythm of the music. Until they could do the steps slowly, they'd never be able to do them at speed.

Everyone grinned and laughed at their own ineptitude as they tried to follow along. Some of them picked it up more quickly than others, but when Alberto sped up to follow the music, it led to laughing protests all down the line. Even Holly and Mike, who were doing better than the others thanks to their lessons, didn't manage entirely.

"Just relax," Alberto told them. "Is not about being perfect. Is about having fun." He grabbed the hand nearest his, not even bothering to see who it was, and spun around. Jess let out a startled exclamation, but Alberto ignored her, guiding her through the steps. It wasn't fancy, but it was fun, and the others all applauded. "See? Like that."

He passed her off to Keith and grabbed Nancy next, repeating the process with each of the women. They could all dance with him leading, but their husbands weren't strong enough dancers to keep it going when he passed them off. "Let's try this," he suggested, lining the women up on one side and the men on the other.

"We're a little uneven here," Don laughed as he stepped to the women's line. "No jokes about fairies or queens, but I'd dance with Shaun anyway."

"I go too," Benicio offered. "Is all dancing."

With the lines even, Alberto began the steps again and did his best not to look pathetically eager to have Benicio as his partner. It was probably a good thing everyone was so caught up in trying to learn the steps, Benicio included, because Alberto was sure his emotions were clear as day on his face. *Madre de Dios*, maybe everyone was right and he needed to just go for it with Benicio. He might get turned down, but he might get lucky and end up with this incredible man in his life.

Deciding to test the waters a little, he grabbed Benicio's hand and spun him like he'd done with the women earlier. Benicio followed his lead with credible grace, and up and down the line, the others imitated them.

Best of all, Benicio didn't pull his hand away and step back to his original distance when they finished the turn. Taking that as a good sign, Alberto kept leading Benicio through basic steps for the other couples to mimic.

As the couples began to gain confidence, the lines broke up and they simply danced. Alberto waited for Benicio to pull away, but he didn't, so Alberto took that as permission to continue. When he no longer had to worry about the others copying him, he relaxed and let his movements fall into sync with the music. Sometimes he would try something too complicated for Benicio to follow, but the music called to his blood, and he let it guide him.

Benicio felt so right in his arms, even when their movements clashed, leading to grins and laughter. The others switched partners as one song followed another, but no one tried to cut in on them. In the back of his mind, Alberto knew he should dance with the others, if only because he and Benicio were supposed to be their hosts, but he couldn't make himself relinquish his hold on Benicio's hand. If someone cut in, he would let them, but he wouldn't let go without prompting.

Best of all, Benicio didn't seem any more inclined to pull away than Alberto. He kept his movements relatively tame since they weren't at the Queen, where anything short of fucking on the dance floor was acceptable, but dancing the salsa without a little contact between the partners' bodies was nearly impossible. Alberto took full advantage to brush up against Benicio at random intervals.

It wasn't the complete mindlessness he sought at the Queen, but when Benicio flashed him a delighted grin, Alberto thought it might be even better. If he could dance like this more often, he might not need the rough-and-tumble grind of the gay bar.

The music finally stopped and Alberto released Benicio reluctantly.

"I'm sorry to be the bearer of bad news," Miguel said from the bar, "but 4:00 a.m. comes early tomorrow. The bus is outside to take you back to the hotel. Benicio and Alberto will meet you in the lobby at four, ready to leave."

Shaun stepped up beside Miguel. "Will you translate for me? I want to make sure our hostess understands me."

"Of course," Miguel said.

"Señora, on behalf of Don and myself, I want to thank you for opening your chicheria to us tonight. Peru already held a special place in our hearts, but you have ensured it will always be on our list of favorite places with your warmth and your hospitality."

Miguel translated Shaun's words. Señora Yupanqui smiled up at him and patted his cheek. "You're good boys," she said in Spanish. "I could see that as soon as you walked in. Enjoy your hike and come see me again before you leave."

"*Gracias*, señora," Shaun said when Miguel had translated her reply. He leaned down and kissed her leathery cheek as everyone applauded. Miguel herded them all toward the door. Alberto hung back and caught Benicio's eye. Benicio let the others pass before walking out with Alberto. When the tourists were all on the bus and it pulled away, Alberto turned to Benicio. He mustered all his courage and lifted his hand to Benicio's cheek.

"Tomorrow we leave for a hike, and we have to focus on that, but when we get back, we need to talk about whatever this is."

"When we get back," Benicio agreed, and if Alberto stored away the breathless sound of his voice to savor in private, that was no one's business but his own.

THEY WERE making their way toward Dead Woman Pass when Don dropped back to walk beside Benicio while Shaun went on ahead. Benicio was surprised; since the first day, they had hiked together the whole time, no matter how slowly or quickly they moved.

"Is all good?" Benicio asked.

"Everything is fine," Don said. "I just wanted a chance to talk to you without anyone overhearing. Some things are easier discussed without an audience."

Benicio wasn't sure he liked the sound of that, but he didn't see a way out of the conversation. "What things?"

"How happy you looked dancing with Alberto the other night," Don said. "You should do that more often."

Benicio would love to dance with Alberto again, but that would depend on Alberto. He swore he could still feel the brush of Alberto's hand on his cheek. He didn't see how it could mean what he wanted it to, and yet he couldn't make it mean anything else. "Is no that easy."

"Of course it is," Don said. "You ask him to go dancing with you. Cusco has a gay club where you could go and not have to worry about anyone saying anything."

"Is no that," Benicio said. "Is…. You see Cancha Cancha. How I do this?"

"You mean a relationship?" Don asked.

Benicio nodded.

"The only difference between a gay relationship and a straight one is the bodies involved," Don said. "You have a relationship with Alberto the same way your parents had a relationship or the way your brother and his wife do. You listen to each other. You talk about problems. You take care of each other. You love each other. Everything else is just mechanics and is easy enough to learn."

Benicio felt a flush rise over his cheeks at the idea of what those mechanics might entail, but he didn't ask Don for details. That wasn't a conversation he wanted to have with anyone other than Alberto, and even having the conversation with Alberto would be beyond embarrassing. Maybe he'd just skip the conversation altogether and go for experiencing them instead.

"And if is no love?"

"Then you go your separate ways and find the man you can love," Don said. "I don't know how it is in your village or even how it is in Peru as a whole, but at home, few people meet the right person the first time out, but they learn from the experience. They learn what works and what doesn't for them. They learn how to treat a partner or how not to, and they learn how they have a right to be treated, and those experiences make them a better partner when the right person comes along. You're a lot older than most people at home are when they start dating, though, so you know yourself a lot better than the average teenager. You know how to treat people already. Just apply that to a lover instead of a friend."

"Is really that easy?" Benicio asked.

"Oh, there's nothing easy about it," Don said with a laugh. "Even when you love someone, you're still human and so are they. They make mistakes, or you do. You argue. You fight. And then you make up and you let it go. That's the hard part, letting it go, but it's also the part that makes it possible to go on. If you hold grudges, you'll end up hating each other as much as you love each other."

Benicio tried to think back to his parents' relationship and apply Don's words to them. He could remember days of tense silence, but they were always followed by the sound of his parents talking late into the night. He preferred not to think about what might have followed those long conversations, but their satisfied smiles the next morning gave him an idea, anyway.

"Only way to know is to try, *sí?*" Benicio said after a moment. "I just ask him to go dance?"

"That's exactly what you do," Don said. "You know he likes to dance. He spent how long teaching us all the other night? So when we get back to Cusco, ask him to take you with him next time he goes. Or better yet, tell him you enjoyed dancing with him and would like to do it again. That way he knows you want to dance with him, not just go to a dance club."

Benicio thought back to the dancing they had done the other night. It had been fun, albeit fraught with a tension he couldn't completely explain away with his own inexperience. He only hoped Alberto wouldn't mind being seen with him when surrounded by dancers who knew what they were doing. His movements weren't exactly polished.

"Whatever you're thinking, stop," Don said. "That's not the expression of a man who's looking forward to a night of dancing with a guy he's attracted to."

"I no dance well," Benicio explained. "What if he no want take me?"

"Benicio, dancing isn't about having all the perfect moves. This isn't *Dancing with the Stars*. Dancing is about the music and your partner and all the ways two bodies can move together outside of the bedroom… or the shower or…. Not the point. Anyway, dancing isn't about what you do, it's about why you do it. Alberto knows that. He didn't let go of you the entire time we were dancing. He's not going to shy away from dancing with you again."

It all sounded too good to be true, but Don's sincerity was obvious. Whether he was right or not, he believed he was right. He wasn't just saying these things to placate Benicio.

"Then I guess I try," Benicio said.

"Good man," Don said. "And I expect regular updates on how things are progressing. You don't have to give me intimate details—unless you want to, of course—but at least let me know that things are working out between you. Alberto has been a friend for a long time, even if I haven't seen him in ten years. You've hiked this trail a few times now. You know what kind of bond it forms."

"Yes," Benicio said. "Is special place."

"It is. Whose idea was it to change the lectures into a story? I thought I'd experienced the trail the first time, but this puts it in a whole new light."

"Is my idea," Benicio said. "My father teach me to tell stories, to value stories."

"He did us all a huge favor. I learned a lot the first time. This time I'm feeling it deep down in my bones."

"You sure is not tired you feel?" Benicio teased. "Bones hurting is no good."

"You know what I mean." Don thumped Benicio's shoulder, bringing an even bigger smile to Benicio's face.

"*Sí*, I know. *Gracias*. Is good to hear from someone who knows both ways. We try with other groups, but they only know one way so no can compare."

"They both have value," Don said. "We got dates and details last time that aren't always repeated in the way you tell the story, but if I had to choose one over the other, I'd choose the emotion. If you want facts and dates, you can read a guidebook, but no book is ever going to bring you the power of the experience the way you do with the story."

"We give dates if tourists ask," Benicio said. "Is no to replace all history, is to make more than history."

"Exactly," Don said. "The Inca Trail is more than a collection of dates or a list of what each building was used for, and that's what your story captures. Shaun commented on it last night as well, so it's not just me. It's good to see a fresh approach, and I know Alberto appreciates it too. He watches you when it's your turn to tell the story. I don't know if you've noticed, but he's as enraptured as the rest of us."

Benicio hadn't noticed. He did his best to block out everything but the story when it was his turn to weave words. He had to concentrate hard enough as it was. Thinking about Alberto watching him would make telling the story in English virtually impossible.

"No, I no notice."

"Look next time," Don suggested.

Benicio nodded, but he already knew he wouldn't. Maybe one time when he could tell the story in Spanish, but as long as he had to worry about his words, he had to think about the story and nothing else.

"Come on," Don said. "The others are getting ahead of us. We should catch up."

Benicio didn't say they were only behind because Don had slowed down. He just picked up the pace until they had caught up with the rest of the group near the top of the pass. He gave them all a few minutes to catch their breath and to take in the scenery, and then he launched into the next portion of their tale.

ALBERTO BROUGHT up the rear of the line as they left camp the third morning. It would be a short hike, and his knees were glad for it. They were bothering him more than usual this trip for some reason. Maybe because it had been colder than usual at the higher altitudes. He'd see how he felt in the morning, when it would be warmer since they'd be back down below three thousand meters. If they were still bothering him, he might have to ask Miguel for a week off. He didn't want to do that if he could help it, though, because it would mean Benicio would go out with a different guide. Alberto had every confidence in Benicio's abilities; he just didn't want to share those talents with anyone else. Not to mention that he'd miss seeing Benicio almost every day while he was gone. He spared a brief thought for the families of the porters, who only saw their loved ones three days for every four they were gone. Yet another reason he wouldn't want to find a partner who couldn't share the trail with him.

"You're thinking awfully hard this morning," Shaun said as he fell into step beside Alberto.

"My knees hurt," Alberto said. "I was thinking about taking a week off, but that wouldn't be fair to Benicio."

"How so?" Shaun asked.

"He can't go on the trail by himself," Alberto explained. "He's still a junior guide, so if I take a week off, he'd have to do the same or go out with someone else."

"I'd think it would be good for him to see how different guides work," Shaun said.

"Maybe," Alberto said, "but I don't want anyone else spoiling my hard work."

"You mean you don't want anyone else trying to steal him from you," Shaun corrected. "Don told me the storytelling was Benicio's idea. I'm glad you listened to him, because it's a great one."

"I've been trying to find a partner who suits me since Miguel retired," Alberto said. "Is it wrong of me to want to keep him now that I've found him?"

"Are we talking about the trail or your life?" Shaun asked.

"I was talking about the trail."

"Uh-huh," Shaun said. "Let's talk about your life, then. You looked good dancing together at the party. Like you fit."

They had fit, Alberto thought. He'd fallen asleep to the memory of their dancing every night since then. Before they could do anything else, though, they had to talk. They fit so well on the trail, but that didn't mean they could fit in the rest of their lives. He had a brief flash of Señora Quispe embracing him before they left Cancha Cancha and telling him to come home with Benicio anytime he needed some home cooking. Alberto wasn't sure how she'd known he didn't have any family left. He didn't think he'd given away how much he longed for the kind of familial warmth he'd felt in her modest home, but maybe Benicio had told her, or maybe she was more perceptive than he thought.

Even if she was willing to welcome him as a guest, that didn't change all the other issues they'd face, both on and off the trail. From Miguel to the porters to Alberto's neighbors, the list of people who might have problems with them being together was as long as his arm. He didn't think Miguel would care as long as it didn't affect their performance on the trail, but if he was wrong, it could cost them their working partnership.

"You don't look convinced."

"It's not that," Alberto said. "It's more a matter of everything being with him would entail. In a perfect world, we could make it work even with the constraints of Andean culture, but this isn't a perfect world. One mistake could cost us our jobs, our homes, his family, or even our lives. Gay bashing happens here too. Not often, but mostly because we all hide too well."

"So you're just going to let the chance pass you by?" Shaun asked. "That doesn't sound like you."

"No, I'm not that stupid. We'll talk when we get back to Cusco and see where things stand. He has to want the same things I do for it to be worth the effort."

"He does," Shaun assured him. "Of all the things on your list of worries, you can cross that one off."

Alberto hoped Shaun was right, because he'd hate to lose Benicio on the trail because he'd misinterpreted his interest off the trail. "Don's going to get to the summit first if you don't walk faster."

That took care of Shaun's interest in Alberto's love life. Alberto grinned. He could always rely on Shaun and Don's competitiveness to get one or the other of them moving.

FIFTEEN

ALBERTO STIFLED a curse as he took off the torn jeans he was wearing. He had another pair with him, but he didn't know if these could be repaired, and they were brand new. It shouldn't have even been a serious situation. Gerald had slipped on the wet stones as they went through the Inca Tunnel, and Alberto had reached out to steady him. They both went down, and Alberto's pants caught on a sharp outcrop of rock, probably the only one in the entire tunnel. It wasn't until the adrenaline had worn off that he realized the sting in his leg went beyond a bruise.

"You should let me help you," Benicio said from outside the tent. "You need to get that clean and bandaged, and it's easier with someone to help."

Alberto groaned. Benicio was right, but that would mean letting Benicio touch his bare skin while he sat there in nothing but his underwear. Not conducive to staying in control and professional while on the trail.

"I need a shower first," he said. "Let me see what it looks like after I'm clean. If it needs more than that, I'll let you know."

"A shower sounds like a good idea," Benicio said. "I'll get my kit and join you. Did you bring soap? You're welcome to use mine if you didn't."

Alberto dropped his head to his knees. This was getting worse by the minute. Wiñay Wayna had two shower stalls in the restroom block, neither bigger than about half a meter square. Anyone who wanted to use them had to dress and undress in the area outside the shower because of the limited space. He could try to delay, but he doubted Benicio would go for it today with him injured. He'd seen enough to know Benicio was a worrier and wouldn't be happy until he'd personally inspected Alberto's leg. At least it was warm enough right now for him to wear shorts after his shower, so he'd have a little protection if he got hard from Benicio's hands on his skin. He'd have to hope the cold water kept him from getting an erection in the shower, because the thin strip of cloth he called a towel wouldn't hide anything.

"Where is it?" Alberto said. "I'll bring it out with me."

"In my pack," Benicio said, "but I need to get a change of clothes too. I'll just come in and get it."

That was exactly what Alberto wanted to avoid, but he could hardly say that. "Give me just a minute, then."

He pulled his shorts out of his own pack and eased them on over his injured leg. Once he was dressed, he unzipped the door to the tent so Benicio could come in. He kept his gaze focused on the wall of the tent and not on Benicio right outside. Falling asleep the last two nights had been a challenge, knowing Benicio was so close but that he couldn't reach out and touch the way he wanted to. He was almost convinced Don and Shaun were right and that Benicio would welcome his interest, but he couldn't act on it while they were on the trail. It wouldn't be professional.

"That looks awful," Benicio said as he ducked into the tent. He started to reach for Alberto's leg, but Alberto pulled away. He wasn't ready for Benicio's hand on his bare skin just yet. Maybe after his shower, when he could be more certain of his self-control. "You may need to see a doctor when we get back to Cusco."

"It's not that bad," Alberto said automatically, but when he looked down at where his calf was still oozing blood, he found it hard to believe his own words. "It's just because I hiked on it all afternoon. Once I get it clean and can stay off my feet for a while, it won't be as bad."

"I'll lead the group to Wiñay Wayna if they want to go," Benicio offered immediately. "You stay here and rest. We have to hike out in the morning, so take it easy this afternoon."

Alberto bristled automatically at the suggestion that he was less than fully capable of doing his job, but he forced the reaction down. Benicio wasn't impugning his abilities; he was acting as Alberto's partner and pulling his own weight. This would hardly be the first time Benicio had taken a group to Wiñay Wayna. The only difference was that when they divvied up duties before this trip, Alberto had taken it and now couldn't follow through.

"Hey," Benicio said, and this time Alberto didn't pull away fast enough when Benicio reached for his leg, "don't be like that."

"Like what?" Alberto asked.

"I can practically see you getting ready to argue with me," Benicio said. "We've swapped duties before for one reason or another. This isn't any different."

Maybe not in Benicio's eyes, but it was the first time Alberto had been unable to carry out something they'd agreed he would do instead of swapping because something in the situation make it more sensible to do so.

"I hate being hurt."

"I don't like seeing you hurt," Benicio said, "but aren't you the one who always tells me that any plan can change depending on the circumstances, and that if it makes sense to switch things up, we should be willing to do so? It doesn't make sense for you to walk over to Wiñay Wayna with your leg cut and bleeding, and don't try to tell me it does. Therefore I will take them over to the ruins, and you will stay here with the ones who don't go and help the porters and if your leg is feeling better, maybe play some bocce ball with the group and with the porters if you can talk them into it, and we will have shared the responsibilities equally and in a way that makes sense in this situation."

Alberto sighed. "I'm going to regret how well you know me one of these days."

"I promise never to use it against you," Benicio said solemnly. "Unless it's for your own good."

And there was the rub, because Benicio's idea of Alberto's good and Alberto's idea of the same would certainly not match up at some point in the future. He wouldn't borrow trouble. The throbbing in his leg reminded him he had enough trouble as it was right now.

"Do you have everything you need for the shower?" Alberto asked to change the subject. "I'm not looking forward to the cold water, but the sooner it's done, the sooner I can sit in the sun and warm up again."

Benicio chuckled. "City boy. The water isn't even all that cold yet. Wait another two months and then see how cold it is."

"No, thank you," Alberto said. "If this happens again, I'll use a basin from the porters."

"Actually, that's a good idea. I'll ask them to boil some water while we're in the shower so we can use that on your leg too, just to make sure it's all the way clean."

Alberto gave up. Benicio was going to have his way regardless of what Alberto said. "Whatever you want. Let's go."

Benicio measured his gait to Alberto's slower limp as they crossed the campsite to the building that housed the restrooms and showers. Fortunately they'd been assigned the campsite closest to it. Usually Alberto would have bemoaned that fact because of the noise of people coming and going at all hours of the night, but this time he was glad of it. Despite his protests, he wasn't sure he could have walked a lot farther than that. He only hoped resting this afternoon helped, because the two-hour hike to Machu Picchu would feel a lot longer if his leg still hurt like this in the morning.

No one was in the shower area when they went in. Alberto figured the porters had already showered if they were going to. Like Benicio, most of them were from the highlands and used to the cold water, plus at the speed they hiked, they worked up quite a sweat even on the coolest days, and a shower was usually the first thing they did when they arrived at the evening campsites. Benicio stripped down to his underwear with no sign of self-consciousness, giving Alberto his first full sight of Benicio's body. He still wore his tight briefs as he stepped into the shower stall and closed the door behind him, but Alberto's traitorous mind had no problem filling in what was hidden beneath the cloth. He groaned and got ready to shower too.

The shower stall was too small to have the water on and avoid the spray, so Alberto braced himself for the cold, got thoroughly wet, and then turned the water off again as quickly as he could. He shivered as the cool air added to the chill from the cold water. He had no idea how Benicio or the porters did this at every stop, and it was warmer today than it had been the previous two nights. For himself, he preferred to wait and shower when he got home unless he had a specific reason to take one on the trail.

As if Alberto's thoughts had summoned him, Benicio started whistling merrily in the stall next to him. Alberto thought no one should be that cheerful while being doused in cold water, because unlike Alberto, Benicio had not turned off the water as he bathed. That image did nothing to settle Alberto's traitorous thoughts. They hadn't even kissed. Alberto should not be imagining Benicio nude in the shower next to him, shouldn't imagine what it would be like to leave his stall and join Benicio in the next one, to press him up against the rough wall and run his hands over Benicio's body. At home, he'd gladly drop to his knees and spend some quality time making Benicio beg. He wouldn't do that on the trail, because he didn't know how clean the floor was and someone might overhear, but he could do other things. He could silence Benicio with a kiss and tease him with his hands until Benicio spilled between them. He could rut against Benicio until he spilled as well. It would be so easy.

"Fuck," he muttered as he turned the cold water back on. He'd need it to walk out of the shower, because his towel would never hide how hard his cock had gotten from his fantasy.

The sound of water in the next stall stopped, and Alberto could hear Benicio humming as he dried off. Alberto waited until he heard the door open and Benicio getting dressed before he turned off his own shower and started drying off. He couldn't do anything about coming out of the shower in a towel, but he could preserve his sanity by not watching Benicio get dressed. After the direction his thoughts had taken during his shower, he wasn't sure he could look at all that bare skin and not touch. He didn't think he would be unwelcome, but they needed to talk first, and that had to wait until they got back to Cusco. The injury on his leg was all the proof he needed of the dangers of being distracted on the trail.

BENICIO WAITED patiently in the shower block for Alberto to finish. He was a little surprised Alberto lingered as long as he did, but maybe he was taking extra care of the gash on his leg. Benicio shuddered at the memory of hearing shouts and turning back to see Alberto and Gerald falling. The trail was often carved out of the cliff face with steep inclines on either side, but this section didn't even have an incline on the low side. The Inca workers had built a foundation several hundred meters up from the valley floor to avoid having another descent and ascent on the other side. There would have been nothing to keep them from the sheer drop if they'd fallen out of the tunnel and over the side of the trail.

By the grace of God or some other miracle, they'd caught themselves while they were still inside the steep tunnel, but it had taken a long time for Benicio's heart rate to return to normal after the surge of adrenaline. He could do without ever feeling like that again.

Gerald had been more shaken up than hurt, fortunately, and Alberto had brushed the fall off like it hadn't been any big deal, but when they had stopped at Intipata for the last story session before making camp, Benicio had seen Alberto favoring his leg. He hadn't asked about it then, but now he realized he should have. The sight of Alberto's leg covered in blood in their tent was one he could have done without. He'd just have to make sure it was cleaned and bandaged so Alberto could make it to Machu Picchu tomorrow. Then he could work on convincing Alberto to ask Miguel for a week off. He suspected that would be a futile effort unless he also said something to Miguel, but he didn't want to go behind Alberto's back that way.

"Alberto, are you all right in there?" Benicio called when Alberto still hadn't come out several minutes after the sounds of running water stopped.

"Yes, just drying off. Why don't you go get the hot water from Arturo and meet me at the tent?"

"I'll get it as we walk back," Benicio replied. "I don't want to leave you to walk by yourself."

"I'm not hurt that badly," Alberto complained. "I can walk back to the tent by myself."

"Okay, okay," Benicio said soothingly. "If you're sure."

"I'm sure."

Benicio wanted to linger, but alienating Alberto was not on his list of things to do, so he walked as slowly as he could justify back toward the cooking tent. Arturo ladled out a basin of hot water as soon as he saw Benicio. Benicio lingered until he saw Alberto come out of the shower block. He was walking slowly, but his limp wasn't as pronounced as it had been earlier. Benicio felt the hard knot of tension and worry in his chest dissolve a little at the sight. They'd see how he felt in the morning, but maybe Alberto was right and it wasn't as serious as it had looked.

"I've got the hot water," he called. "I'll just get the first-aid kit. Would it be easier to do sitting on a stool in the dining tent?"

"Probably," Alberto said. He took a seat at the entrance to the tent while Benicio got the first-aid kit. It wasn't anything fancy, but it had antibiotic ointment and a pressure bandage he could wrap around Alberto's calf to keep the dirt out and provide a little support as he hiked.

He knelt down at Alberto's feet and picked up a towel and the sliver of soap the porters had provided along with the hot water. He focused on Alberto's legs, refusing to look up at his face, suddenly aware of the intimacy of what he was about to do. It needed to be done, and it would be done better if Benicio did it than if Alberto tried to do it for himself, but this was the man Benicio was falling for and who, by some miracle, seemed to return his interest, and he was kneeling at Alberto's feet and touching his bare skin for the first time, and, oh fuck, he was never going to survive this if he looked at Alberto's face.

He kept his hands from shaking by sheer force of will as he lathered the soap and cleaned the cut on Alberto's leg. It was long but not as deep as Benicio had feared, and with the blood washed away, it didn't look nearly as bad as it had when he'd walked into the tent and seen Alberto's leg covered in blood.

Above him, Alberto hissed at the soap on the open wound.

"Who knows what was growing on that rock," Benicio said. "I've got to make sure it's clean before I wrap it up, or it could get infected."

Neither of them needed to say how bad that could be. Alberto's career on the trail required two good legs. If he couldn't hike, he couldn't work.

Alberto's skin felt hot beneath his hands, especially considering he'd just taken a cold shower, but Benicio pushed aside his worry. He had one job to do, and one job only: to clean and bandage Alberto's wound. Alberto could take some paracetamol himself if he had a fever. He reached for the antibiotic ointment and smeared it along the cut. Alberto's skin was smooth beneath his fingers except along the jagged edge of the injury, and Benicio wished he had the right to explore more of it. He'd always been a tactile person, lingering over the feel of his mother's alpaca sweaters and blankets or the roughness of the mud bricks that made up their walls. Alberto's skin was a brand-new playground for him, but he couldn't do anything about it now. They were sitting in the open where anyone walking by could see them, they were on the trail where professional behavior was expected, and most importantly, Alberto hadn't given permission for him to do anything more than bandage his leg.

"I think that's enough ointment for a cut three times that size," Alberto said in a hoarse voice. Benicio made the mistake of looking up at Alberto. He squirmed beneath the intent gaze, hoping he was reading the emotions there correctly. If they'd been at Alberto's apartment, maybe even if they'd been alone in their tent, Benicio would have pushed up from sitting on his knees so he could reach Alberto's mouth. If they'd been somewhere private, he wouldn't have waited anymore. The need on Alberto's face answered the final questions that had lingered in Benicio's mind. All they needed now was the time and space to explore what had been growing between them unspoken all this time.

"I don't want it to get infected," Benicio repeated. "I'll just wrap it up now, shall I?"

Alberto nodded, and Benicio forced his attention back to Alberto's leg. He wrapped the bandage around Alberto's calf until the cut was completely covered in several layers of gauze. "Is that too tight?" he asked, running his fingers along the edge of the bandage to check the tension.

"No," Alberto said. "It's fine, but you need to stop now. You need to get up and take the group to Wiñay Wayna."

"But—"

"Benicio," Alberto interrupted, "I'm hanging by a thread here. Maybe Shaun and Don and the others wouldn't mind if I grabbed you and kissed you and dragged you off to our tent to do wicked things to you, but the porters might, and most importantly, Miguel might. Please, do what I asked you to."

Benicio swallowed hard and stood up shakily. Alberto's words evoked such a vivid longing in him that it took all his self-control to back away when all he wanted was to beg Alberto to do exactly as he'd said. He cleared his throat to speak but decided against it. Nothing he could think of to say would make the situation any better, and most of the things that raced through his head would only enflame it more. They still had to share a tent tonight, still had to finish the hike tomorrow, and take the train back to Cusco. They had to check in with Miguel before they were off for four days. Benicio would gladly spend all four of those days in Alberto's bed if Alberto was willing.

"Tomorrow," Alberto promised as if he could read Benicio's mind. "When we get done with Miguel tomorrow, we'll talk, and then we'll see what else we want to do."

"Tomorrow," Benicio agreed and pivoted on his heel to summon the tourists who wanted to walk over to Wiñay Wayna.

ALBERTO WAITED until Benicio and all twelve of their tourists had left for Wiñay Wayna before standing up. It had taken that long for his erection to go down to tolerable levels. He limped back to the tent and climbed inside. His leg throbbed still but much less than it had before Benicio had cleaned and dressed it. He'd have to say thank you later, if he could get his mouth to say anything but dark whispers of what he wanted to do to Benicio in the privacy of his apartment.

He grabbed his water bottle and gulped down half of it, trying to quell the heat in his blood. Benicio's hands on his skin shouldn't have left him so discombobulated. He was no innocent, and Benicio had just been doing a job, not trying to seduce Alberto. He had done that anyway. He didn't know why Benicio's hands felt different than anyone else's ever had, but they did. The simple brush of Benicio's fingers along the edge of the bandage had left every nerve in Alberto's body singing with delight and need. He told himself Benicio was just checking to make sure the bandage wasn't too tight, but it didn't make a whit of difference. Alberto wanted those fingers all over him, wanted Benicio spread out beneath him so he could explore in return. He needed….

It didn't matter what he needed. They were on the trail. Until they got home, he was stuck with his own hand or another cold shower or willing it away. If he took another shower, he'd ruin the bandage Benicio had put on and would have to go through another session like the one that had gotten him in this state in the first place. If he dealt with it himself, the tent would smell like sex all night, and he'd have to sleep next to Benicio with the scent of his own need in the air. That left ignoring it until it went away. With a groan, he dug through Benicio's pack for the bocce ball set Thomas had left with Benicio that first hike and stepped back out of the tent.

"Anyone want to play?" he asked the porters. Most of them still wouldn't play with the tourists when Benicio pulled it out at the final campsite, but they'd become avid players while the tourists were at Wiñay Wayna. It was as good a distraction as any, even if the game was wrapped up in thoughts of Benicio.

SIXTEEN

BENICIO RESOLUTELY didn't look at Alberto as everyone gathered around Shaun and Don. They had waited at the Sun Gate for all the other groups to pass and then had taken their time walking down to the last overlook before entering the city itself. It was still early enough that none of the tourists coming to Machu Picchu just for the day had started up the trail to the Sun Gate, so they had the space to themselves. Benicio knew what Shaun and Don had planned. They'd discussed it several times over the course of the hike, but now that the moment had arrived, Benicio was itchy with nerves. It would have been easier if he hadn't had to bandage Alberto's leg yesterday. If he could have continued in blissful ignorance of how hot Alberto's skin was and the kind of effect he could have, he might have stood here and simply been happy for Shaun and Don. Now, though, his thoughts were consumed with the tension that stretched between him and Alberto like an invisible chain, binding them together, pulling them inexorably toward each other even when they could do nothing about it.

Shaun took both Don's hands in his, holding them tightly as he looked at the people surrounding him. "Thank you for being here with us," he said. "It meant everything to us to come here on our honeymoon and to be met with such an accepting group of people. To have stayed friends and to have you come back with us now is a gift we could never have anticipated but one we will always treasure. We can't think of anyone we'd rather have witness the renewal of our vows than you."

Benicio found himself holding his breath as Shaun turned back to Don. The smiles on their faces were so peaceful, so loving, so perfect that he knew he would remember them forever.

"Ten years ago, I stood before a justice of the peace in San Francisco and bound my life to yours," Don said reverently. "Ten years ago, I promised to love, honor, and cherish you all the days of my life. Today I stand before our friends to renew those promises. Shaun Taylor-Perkins, I take you to be my husband, to have and to hold, for richer or for poorer, in sickness and in health, for as long as we both shall live."

Benicio swallowed around the tightness in his throat as his emotions rose to the surface at the traditional vows. A sense of rightness pervaded the overlook. No matter what anyone said about right and wrong, natural and unnatural, Shaun and Don belonged together. He defied anyone to witness this moment and doubt that.

"I grew up on fairy tales," Shaun said when he could find his voice. "My mother loved them and read them to us every night before bed. I grew up believing in true love and happily ever after. Like the princesses in the tales, I knew one day my prince would come. I just had to be patient until I found him or he found me. I never dreamed I'd meet him in a museum, but I recognized you the moment I saw you. Ten years ago I married the prince in my very own fairy tale and have lived my happily ever after since. Don Taylor-Perkins, I take you to be my husband, to have and to hold, for richer or for poorer, in sickness and in health, for as long as we both shall live."

They leaned into each other, foreheads resting together for a moment of communion before they tilted their heads for a kiss. Benicio had to look away, so unbearably intimate was the kiss, tender and full of devotion bordering on reverence. As he turned his attention to the other people in the group, he saw tears on the lashes and cheeks of all of the women, and more than one of the men wiped his eyes surreptitiously. Benicio took some comfort in not being the only one moved to his core by the scene they had just witnessed. Then he met Alberto's gaze, and the longing he saw there nearly sent him to his knees. This… this moment of perfect communion… they might never have the legal bonds between them that bound Shaun and Don, but Benicio longed for the emotions that surrounded them. He cleared his throat and looked away. They needed to talk, but that wouldn't happen for another untold number of hours. They had a visit to Machu Picchu to conduct first. He only hoped he could remember how to speak English.

BENICIO HAD said good-bye to a number of tour groups since he'd started hiking the trail with Alberto. He had been sorry to see some go and beyond ready to get rid of others, but none of the good-byes had been like this one. The others had been acquaintances of four days, no matter how intense the bonds had felt at the time. With this group, though, it went beyond that. They had been guests in his home. They had opened his eyes to everything he could possibly have with Alberto. They had truly become friends.

"We won't wait another ten years before coming back," Jess promised as she hugged Benicio in the canteen area outside the gates of Machu Picchu. "Whatever it takes, we'll make it happen. I promise."

He even believed her.

"Keep in touch," Ed said as he clapped Benicio on the shoulder. "Make Alberto let you use his computer if you don't have one of your own. He manages to keep in touch. You can too."

"I will," Benicio said.

Then Don and Shaun squeezed in on either side of him. "You will talk to Alberto, right?" Shaun said.

"As soon as we get back to Cusco and have a few minutes," Benicio replied.

"And you'll tell us how it works out," Don added.

"But no details," Benicio said. "Is private."

"Just tell us if it works out," Don said. "That's all that matters."

"Yes, I let you know," Benicio said.

They hugged him again tightly, and then it was time to go or they'd miss their train back to Ollantaytambo. Benicio looked back as they started down the steps to Aguas Calientes—the line for the bus was too long to wait now—and found everyone still gathered, ready to wave one last time. He hadn't expected it to be this hard to say good-bye.

"Does it get easier?" Benicio asked.

"Only because I know they'll be back again," Alberto said. "Not next week or maybe even next year, but we'll see them again."

Benicio wasn't sure it was much consolation, but it was better than nothing.

ANTICIPATION TINGLED along Benicio's skin as he walked with Alberto toward Alberto's apartment. The debriefing with Miguel had been quite short, a relief after the mercilessly long train and bus ride from Aguas Calientes. Words crowded on Benicio's tongue, but the street was not the place for the conversation they needed to have.

They climbed the steps to Alberto's apartment, and Benicio tapped his fingers nervously on his thigh as he waited for Alberto to unlock the door. The moment they were inside, Benicio opened his mouth to speak, but Alberto beat him to it.

"Wait," he said, crowding into Benicio's personal space. "Just… wait."

Benicio froze, not sure what to make of Alberto's words, but before his usual self-doubt could return, Alberto cradled his cheeks in hot, roughened hands and leaned in to kiss Benicio. Benicio sagged into the embrace, every nerve in his brain short-circuiting at the delicious contact. He was sure his knees would have given out if that hadn't meant losing the touch of Alberto's lips against his own.

When Alberto lifted his head—seconds or hours later, Benicio didn't know—Benicio murmured in protest, trying to recapture the kiss. Alberto rested their foreheads together, so close to the way Shaun and Don had stood that morning that Benicio's heart clenched in his chest.

"When we left the chicheria before the hike and I said we would talk, I was going to talk you into bed," Alberto said hoarsely.

That sounded perfect as far as Benicio was concerned. Tension had been simmering between them for weeks and had reached the boiling point the day before. He ached with a desire he couldn't formulate and didn't really know how to fulfill, but he knew the solution lay in Alberto's arms. He just had to convince Alberto to show him.

"I think bed sounds perfect," Benicio said as he pulled Alberto in for another kiss.

Where the first kiss had been all tender promise, this one was raw need, and Benicio felt his own desire rising to meet it. He opened his mouth beneath Alberto's onslaught and offered everything he had.

Alberto tasted of coca leaves, though Benicio hadn't seen him chewing any that morning. The flavor made the moment that much more real. In all his fevered imaginings, Benicio had never thought to ascribe a taste to Alberto's kisses.

Alberto's hands mapped Benicio's skull and then down his back, steadying him as he moved them toward the couch. Benicio followed Alberto's lead eagerly. As desperate as he was, he'd take the wall or the floor if it meant finally getting to touch Alberto and be touched in return. The couch was an added bonus. They had nearly reached it when Alberto broke the kiss. Benicio started to protest, but Alberto grabbed his hand and led him toward the bamboo screen that separated his bed from the rest of the apartment—the one place Benicio had never seen. He tugged off his sweater as they rounded the screen. Alberto's bed was as simple as the rest of the apartment, a brightly colored handwoven bedspread the only thing to make it feel like a home instead of a hotel, but Benicio understood the import of the gesture, nonetheless. This wasn't some casual fuck on the couch or against the wall. Alberto had brought Benicio to his bed. Whatever this was, casual didn't apply.

Benicio reached for the hem of his T-shirt, but Alberto beat him to it, stripping it over Benicio's head and tossing it in the general direction of his sweater. Benicio stepped back into Alberto's embrace and renewed their kiss. He didn't really know what came next, but he figured kissing showed his willingness for Alberto to proceed.

"I don't"—Alberto murmured between kisses—"bring"—kiss— "men"—kiss—"in here."

The words confirmed Benicio's guess and only fired his blood more. He grabbed Alberto's head and ended their conversation with his tongue. Alberto groaned into the kiss and nudged Benicio toward the bed.

Benicio went willingly, only breaking the kiss when the backs of his knees bumped the edge of the mattress. Alberto stared at him for one fraught moment and then ripped his own sweater and shirt over his head. Benicio reached for him and fell backward onto the bed, pulling Alberto down on top of him.

"Sweet Mother of God," he breathed reverently when he felt the weight of Alberto's body along the length of his own. They were of a height, but pinned beneath Alberto, Benicio felt surrounded, like the world had shrunk to the confines of Alberto's bed and the contact of skin against skin.

"Is that good?" Alberto's chuckle at the mild invective resonated through Benicio's chest as well, sending another shiver of need through him.

"Yes!" Benicio grabbed Alberto's hips as if he might move away. Alberto chuckled again and rutted down against Benicio. "Oh fuck!"

Alberto attacked Benicio's bare skin with teeth and lips. Benicio was sure he'd be covered in marks, but that only made him want it more. Maybe no one would see them but him—he wasn't in the habit of walking around shirtless, and Alberto's teeth were currently attached to his collarbone—but Benicio would know they were there, tangible proof that this had happened, that he had spent an afternoon in Alberto's bed, the sole object of his attention and affection. He didn't know what would happen when they came down from this high and had to face reality again, but nothing would ever be able to take this perfect moment from him.

When Alberto shifted to Benicio's other shoulder, the change in weight pressed their hips even more tightly together. Benicio threw his head back with a wordless moan and rocked into the contact. He needed more, needed now, harder and faster and just fuck him already. He dug his fingers into Alberto's back, silently begging for everything he could get. Alberto must have understood the wordless plea because he rutted harder against Benicio's groin, dragging their cocks together through the layers of fabric that separated them. Benicio wanted the cloth out of the way, but that would have meant stopping and pulling apart to remove them, and he couldn't, even sure as he was that doing so would make the experience that much better.

It couldn't get any better. His head felt like it was going to explode as it was, all the sensation and emotion pushing against his skull and his skin, a torrent of need and want roiling around in his body, determined to break out of the banks and flood the bed, the room, the world. It couldn't be contained, not with Alberto continuing the rough frottage and kissing him like he would devour him whole.

"I need…." Benicio couldn't put words to what he was feeling beyond that.

"I know," Alberto said. "Me too."

Then give it to me, Benicio wanted to shout, but Alberto kissed him again, taking possession of his mouth and his senses in one fell swoop. The driving pressure against his erection increased until he lost all track of everything except the points of contact between them. The feelings bubbled and frothed inside him until they consumed him. With a wordless shout, he arched off the bed as his vision whited out with ecstasy.

He slumped back onto the bed, breathless, as Alberto rutted against him a few more times before stiffening and letting out a harsh groan. He collapsed on top of Benicio, panting harshly. The gust of breath over Benicio's sweaty skin sent another shiver through him, almost painful on his overstimulated nerves.

Alberto nuzzled Benicio's neck and buried his face in the pile of Benicio's hair where it had come loose from its usual neat queue. "I love your hair."

"My mother hates it. It was my one rebellion growing up. I used to worry she'd come in my room one night and cut it while I was asleep."

"Are you going to tell your family?" Alberto lifted his head and propped himself on his elbows so they could look at each other.

"I don't know," Benicio replied honestly. "I guess it depends on what there is to tell them. I mean, if this is just messing around—"

"It's not," Alberto interrupted. "You know it's not."

"I hoped," Benicio said, "but you hadn't said, and I certainly don't know what I'm doing, so how would I know the difference?"

"I'm not going to lie and pretend I haven't been with other men, but I was telling the truth when I said I've never brought them in here," Alberto said. "We went to their place or we used the couch or wherever, but not in here. You're the only one I've ever had in *my* bed."

That reassured Benicio to a certain extent, but his remaining doubts must have shown on his face, because Alberto leaned down and kissed him tenderly.

"I told you I'd planned to talk you into bed, but I didn't get to finish what I was going to say. We got a little sidetracked. I was going to tell you that being casual lovers isn't going to be enough now. I want what Shaun and Don have. I know it's too soon to talk about happily ever after the way they did this morning, but that's what I want to work toward. If you're willing to give it a go, that is."

The raw sincerity in Alberto's voice did what all the fevered groping had not. It soothed Benicio's deep-seated fears. "I'm willing." His voice broke on the words, but he couldn't be bothered to care. He'd mostly believed it would happen after the fraught moment yesterday and the simmering tension between them in the tent and during Shaun and Don's renewal of vows this morning, but to hear the words still left him humbled with gratitude. "I don't know how it will work, but I want to try."

Alberto kissed him again, so tenderly this time it made Benicio want to shout with happiness. He ran his fingers through Alberto's short hair and basked in the rightness of the moment.

"So how will this work?" Benicio asked when Alberto finally released his mouth again.

"However we want it to," Alberto said. "We can define our relationship any way we want, because we don't have to live up to anyone's ideals but our own."

"Aren't those the hardest ones to live up to?" Benicio asked. "No one else will ever be as harsh as I am on myself."

"It's not that," Alberto said. "It's that we don't have to conform to anyone else's ideas of what our relationship should look like, because we're the only ones with opinions on the matter. Straight couples have societal expectations to live up to. We don't."

"Except the expectation that we're straight and just haven't met the right girl yet."

"That's your village talking. I know lots of single straight guys who are perfectly happy that way," Alberto said, "but if they do meet a girl someday, there are expectations. We're never going to even start down that path, so we can set our own expectations and goals. That's all I'm saying."

Benicio wasn't sure he saw the distinction, but he let it go. They had more important things to worry about.

"We're both going to be really uncomfortable really quickly if we stay like this," Alberto said. "Take a quick shower. I'll clean up too, and then we can talk. And maybe you'll let me make love to you properly next time."

"I'm pretty sure you can't take me apart any more than you already did," Benicio said.

Alberto grinned, the expression so full of hunger that Benicio felt his spent cock stir in his pants.

"That's a challenge I'll look forward to meeting." Alberto pushed to his feet. "After we clean up and talk."

Benicio pouted, but his heart wasn't in it. Already his clothes were sticking to him, and the cooling mess was decidedly uncomfortable. He'd take Alberto up on the offer of a shower, and then they'd see.

ALBERTO PACED the living room of his apartment, waiting for Benicio to come out of the bathroom. He'd wiped himself clean with a towel and water from the kitchen sink and changed into clean clothes, and Benicio still hadn't come out. He'd started for the door more times than he could count, just to make sure Benicio was all right. He'd let his cock do the thinking for him earlier and had jumped Benicio practically the minute they walked in the door. He wouldn't be surprised if Benicio was hiding in the shower to avoid telling Alberto to go to hell.

He forced his mind away from that train of thought. Benicio had kissed him back, had urged him on, had been a full and willing participant in their crazed rutting. He'd said he wanted Alberto, not just for that moment, but in his life. All they had to do was negotiate the details. So why did he feel like everything was about to go sideways?

"Whatever you're thinking to have that scowl on your face, please don't tell me about it," Benicio said from the bathroom doorway. "I'm feeling too good to have it spoiled right now."

"As long as you still want to be here with me, it's nothing important," Alberto said immediately. Benicio still wore the same clothes he'd had on earlier, but his hair was wet and leaving dark marks on his T-shirt, and he had a beautiful smile on his face. Alberto thought he'd never seen anything more delectable. He could imagine a few things that would be—Benicio naked in his bed wearing that same glorious smile, to name just one—but he hadn't seen them yet.

"I still want to be here." Benicio crossed the room to Alberto's side. "You're not having second thoughts, are you?"

"More like worried you were having them," Alberto admitted. "I'm standing here on the verge of having everything I never knew I wanted, and a part of me is afraid it's too good to be true."

"Maybe it is," Benicio said. "Maybe we're on the fast track to disappointment, but it doesn't feel like that. It feels like we're on the cusp of something amazing. We just have to make it real."

"When did our roles get reversed?" Alberto asked with a small smile. "A few minutes ago, I was reassuring you."

"You said you wanted to try," Benicio replied with a shrug. "I was so afraid this was just a passing thing, and you said it wasn't. As long as it's not, everything else can be worked out. Isn't that what you told me? That we get to define the path we take from here?"

Alberto thought briefly of Benicio's mother, of the perplexed, not quite disapproving look she'd given Shaun and Don. He thought of the profound devotion implicit in Benicio's invitation to the village in the first place, and the way his family rallied around him to provide a warm welcome to their guests. He remembered the way Señora Quispe had patted his cheek and told him to come back with Benicio any time, that any friend of her son was welcome in her house. Did Benicio realize he could lose all that?

"We'll never be able to be open about it like Shaun and Don are," he blurted out.

"I live here too," Benicio said with an indulgent smile. "I knew that already." He sat on the couch and patted the cushion beside him. "Who can we tell and what do we tell everyone else?"

"Miguel knows about me," Alberto said. "He found out when Shaun and Don were here the first time. When we were all talking about our families, Ed asked if I was married or had a girlfriend, and when I said no, Don asked if I had a boyfriend. I was flustered already simply because we had a gay couple on the trail with us, and then he said that. I had no idea how to react, and that clinched it for them. I don't know how he'd feel about us working together if he knows we're sleeping together, but you don't have to worry he'll fire you because you're gay."

"That's a start," Benicio said, "but I don't want to stop working with you. I'll agree to whatever terms he wants on the trail in order to stay as your partner. What we do together between treks isn't his business as long as we're professional on the trail."

"The simplest solution is to not tell him unless we have to," Alberto said. "But you're right about the trail. The job has to come first out there."

"It will," Benicio promised. "We'll be too tired, and the tent walls are hardly soundproof. I don't want to share even the sounds of our lovemaking with anyone else."

"Not like that one couple, right?" Alberto said, a grin spreading on his face at the memory of a couple on the trip before this one who'd had sex—very loud sex—all three nights on the trail, to the great amusement of the porters. Alberto had grinned right along with them, but he wouldn't be providing fodder for them if he could help it.

"No, definitely not. A kiss before bed or when we wake up would be okay, though, as long as no one sees us, right?"

"I'd be upset if I didn't get a kiss at night before bed," Alberto replied. "Now that I know what you taste like, it'll be hard not to sneak in a kiss anytime we stop."

"Are you sure that's a good idea?"

It probably wasn't, but Alberto bristled a little at the idea of going without. "I guess it would depend on the group, both tourists and porters," he replied. "If we knew they wouldn't care, I wouldn't mind them knowing, but I've kept it secret for so long that I don't even know how I'd start telling people."

"So what do we tell people?" Benicio asked. "I mean, someone's bound to ask at some point."

"Maybe, maybe not," Alberto said. "Nobody's asked so far. They know we're friends, they know we work together so we spend a lot of time together getting ready for hikes or going over the previous one. We'll still do those things, we'll still play football with the guys when we're in town on the weekend, we'll still have lunch at Señora Vargas's café or go to see Señora Yupanqui for chicha. Nobody will blink at that as long as we don't suddenly start holding hands or kissing where they can see us. And if we decide to go to the Queen some night to dance, nobody there will care because they're all gay too. If anything, they'll be jealous that we're together instead of still looking for someone, like most of them are."

"So we just let people draw their own conclusions?"

"We *are* friends and we *are* colleagues, so it's not like we'd be lying about that part," Alberto said. "All we'd be doing is not telling them the rest of it. It's like what you said about Miguel. It's not their business."

Alberto didn't address what they might have to say if someday Benicio decided to move in with him or how they'd deal with problems that arose if ever one of them needed to speak for the other. They weren't at that point yet, and there was no use borrowing trouble.

It took Benicio so long to answer that Alberto worried he'd said something wrong. Finally, though, Benicio nodded. "I guess it really is that simple."

"We could always go to Lima for a few days if we get tired of hiding in plain sight here," Alberto offered. "Nobody knows us there, so even if people disapproved, it wouldn't matter, and I've heard there are a lot more clubs and places where we could go out together without worrying about people's reactions."

"No, it's fine," Benicio said. "It's not like I'm used to going out places anyway. You saw the village where I grew up. There wasn't anywhere to go, and you grew up in Urubamba, so you know it's no better."

That put things back in perspective for Alberto. Sure, they would have limitations on what they could do when others were around, but they were still better off than countless others because they had each other for when others weren't around. Unlike so many of the other gay men Alberto knew, they had found someone they wanted to be with beyond a random hookup at a club. They might not be able to tell many other people that, but nothing could take away the fact that they had each other now, and that was exactly the same thing they had celebrated with Shaun and Don that morning, only less overt.

"You're right, it is fine," Alberto said. "It's more than fine. It's perfect. We're perfect. We're together. Everything else is secondary." He scooted closer to Benicio and put his arm around Benicio's shoulders.

Benicio leaned against him immediately, making Alberto realize how much Benicio needed the reassurance the contact brought. He couldn't fix a lot of things, but he could fix that. "I think I promised to make love to you properly. Let me show you how perfect we can be together?"

SEVENTEEN

"I THOUGHT we had already decided it couldn't be any better than the first time," Benicio said.

Alberto heard the bravado in his voice and the nerves it tried to hide.

"Only what you want," he promised. "We don't have to do anything you don't want. We don't have to do anything at all if you don't want."

"No, it's not that. It's just…."

"You've never done this before," Alberto finished for him. "I know. It's nothing to be embarrassed about. Everyone has a first time."

"Not usually at my age," Benicio muttered.

"You know what that says to me?" Alberto asked. Benicio shook his head. "It says you were honest enough with yourself not to pretend something you didn't feel in an attempt to deny who you are. There's a strength in that I admire."

"Or I grew up in a village where sleeping with a girl meant marrying her," Benicio muttered.

"You resisted that too," Alberto said. "I know highland mothers, even if mine died before I grew up. If yours hasn't suggested at least three or four girls to you, something's wrong."

"No, she did, but my father was ill, my older brother already married, and my younger brother still in school. It gave me an excuse she would accept, because she couldn't have taken care of him by herself, especially toward the end."

"But you found an excuse—you resisted the pressure to conform," Alberto said. "The fact that you haven't been with anyone else isn't something to be ashamed of." He didn't say what an incredible turn-on it was to him. He didn't think Benicio would appreciate it.

"If you say so."

"I do," Alberto insisted. He leaned over and nuzzled Benicio's neck. "Let me take you to bed. Let me make you feel good. Let me make you scream."

Benicio's breath hitched at that. Alberto smiled against his skin. "Please?" He nibbled at Benicio's earlobe, eliciting another unsteady breath. When Benicio tilted his head to give Alberto better access, he knew he'd succeeded. Even then, he didn't press. Benicio had given him a gift, and he had no intention of squandering it. Not even if Benicio wanted him to. He wouldn't rush this time. He'd savor every step and make sure Benicio did the same. If it meant Alberto would get to hear more of the delicious begging sounds Benicio made, that was a bonus. The important thing was making sure Benicio enjoyed everything they did, whether they stopped at kissing or went all the way. The fast, furious round before had taken the edge off for Alberto, and that, combined with the conversation, had eased the tension plaguing him these past weeks. He could be patient now because he had what really mattered. Benicio trusted him, and that was far more important than what they did in bed together tonight or this week or ever.

"Yes," Benicio said finally. "Just…."

"Nothing you don't want," Alberto promised. "All you have to say is stop." He'd rather lose a hand than violate Benicio's trust in any way, but this one most of all. He stood and offered his hand to Benicio. "Come to bed with me."

Benicio stared at him for a moment, just long enough for Alberto to wonder if he should have stayed on the couch, but Benicio must have found comfort in whatever expression graced Alberto's face because he nodded finally and took Alberto's hand.

Alberto pulled Benicio to his feet and into his arms. He kept the kiss gentle—they'd rushed enough the first time around—and did his best to pour all his emotions into the touch of lips to lips. Benicio sighed into the kiss, and Alberto drank down the gentle puff of air. He wanted to capture every sigh, every whimper, every moan, and later, if he got his wish and made Benicio come apart beneath him again, he'd capture every sob and scream. He'd make tonight as perfect for Benicio as he could. For himself, it was already perfect because Benicio was here with him, wanting the same things he did.

He ran his fingers through Benicio's long hair, marveling at how soft it was. Even still wet, the strands caressed the back of his hand and wrapped around his fingers like they wouldn't ever let him go. Alberto could live with that if it meant having Benicio close always. He ran his other hand down Benicio's back to his waist. He wanted to go farther, but he didn't want to rush. Instead he tugged lightly at the hem of Benicio's shirt. "Can this come off?"

"You've already seen me in less," Benicio replied.

"But you took it off last time," Alberto reminded him. "I don't want to presume."

"Please presume," Benicio said. "If you don't, how am I supposed to know what to do?"

"I don't want to make you uncomfortable," Alberto said. "I know this is all new to you."

Benicio grinned at him, the expression indulgent and yet somehow wicked. "Are you worried or aroused by that fact? Because let me tell you, I'm far more turned on by the thought of finally getting to touch you than I am worried you'll do something I won't like. So if that's what's holding you back, you can stop worrying."

"It's not that." It was exactly that. "You only get one first time. I want it to be special."

"It will be," Benicio said. "It will be special because I'm with a man I trust and admire and desire. The rest is just details."

"Details matter. Isn't that what you're always telling me about our stories?" Alberto said. He didn't even know why he was arguing when Benicio was giving him free rein, but this was important.

"Do you really think you're going to do something I won't like?"

"I hope not."

"Then stop worrying and trust me to tell you if I don't like something. I want your hands and mouth on me again, maybe even in me if that's where things go, although I probably won't last that long."

Alberto wouldn't either if Benicio kept talking like that. To save what sanity he had left, he caught Benicio's mouth with his once more, stopping the flow of words with his tongue. Benicio opened so beautifully into the kiss that Alberto deepened it, running his tongue over Benicio's teeth and then into his mouth to lay claim to it.

Benicio gripped his arms tightly, digging his fingers into the muscles, but when Alberto would have pulled back to check on him, Benicio followed him, keeping the kiss going and even chasing Alberto's tongue back into his mouth. Alberto gave up trying to think for Benicio and focused on trying to make him feel as good as possible instead. He urged Benicio toward the bed and had to hide his amusement at Benicio's enthusiasm as he turned and practically pulled Alberto behind the screen. He'd never manage to hide his erection, so he didn't try. He wanted Benicio to know how much this turned him on.

He caught Benicio's hands when he would have started stripping again. He certainly wanted Benicio naked if he could arrange it, but he wanted to be the one to do it. Benicio gave a wordless whine at the delay, but Alberto ignored him in favor of pressing against Benicio's back and holding him tight. He rocked against Benicio's ass and was rewarded with another needy rasp. He nipped at Benicio's earlobe and slid his hand beneath the edge of Benicio's shirt to find smooth, warm skin. "We'll get there," he promised, "but we don't have to rush."

Benicio looked like he was about to protest, so Alberto smoothed his hand farther beneath the shirt and up over the muscles of Benicio's stomach. He wasn't bulky like some of the tourists were, buffed to the point of ridiculousness, but he didn't have an ounce of fat on him. Alberto took his time with his exploration, feeling the heat rise between them. Benicio smelled of soap and spring water and just a hint of musk. Alberto could imagine him growing hard beneath his shorts, his cock leaking just a little at the tip to give off that fragrance. The thought made him groan and rock against Benicio again. Benicio moaned and pushed back, rubbing his pert ass against Alberto's cock. Fuck, he hoped that meant Benicio would be willing to bottom for him at some point. Alberto could already imagine how good it would feel to sink into that tight heat. He'd be the first one inside Benicio, and if he was lucky and played his cards right, the only one to ever know just how good Benicio felt when he came on a hard cock. Need swamped him, and he had to grab Benicio's hips to stop them from ruining the moment. He hadn't realized he had a virgin fetish. Or maybe it was just Benicio who made him feel this way, because the thought of making love with anyone else didn't have anywhere near the appeal as the thought of Benicio did.

"You stopped," Benicio protested.

"You've already made me come in my pants once tonight," Alberto said. "I was hoping to actually get us undressed before I came again."

Benicio turned in Alberto's embrace. "What are you waiting for, then? I'm all yours, remember?"

He remembered. Oh, how he remembered! That was part of the problem. He wanted this too much, but he'd just have to keep himself under control. Deciding not to delay at least this much any longer, he pulled Benicio's shirt over his head and paused to lick the bite marks along his collarbone.

"Yes, you marked me," Benicio teased. "Mark me some more so I can't help but remember tonight when I'm back in my apartment alone."

It was on the tip of Alberto's tongue to tell Benicio to stay, to get his things and move in here, but they hadn't talked about that yet. They hadn't even managed a real date yet, despite what they were about to do. Instead he unfastened Benicio's shorts and pushed them off before taking a moment to savor his first glimpse of Benicio naked. It didn't matter that he'd seen Benicio in his underwear going into the shower. This time Benicio was completely bare for Alberto's delectation. He didn't know how long he stared before Benicio shifted uncomfortably.

"Do I get to see you too?"

Alberto had never stripped so fast in his life.

Benicio stretched out a hand, stopping just shy of touching Alberto's erection.

"You can touch if you want," he said hoarsely.

Benicio's hand was hot on his cock as he closed his fingers around Alberto's length. It was a firmer touch than he'd expected, given Benicio's initial hesitation, and the lash of sensation caught him unprepared. He dropped his head to Benicio's shoulder with a long, low groan of delight. The stroke up his shaft and back down was awkward, but finesse would come with familiarity.

"Bed." Alberto followed his own order and moved to the bed to pull the blanket his mother had made him out of the way. They'd snuggle together beneath it when they were done, but Alberto didn't want anything impeding his sight or touch right now. He settled onto the mattress and patted the space beside him. Benicio stretched out next to him eagerly and reached for Alberto again. Alberto didn't know how long his control would last, but he lay back to let Benicio play while he still could.

Benicio stared at him with such a hot, needy expression that Alberto almost moved things along just to satisfy him, but rushing wouldn't do either of them any favors. Then Benicio began exploring, running the tips of his fingers over Alberto's skin. It was so light as to be almost ticklish. Alberto's skin tingled as goose bumps rose wherever Benicio touched. To his surprise, Benicio didn't go straight for the obvious erogenous zones, choosing instead to trail his fingers over as much of Alberto's skin as he could reach.

"Are you sure you've never done this before?"

"Would I matter if I had?"

"No, but you aren't touching me like someone who doesn't know what they're doing," Alberto said.

"You don't grow up in a village as small as mine without figuring out how sex works," Benicio said. "We raised llamas and alpacas. We learned how that worked at an early age. When we were a little older, my cousins decided we needed to know how it worked with people too. My oldest cousin had a girlfriend in Calca and could sleep with her without ending up married right away. He took great pleasure in describing their encounters in intimate detail. I was more interested in what she did to him than the other way around, but it served its purpose. I might not have any hands-on experience, but I've had years to fantasize about what I'd do with a lover if I ever had one."

"One of these days you'll have to tell me your favorite fantasy," Alberto said. "We'll see if we can make it come true."

Benicio flushed enough for it to show even against his coppery skin. "We already have."

Alberto raised an eyebrow. "Which part? The rubbing off against each other or being here like this now?"

"Neither, or maybe both," Benicio said. "My favorite fantasy was always just having a lover to call my own. My cousins got married and then my older brother did, and it was just me and my younger brother, but he was away at school. I used the need to help my mother take care of my father during his illness as the excuse not to marry, but I always expected to give in someday and end up tied to some poor girl I couldn't love and probably couldn't even have sex with. My dream was always just this: to be with a man because I wanted to instead of married to a woman because I had to."

"You amaze me," Alberto said, humbled by Benicio's reply. "I keep thinking I know what to expect from you and you keep surprising me."

"I'm sorry."

"Don't be," Alberto said as he leaned over to kiss Benicio. "It means I'll never be bored. I expected no answer or something sexual. I was trying to tease you, get you worked up with the thought of lying in bed dreaming. Instead I get this beautiful, heartfelt answer. It's a good reminder of how lucky I am to be here with you."

"There was plenty of sex in the fantasies," Benicio admitted, "but that was a side benefit of the relationship. The fantasy always started with a relationship. I'd imagine him coming home at the end of the day, asking about my day, kissing me and holding my hand as we talked before he took me to bed and made love to me. It was never one without the other."

"We debriefed with Miguel this afternoon. Does that count as asking about your day?" Alberto wanted to get to the making love part of the program, but he'd wait and talk for hours first if it meant living up to Benicio's fantasy.

"It was a dream. Reality is so much better," Benicio said.

Another time Alberto would press for more details of the fantasy lovemaking. For now, he had a reality to make better than any dream. He pushed up on one elbow so he could reciprocate the tender exploration Benicio had lavished on him. Benicio groaned and rolled into the contact, aligning their bodies for the first time without clothes between them. Alberto shifted until their cocks lay nestled side by side. He reached between them and took them both in hand. Benicio threw his head back with a shout.

"Told you I'd make you scream," Alberto said smugly. Benicio opened his mouth to retort, but Alberto didn't give him the chance, stopping whatever Benicio might have said with a kiss. Benicio sucked Alberto's tongue into his mouth, making Alberto wonder how it would feel to have Benicio's mouth elsewhere, but for now, he'd settle for his tongue in Benicio's mouth and his hand on Benicio's cock. He shifted so he held only Benicio's erection and worked it slowly, lingering over the sensitive head hidden beneath its fleshy hood. Benicio cried out again, the sound disappearing into their kiss. Alberto shifted his weight so he had both hands free. It meant breaking the kiss, but it was worth it to watch the look on Benicio's face as Alberto moved his hand more deliberately and cupped Benicio's sac with his other hand. The look of sheer bliss on Benicio's face more than made up for the loss of contact between their bodies. Alberto was tempted to slip his hand even lower and see how Benicio reacted to a touch to his perineum or even his entrance, but he'd save that for another time. Benicio already looked totally wrecked, and from the way his cock was leaking, it wouldn't take him much longer to find release.

"Come for me," he murmured. He moved his hand faster, the fluid from Benicio's erection easing the slide. "Let it go."

Benicio's breath stuttered once and then again. Alberto pumped faster until Benicio's whole body tensed. He kept his eyes on Benicio's expression, watching wonder and satisfaction chase each other across his face. His hand grew sticky as he slowed his stroke, trying to draw out Benicio's pleasure as long as possible. Finally Benicio reached out for his hand. "Enough."

"Too sensitive?" Alberto asked.

Benicio nodded. Alberto smiled and bent down to kiss him. Benicio returned the embrace languidly. Alberto pushed aside his own need for release in favor of savoring the moment. Benicio broke the kiss after a few moments and ran his hand over Alberto's chest. "What can I do for you?"

"What do you want to do?" Alberto asked in reply. Anything Benicio wanted would be perfect as far as Alberto was concerned, and if he wasn't ready to do anything. Alberto would get off in a matter of minutes thinking about the look on Benicio's face as he came.

"Can I touch you the same way?"

"You can do whatever you want, lover," Alberto assured him. "Or you can do nothing at all."

"I couldn't. That wouldn't be fair."

"Neither would pressuring you to do something you aren't comfortable with," Alberto insisted. He rolled onto his back and grabbed Benicio's hand to kiss his fingers. "Whatever you want."

BENICIO STARED at Alberto spread out on the bed for his enjoyment. It was a selfish way to look at it—and Alberto had just proven how very much the person on the receiving end enjoyed it too—but it felt that way nonetheless: that Alberto was offering himself for Benicio's pleasure. He felt a fresh tingle of desire. His cock was too spent to rise again so soon, but he didn't need that physical sign of his interest. Whatever you want, Alberto had said. The problem was that Benicio didn't even know where to start. His cousin's whispered descriptions had left him more with vague yearnings than actual information, beyond a few details. The time spent in Alberto's bed with Alberto's hands driving him wild had filled in a few of the blanks, but he was still left with the feeling of ignorance.

"Stop thinking so hard and just touch me," Alberto cajoled. Benicio flushed at the gentle reminder that Alberto was still hard and practically untouched other than the few moments when he'd held both their cocks together in his strong hand.

"I don't know what to do," Benicio said.

"Jerk me off, suck me off, fuck me into the mattress, if you can get it up again," Alberto said. "Or sit back and watch while I take care of myself. That would be hot too, your eyes on me as I jerked off. Or maybe you'd like it better if I finished myself with my fingers. You could imagine it was your hand opening me up for your cock."

Benicio's breath caught in his throat at the sinful image conjured by the words. Jesus Christ, he wanted to feel Alberto's body opening for him. "Show me how," he said hoarsely. "I want to do it."

He saw the surprise that crossed Alberto's face before his pupils flared with need. Benicio almost called it off, afraid he'd crossed a line, but Alberto rolled to the side and rummaged through a drawer. "You'll need this," he said, tossing Benicio a bottle of clear fluid. "I don't fancy being taken dry."

Benicio frowned.

"Put it on your fingers," Alberto instructed. "It'll make them slippery so they'll go in more easily."

Benicio swallowed hard and did as Alberto instructed, coating his fingers in the oily fluid. When he was done, Alberto took the bottle from him and dribbled a little on his own hand. He palmed his cock briefly, leaving it glistening in the lamplight, and then moved lower between his legs. "Watch," he said. As if Benicio could do anything else.

The angle made it hard to see exactly what Alberto was doing, but the look on his face assured Benicio it was enjoyable. Wanting to be the one putting that look on Alberto's face, he slid his hand next to Alberto's and waited for directions. Alberto didn't provide any immediately, removing his hand instead. Benicio hesitated for a moment, but logic provided only one course of action if he intended to do what he'd said, so he fumbled around until he found the crinkled skin of Alberto's entrance. Alberto's breath hitched when Benicio touched him, which Benicio took as encouragement. He circled the tight ring slowly as he wrapped his mind around what he was about to do. He'd never expected to—

"Stop thinking so hard and press them inside me," Alberto interrupted. "Please, Benicio. I need you inside me."

Oh fuck, that was almost enough to get him hard again, the idea that Alberto needed him this way. He pressed tentatively against the resisting muscle.

"Go on," Alberto said. "You won't hurt me, not with just one finger. It'll feel so—"

Benicio didn't wait for him to finish his sentence. He followed Alberto's instructions instead, gratified when a sharp moan ended Alberto's sentence. Alberto clenched on his finger so tightly Benicio wondered how anything more would ever fit, but Alberto shifted on the bed, planting his feet and lifting his hips. Benicio gave up trying to figure it out ahead of time and focused on Alberto's face and ass, doing his best to make as it good as Alberto had made Benicio feel earlier.

Alberto lifted one hand to lightly stroke his cock in time with the movement of Benicio's fingers, and Benicio suddenly understood the appeal of watching, because, damn, Alberto was beautiful like this. Maybe another time when he knew what he was doing a little better, he'd knock Alberto's hand away and see to his pleasure both ways, but he was already overwhelmed nearly to the point of floundering. He would let Alberto take care of himself that much. He pulled back and pressed in again, reveling in the way Alberto's dark eyes flared to black.

"Add another finger," Alberto begged. "Make me feel it."

Benicio shuddered with the possibilities. It wouldn't happen tonight, but soon, and maybe he'd convince Alberto to reciprocate. Alberto had been so careful with him, not wanting to spook him, and Benicio appreciated it, but he wasn't spooked anymore. He was wound so tightly he thought he'd explode, and he'd come only moments ago. He had no idea how Alberto could stand it. He had no standard to gauge his actions by except his own memories of the past few hours, but he knew Alberto and his expressions now, even if he had never dared to dream he would see the look currently gracing Alberto's face, such a mixture of need and desperation that Benicio had to kiss him. Alberto threw himself into the kiss, attacking Benicio's mouth desperately. Benicio thought he could kiss Alberto forever, but he owed his lover—his lover, *Madre de Dios*, what a thought!—better than just a kiss. He added a second finger as Alberto had requested and then a third when Alberto didn't seem satisfied. Alberto's eyes rolled back in his head, and he lifted his hips to meet Benicio's hand.

"Please," Benicio whispered against Alberto's lips, "tell me how to make you feel good."

"Any better and you'll kill me," Alberto groaned. "C-crook your fingers. There's a bump. Play with it."

Benicio followed Alberto's instructions, crooking his fingers and searching for the spot. When Alberto nearly came off the bed, Benicio assumed he'd found it. If Alberto tried to say anything after that, Benicio couldn't make sense of it, but he didn't need words to guide him now. Alberto's body reacting to Benicio's fingers, Alberto's white knuckles as he clutched the sheets, gave Benicio all the guidance he needed. Then Alberto tensed from head to toe, a strangled shout leaving him, and his body clenched so hard around Benicio's fingers it almost hurt. Almost, because a part of him imagined how that would feel around his cock, and he found himself getting hard again.

Carefully he withdrew his hand from Alberto's passage and lay down next to him. Alberto stretched languidly, reminding Benicio of the jaguars he had caught glimpses of sometimes in the mountains as a child.

"If that's what you do to me with no experience, I might be the one in need of lessons instead of you."

It took Benicio a minute to catch up mentally before he remembered everything Alberto had said about how making love was even more powerful than the rutting when they first came together. Now that he'd had more of a taste, he couldn't wait to see what else Alberto could show him.

"How about we stop worrying about that and just enjoy each other?"

"Sounds perfect." Alberto pulled Benicio into his arms. "Sleep."

Benicio wasn't sure that was a good idea. He needed to go back to Pisac tonight and he didn't want to miss the last bus. At least if he did, though, he wouldn't be afraid to share Alberto's bed.

EIGHTEEN

"HEY, BENICIO," Joaquin said as they sat around the table at the chicheria, "watch your time. You don't want to miss your bus."

Benicio froze, a chinchilla caught by the approach of a condor. A week ago, he'd have thanked Joaquin, gathered his things, and gone to catch the bus, but Alberto had convinced Benicio to spend the night in Cusco tonight instead of going home—to spend the night with him. Benicio had agreed eagerly, but he hadn't prepared an explanation for their friends. "I'm… um… I'm staying in Cusco tonight. I get tired of leaving early."

"You need a place to crash?" Leonardo asked. "I've got an extra mattress if you need it."

"No, but thank you," Benicio said. "Alberto offered to let me sleep at his place. We spend more nights together than not on the trail anyway."

Alberto came back with another pitcher of chicha. Benicio looked at him frantically, but Alberto didn't seem to understand what he needed.

"Going to make Benicio sleep on your couch?" Joaquin teased. "You did warn him it's hell on your back, right?" Benicio feared Joaquin knew from the smile on his face, which only left him more panicked.

"He's slept on my couch before," Alberto said with a shrug. "He hasn't complained yet."

"It's better than a cold bus ride home at this hour of night," Benicio chimed in. It was even the truth. He didn't mind the hour's bus ride most of the time. He enjoyed the opportunity to unwind from the day, to reflect and relax before he got home and had to think about food or anything else, but the last bus of the night was different. Maybe because he was tired or because it was dark and cold once the sun went down, or maybe it was because when he caught the last bus, he had to tear himself away from Alberto to do it.

"You ought to move to Cusco," Joaquin said. "It's got to be easier than traveling back and forth all the time."

"Cusco's too big and too expensive," Benicio said. "Pisac is more my speed." He didn't look at Alberto as he said it. He couldn't or he'd give himself away. Alberto couldn't do anything about the size of the city, but if he asked Benicio to move in, Benicio would do it in a heartbeat. Benicio couldn't bring it up, though. That had to come from Alberto.

"You need a girlfriend," Leonardo said. "If you shared the rent with her, it wouldn't be so expensive."

"Now you sound like my mama," Benicio said. Everyone laughed, as he'd intended, but the panic was growing, so he tried to deflect their interest. He risked a glance at Alberto, but it only flustered him more to see his usually unflappable lover looking as frazzled as he felt. It wasn't supposed to be this hard.

"Not everyone is looking to shack up with a girl and have a brood of kids before he's thirty," Joaquin interrupted. Benicio didn't know what had motivated him to come to Benicio's defense, but he was grateful for it. "Just because that's your goal in life doesn't mean it's Benicio's. He's gone on the trail so much he'd have a hard time keeping a girl anyway."

"I'm perfectly happy without a girlfriend," Benicio said. "If I'd wanted to get married and have kids, I would've stayed in Cancha Cancha. I like having the freedom to come and go as I please."

"A lot of the porters are married," Leonardo said.

"Yes, but their families are in villages where they have support while the porters are gone," Alberto said. "It's not the same at all as having a girlfriend or even a wife in the city. You know what girls in town are like, always wanting to go out dancing or to a fancy restaurant. No, Benicio's right—it's easier to not have a girlfriend when you work the Inca Trail as much as we do."

Leonardo let it go and conversation moved on to other topics, but Benicio couldn't get past his panic. He excused himself and went out the back to the toilets. He didn't need them, but it gave him an excuse for momentary solitude.

"Benicio?"

"I'm here, Joaquin," Benicio called back. "I'll be out in a minute."

"I'm sorry about Leonardo back there. He means well, but he doesn't always think."

"You're not responsible for him," Benicio replied, "but thanks."

"If you want to keep your secrets, though, you're going to have to get better at deflecting those kinds of questions. I don't think the guys would care, but it's your decision."

"Wh-what secrets?" Benicio stuttered.

Joaquin didn't say anything right away, but when he did, it was the last thing Benicio expected. "Ask Alberto to take you dancing at the Queen. You'll enjoy it. I always do."

Benicio heard footsteps on the cobblestone courtyard and then a door slamming shut on its spring. He took a minute to breathe, ignoring the smell that accosted his nose. It wasn't any worse than the llama dung back home. He couldn't have heard what he thought he'd heard, or if he had, Joaquin meant something else by it. He hadn't really just told Benicio he was gay and that he knew Alberto and Benicio were together. He couldn't have meant that.

"Benicio, are you all right?"

"Can't a guy take a shit in peace?" Benicio snapped, even though thought Alberto didn't deserve his anger.

"If I thought that's actually why you came out here, maybe," Alberto replied. "Come out and talk to me, even if you aren't ready to go back inside."

Benicio pulled the chain to flush the water through the hole to maintain some pretense of actually needing the facilities and stepped outside.

"I didn't mean to panic. I haven't ruined anything, have I?" Benicio asked.

"No," Alberto said, "you haven't ruined anything. If anyone did, it was me, not helping you out when Leonardo tried to pin you down."

"I think Joaquin knows about us," Benicio said.

"He might," Alberto replied, "but since I first met him at the Queen, the local gay club, ten years ago, I don't think it'll hurt anything if he does. He won't give us away because he'd have to explain how he knows, and that would out him too."

"He did say he didn't think the guys would care."

"I don't know if they would, but do you really want to take that chance?"

"No," Benicio admitted. "I just have to figure out what to say next time."

"Go on back in," Alberto said. "I'll be back in soon. We'll talk about it tonight and come up with a better way to explain things."

Benicio nodded and went back inside. Señora Yupanqui cornered him before he could rejoin his friends. "They are good boys," she said in Quechua, "but they aren't highland boys. They don't understand."

"Understand what?" Benicio asked.

Señora Yupanqui smiled her toothless grin and patted Benicio's cheek. "That not every path has to lead to the same place or to the place they think it should go. Your heart will show you your path or the mountains will show it to you. Follow it, not the one they think you should take."

"Thank you, *abuela*. I needed that reminder."

"I'm not old enough to be your *abuela*," she cackled. "Maybe your *tia*, but not your *abuela*. Go on, drink your chicha with your friends."

Benicio was pretty sure she was older than his grandmother would have been if she were still alive, but he didn't argue. "Thank you, *Tia*," he said instead and went back to join his friends.

"I DIDN'T hear what started the conversation tonight," Alberto said after they'd hung their coats up. "What did Leonardo say?"

"Buzzkill," Benicio muttered. He'd spent the bus ride back to Alberto's apartment thinking of ways to forget about the evening, most of which had involved getting Alberto naked and into bed as soon as possible. That would have to wait until after they'd talked. As if sensing Benicio's dour thoughts, Alberto clasped their hands and drew Benicio to the couch, where he tangled their legs together as well. The contact reminded Benicio he wasn't as alone with this as he'd felt at the chicheria.

"Leonardo didn't actually start it. Joaquin reminded me to watch my time, which led to me saying I was staying with you tonight, and that led to the whole 'girlfriend' conversation. The part they don't get, besides the whole issue of being gay, is that I didn't grow up with the idea of moving in with a girlfriend like that. You lived at home until you got married, and then you moved into a bigger bedroom. You didn't always even get your own home right away."

"Then that's what you should tell them," Alberto said. "The trick, as much as you can manage it, is to tell the truth, just not *all* of the truth. The tourists ask if I'm married or if I have a girlfriend. I used to say no, I was single. Now I'll say not married, no girlfriend. It's the truth. I don't have to worry about remembering what I said or about contradicting stories because I've given the real answer to the question."

"And if someone asks you point blank if you have a boyfriend?" Benicio asked. "Shaun and Don did. Isn't that what you told me?"

"They did, and at the time, I told them the truth too," Alberto said.

"And now?" Benicio asked. "If they asked you again or if someone else asked, what would you say?"

"If someone asked me in a way I couldn't deflect, I would say yes," Alberto replied. "I wouldn't say who without your permission, but I would say yes. The thing is, I don't think anyone will ask. Well, Joaquin might now, and Miguel might at some point, but they already know I'm gay, so answering them honestly wouldn't change anything."

"They would want to know who."

"They might. Joaquin would probably figure it out, if he hasn't already. I'd tell Miguel I'd rather not say without talking to my boyfriend first, that him knowing about me only affected me. Telling him about my boyfriend would affect him too."

"Would he let it go at that?"

"I think so. He's always encouraged me not to mention it so I don't make anyone—tourists or porters—uncomfortable," Alberto replied.

"This wasn't supposed to be this hard," Benicio complained. He knew he was being childish, whining about something Alberto couldn't change and that he'd known would be this way before they'd even started, but it was more of a challenge than he'd expected.

"Nothing worth having is easy," Alberto replied philosophically. He ran his hand through Benicio's long hair and twirled the ends around his fingers. "Don't let it spoil tonight. I want to sleep with you in my arms and forget about the world for a while."

"I don't want it to spoil anything," Benicio replied. "It just caught me off guard, and I don't like feeling that way."

"It'll be easier next time," Alberto promised, "and every time after that will be even easier."

Benicio hoped Alberto was right. He could deal with a lot if it meant being with Alberto, but he'd have to cope better than he had tonight or they wouldn't be a secret for long.

"Hey," Alberto said, lifting Benicio's chin so their eyes met, "whatever happens, we'll deal with it. We're in this together."

Benicio wondered how true that would be if he cost Alberto his friends, but he didn't bring it up. He didn't want to hear the answer, and he wasn't sure he'd believe it even if Alberto said what he wanted to hear. He simply nodded instead and leaned into the kiss when Alberto coaxed him into it. He wanted the reassurance implied in the simple contact.

"This isn't how I wanted tonight to go," Alberto said after he broke the kiss. "I didn't want the first night we spent together to be anything but perfect."

"We've been spending nights together for months now," Benicio said, trying to lighten the mood.

"Not like this," Alberto insisted. "Not as lovers."

"It's not important," Benicio said. "We're still here, still together, and still going to share your bed for the night. It doesn't have to be perfect. It's enough that it is at all."

"You amaze me," Alberto said.

Benicio didn't feel particularly amazing, but he wouldn't complain about Alberto feeling that way. "Let's just go to bed," Benicio said. "Everything else can wait until tomorrow."

"I like the idea of taking you to bed," Alberto said with a grin that sent lust shooting through Benicio.

"What do you have in mind?" Benicio asked. Possibilities raced through his mind, each one more tempting than the last. The touch of Alberto's hands, the taste of his mouth, had grown familiar over the past few days, which, if anything, added to his anticipation. He knew what to expect now, knew how good Alberto could make him feel, and that made him want it all the more.

"That depends on what you want," Alberto replied.

"What do *you* want?" Alberto had been so careful not to push, but Benicio was tired of him holding back.

"Don't tempt me," Alberto warned. The dark, needy tone of his voice only egged Benicio on.

"Tell me," he urged. "You never know. I might want it as much as you do."

"Your knees over my shoulders as I drive you wild with my fingers in your ass and my mouth on your cock," Alberto replied hoarsely.

Benicio's mouth went dry at the words alone. "What are you waiting for?"

"For you to say yes."

"Yes," Benicio practically shouted. "Christ, yes!"

Alberto had him behind the screen so fast his head spun. He tore at his clothes, fully expecting Alberto to try to slow him down, but Alberto mimicked him and stripped swiftly. He grabbed Benicio into a rough, hungry kiss as he tipped them onto the bed. They landed with Alberto's weight pinning Benicio to the mattress. He cried out into the kiss. He spread his legs so Alberto could settle between them. Alberto shifted a little and his cock bumped against Benicio's ass. Benicio tensed even as he moaned.

"Not tonight," Alberto said, "but soon. When you want it so badly you can't think of anything else."

Benicio groaned. He hadn't thought of anything other than what Alberto did to him in days, and they left on the trail again in two days. Tomorrow he'd have to go to his cousin's to keep up appearances, and then it would be three long nights of sleeping an arm's length away and not being able to touch. They were going to be the longest five days of his life.

"I already want it that much," Benicio said, hoping to goad Alberto into action, but Alberto ignored his words in favor of kissing his way down Benicio's chest. He lingered over Benicio's nipple, a spot he had learned was exquisitely sensitive. When Benicio was writhing on the bed and the sounds spilling from his mouth had degenerated to wordless babble, Alberto moved lower. Benicio spread his legs even more to make room for Alberto's shoulders. Alberto settled comfortably between them and pressed a tender kiss to the inside of Benicio's thigh. He nibbled his way upward toward Benicio's groin until his nose nuzzled Benicio's sac, and Benicio started to wonder where Alberto's real target was. He jerked when he felt Alberto's tongue swipe across the skin beneath his balls. Surely Alberto wouldn't…. He didn't get the chance to finish that thought before he felt Alberto's hot mouth moving up his shaft. For a moment, he couldn't decide if he was relieved or disappointed Alberto hadn't continued, but even that thought fled when Alberto took Benicio in his mouth. He arched off the bed, pushing deeper into Alberto's mouth. Alberto swallowed him down immediately, making Benicio suddenly jealous of everyone Alberto had practiced on to lose his gag reflex that completely. Before he could follow that train of thought to its conclusion or form any kind of question, Alberto pressed Benicio back to the mattress with one hand. When Benicio moved as urged, he discovered the location of Alberto's other hand—perfectly placed beneath him to wedge his fingers into Benicio's crease and tease his entrance. He flinched reflexively, even knowing Alberto had this very end in mind. Instantly Alberto lifted his head.

"All right there?" he asked.

"Fine," Benicio gasped. "Just getting used to the feeling."

Alberto brushed his fingers over the tight muscle again. "Take all the time you need. We don't have to do this tonight."

They sure as hell did as far as Benicio was concerned. "You don't get to tease me and then not follow through."

"If you aren't comfortable—"

"I'll be fine," Benicio interrupted. "You surprised me, that's all."

"Should I announce what I'm doing ahead of time?" Alberto teased.

"If you're going to stop every time you surprise me, maybe you should," Benicio grumbled.

Alberto laughed and leaned up to kiss Benicio. He could taste salt and musk on Alberto's tongue as he sucked it into his mouth. Alberto gave him control of the kiss, settling Benicio's nerves again. Yes, Alberto had surprised him, but the touch wasn't unwelcome. He wanted everything

Alberto had described and more. He'd just been caught off guard. Alberto's reaction proved once again that Benicio's trust was well placed. Now he just had to convince Alberto to stop being quite so careful. He wanted Alberto's fingers inside him, driving him out of his skull. He knew they could do it. Every time Alberto touched him, Benicio felt it, the hints of a passion strong enough to wipe everything else away, but Alberto always held back a little, like he was scared of running Benicio off if he didn't keep everything under control. Benicio wanted to know what it felt like when he finally lost control.

This time, when he felt Alberto's hand moving up his thigh, he spread his legs and lifted his hips in silent invitation. That seemed to appease Alberto's worries, because he didn't hesitate this time before dragging the dry pads of his fingers across Benicio's entrance. Benicio clenched reflexively.

"Relax," Alberto murmured against Benicio's lips. "I don't want to hurt you."

Benicio took a deep breath and consciously relaxed his muscles. The moment he did, the zing of pleasure returned as Alberto massaged the spot between his sac and his hole. He took another deep breath and drew Alberto back into a kiss. He could do this as long as he had that connection. He could do anything as long as he had that connection.

Alberto teased Benicio's mouth with the same careful control that he used as he teased Benicio's ass, brushing his tongue over Benicio's lips as he brushed his fingers over Benicio's entrance. Benicio chased Alberto's tongue, but Alberto pulled out of reach. In frustration Benicio grabbed his head and crashed their lips together. Alberto gave in and took Benicio's mouth in a deep, hungry kiss that stole Benicio's wits so thoroughly that he nearly missed Alberto pressing a slippery finger inside of him. He might have missed it entirely if Alberto hadn't found his sweet spot.

"Shit, what is that?" Benicio gasped.

"Your prostate," Alberto said with a smug grin. "Should I demonstrate?"

Benicio knew vaguely what to expect since he'd watched Alberto come apart beneath his hands a few days earlier, but that hadn't prepared him for the intensity of the sensation. He clung to Alberto's shoulders, desperate for some stability as his body buzzed with all the force of a

February storm in the mountains. Alberto kept his fingers pressed against the sensitive gland, never giving Benicio a moment to catch his breath.

When Alberto lowered his head back to Benicio's cock, Benicio was a goner. All coherency deserted him, leaving him a writhing mess on the bed. The storm built and built until he was sobbing with need, unable to ask for more or to call a break. He gave himself over to Alberto's hands and mouth and let rapture steal his consciousness.

He must have blacked out because when he could force his eyes open again, Alberto lay on the bed next to him, a look of pure masculine satisfaction on his face. He kissed Benicio lightly. "I should clean us up."

Benicio lay where he was and let Alberto wipe his stomach clean. "What about you?" he asked finally.

"Half that mess on your stomach was mine," Alberto admitted. "I couldn't help it."

Benicio liked the sound of that. He pulled the rag from Alberto's hand and tossed it to the floor. Then he snuggled into Alberto's embrace and rested his head against Alberto's chest, letting the sound of Alberto's heartbeat lull him to sleep.

NINETEEN

BENICIO SAT on his sleeping bag and brushed out his hair. He'd taken a shower when they got to Wiñay Wayna, as he always did. It had been warmer than usual, a reminder that winter was almost over and that summer temperatures—and the wet season—would be there before long, and he'd worked up quite a sweat even though most of the hike had been downhill. Alberto had taken the group to see the ruins near the campsite, so Benicio had the tent to himself for the moment. He took full advantage of it. He'd tossed the bocce ball set to the porters before he took his shower, and all the tourists had gone with Alberto, so he could let down his guard—and his hair—for a time and relax.

The trip had been both harder and easier than the previous ones. The tourists had been an easy group, and everything had gone according to plan. The uncertain tension between Alberto and himself had disappeared now that they knew where they stood with each other, only to be replaced by a different kind of tension as they worked and slept side by side without being able to acknowledge everything between them in any overt way. How many times had Benicio caught himself reaching out to touch Alberto only to think better of it at the last minute? Even the kisses they'd exchanged before bed and in the morning when they awoke were little more than swift pecks, not the deep, hungry kisses Benicio had come to crave in the time since they had become lovers.

Lovers. The word brought a smile to his lips. They might have to be discreet about it, especially on the trail, but it still made him happy. He had a lover of his own, someone to share his days—and occasionally his nights—with, someone to talk to about anything and everything on his mind, someone to build a life with. And then there were the hours they had spent in Alberto's bed.

He hadn't known he could feel as good as Alberto had made him feel. He hadn't known how powerful pleasuring Alberto in return would make him feel. He still felt like pinching himself some days to make sure he wasn't dreaming, but then Alberto would lean over and kiss him and all his doubts would flee again in the face of Alberto's affection. If he still wished they could be more open about it in public, that was his problem and something he'd have to learn to live with. He'd overheard two of the porters making derisory comments about one of this week's tourists, a single man they considered effeminate. Arturo had shut them up as soon as he heard them, but it had served as a reminder to Benicio of why Miguel had counseled Alberto to keep his secret ten years ago. None of the tourists seemed bothered by Sam, if he was in fact gay, like the porters believed, but Benicio was more concerned with the porters' reactions than the tourists. The tourists would go home at the end of the hike. He had to work with the porters week after week, and having their respect and cooperation was essential.

The sound of the tent flap being unzipped pulled Benicio out of his thoughts. He smiled as Alberto ducked into the tent beside him.

"Did it go well?" Benicio asked.

"They loved it, as always," Alberto said. Benicio smiled. He was particularly proud of the portion of their story centered around Wiñay Wayna. Unlike so many of the tambos that were little more than shelter for a night, Wiñay Wayna had been a thriving village in its own right, home to several hundred people and the last stop for pilgrims on the way to Machu Picchu. From Wiñay Wayna, they could leave before dawn and hike the last few kilometers by torchlight to arrive at the Sun Gate in time to see the sun break over the horizon and bathe Machu Picchu in golden light. It had been a place of preparation for the pilgrims, but it had also been a home, something they took great pains to stress when they took groups there.

"Luis has tea almost ready. Are you going to join us?"

"Of course. I wouldn't miss Luis's popcorn for anything," Benicio said. Alberto started to back out of the tent again, but Benicio grabbed his hand. "Actually, there is one thing I might miss Luis's popcorn for."

Alberto cocked an eyebrow at him. Benicio ignored the questioning look and pulled Alberto toward him for a kiss. Maybe it was unwise on the trail, but they were in the privacy of their own tent with everyone else occupied for the moment. The tent wouldn't keep any noises inside, but it did provide a visual barrier, and Benicio needed a real kiss after three days of almost no contact.

Alberto hesitated for only a moment before diving into the kiss with the same longing Benicio felt. *Madre de Dios*, Alberto could kiss. Benicio leaned into him, desperate for more contact. Apparently of the same mind, Alberto pressed Benicio backward onto his sleeping bag, covering Benicio's body with his own. Benicio groaned into the kiss.

"Shhh," Alberto murmured in his ear. "Don't make any noise or we'll have to stop."

Benicio bit his tongue to stop the groan of frustration because he loved the noises Alberto made when they were together, and Alberto had told him more than once that he felt the same way. If the choice was silence or stopping, though, it was no choice at all. He'd bite his tongue until it bled if it meant Alberto would keep kissing him.

Alberto had other ideas for keeping him silent. He captured Benicio's lips with his own and took possession of his mouth. Benicio grabbed Alberto's shoulders and threw himself into the kiss for all he was worth, tangling their tongues together even as he struggled to stay quiet. He nearly lost that battle when Alberto shifted so Benicio could feel his erection against his hip. Fuck, he wanted to reach for it and jerk Alberto off, but he wouldn't be able to do it silently

"Benicio! Alberto!"

"Fuck," Benicio muttered as Alberto rolled off him at the sound of Arturo calling their names.

"I'll be right there," Alberto called back. "Is tea ready?"

"Luis is serving it now," Arturo replied.

"Okay. Let me finish changing and I'll be out."

"I'd better go now," Benicio said after Arturo's acknowledgment. "I can't stay in here while you change clothes. Not now."

Alberto nodded and rummaged in his pack for a change of clothes. "We'll finish this when we get home tomorrow."

"I can't wait," Benicio said, and for once, it was more than an expression. He really wasn't sure he could wait, but they didn't have much choice.

"WHEN ARE you going to take me to the Queen?" Benicio asked as he and Alberto got ready for bed that night. Benicio figured it was safer to discuss their plans for their days off than it was to watch as Alberto got ready for bed. Some things simply weren't good for his self-control.

"What brought that on?" Alberto asked.

"Joaquin said you met there and that I should ask you to take me there," Benicio said. "I know I'm not much of a dancer, but I had fun dancing with you at Shaun and Don's party."

"Dancing at the Queen isn't like dancing at their party," Alberto warned. "For a lot of the men there, it's a way to find a partner for a quick fuck for the night, and even if it's not, it's still a lot more physical."

"Does it matter why everyone else is there?" Benicio asked as he crawled in his sleeping bag. "I mean, I'd be there to dance with you, not with anyone else, and it's not like it would bother me if you danced close to me. Not after everything we've already done."

"No, I guess not," Alberto said. "It can be a bit of a shock the first time, that's all."

"In what way?" Benicio asked.

"We're so used to having to hide that it's always a bit odd at first to go into a room full of people so deliberately not hiding," Alberto explained. "And then there's the fact that short of stripping completely, pretty much anything goes. I've seen guys with their hands down each other's pants. I've seen guys rubbing off against each other under the guise of dancing. As long as nobody complains, the management turns a blind eye, and believe me, nobody wants to be the one who complains."

"I'm an adult," Benicio reminded him. "I think I can handle it. Will you go dancing with me tomorrow night, or the night after at the latest if we're too tired tomorrow?"

"If you want to go dancing, I will go with you," Alberto said. "Just don't say I didn't warn you if it isn't what you expect."

Benicio hoped it was exactly what he expected, because if he had his way, Alberto would be so worked up by the end of the night, he'd take Benicio home and fuck him properly instead of stopping with fingers and mouths. Benicio wanted Alberto inside him, and he was tired of waiting.

THE POUNDING beat of the salsa music reverberated down the street before they ever entered the Queen. Benicio's heart thumped in time with the sound as they approached. He had looked forward to this since Alberto told him about it two days ago. They'd been too tired to go out last night after coming off the trail. They'd spent most of today resting and recovering. Alberto's knees had been sore more than usual, so Benicio had done the shopping and laundry for both of them, but a day of rest had been enough for Alberto to suggest dancing tonight, and Benicio was just selfish enough to agree.

He'd fretted over what to wear until Alberto had tossed a shirt and pants at him and told him to get dressed. They were no different than the clothes he wore anytime he wasn't on the trail, but Alberto hadn't dressed any differently either, so Benicio had gotten dressed, pulled his hair back into its usual queue, and accepted that he was the only one who saw this outing as anything special. For Alberto—and presumably the rest of the club's patrons—this was just another night out. For Benicio, though, it felt monumental.

"Relax," Alberto said as they neared the entrance. "You're strung tight as a wire."

"I know this isn't anything special for you, but it's my first time doing something like this."

"It's my first time too," Alberto said. "I've never gone dancing with anyone special before. It's always just been a question of going and dancing, not of going with someone."

Benicio couldn't decide if that helped or made matters worse, but like everything else they did together, he'd trust it was right. They walked into the club and the noise hit Benicio like a wall, voices and music and laughter all swirling together in an almost overwhelming mix. Lights flashed above the writhing mass of bodies on the dance floor, giving Benicio glimpses of men entwined as they moved in time with the music. "Wow."

"I told you," Alberto said.

"I know you did, but seeing it isn't the same as imagining it."

"Is it better or worse?"

"Better," Benicio said. "Definitely better."

"You want something to drink before we go out there?"

Benicio shook his head. He only wanted one thing right now: to be on that dance floor with Alberto.

"Let's go, then."

Alberto took Benicio's hand, a luxury in itself, and pulled him toward the dance floor.

The mood on the dance floor, as Alberto had warned, was far more carnal than the salsa dancing they'd done at Shaun and Don's party, but that only added to the glut of sensory input for Benicio. He moved into Alberto's arms and let Alberto's movements guide his, but even then, he watched the other dancers and the way they moved together. He was here to dance with Alberto, but he had plans for the rest of the evening, plans that required a level of seduction he wasn't sure he could pull off on his own. If he could get ideas from the men around him, men clearly set on tempting their dance partners into more than just dancing if the way they flirted and moved against each other was any indication, he'd be that much closer to reaching his own goal for the night.

ALBERTO COULDN'T count the number of times he had gone dancing at the Queen. He had been coming here for over ten years, sometimes alone, sometimes with Joaquin. The evenings ran together in their uniformity. Even the times he'd met someone to go home with for the night didn't stand out in any particular fashion.

He could say with complete certainty that he'd never had a night like this one. He'd never come to the Queen with a date, and he'd never danced with someone he was involved with, and that changed the game completely.

Benicio was a living flame in his arms. His movements might not have been as practiced as some of the other dancers, but everything about him enflamed Alberto's senses. He'd expected to take the lead with dancing as he had with making love, but Benicio surprised him with his boldness. Instead of waiting for Alberto to lead him, he took the initiative, pressing against the length of Alberto's body and moving with him in time with the music. His breath caught in his throat as Benicio ran his hands around Alberto's waist, toying with the hem. The shirt rode up easily, leaving a swath of flesh bare for Benicio's fingers. It shouldn't have been any different than anyone else he'd danced with, any other touch to guide a partner or be guided by one.

It shouldn't have been any different, but as Benicio leaned in closer to say something that even at that distance got lost beneath the music, Alberto gave up the idea that tonight would be anything but a completely new experience.

"I can't hear you," he shouted back, his mouth against Benicio's ear as he spoke. He felt the shiver that ran through Benicio and grinned. Talking wasn't really an option, but he blew across the shell of Benicio's ear to see if it would have the same effect.

It was even better. Benicio shuddered in his arms and pressed even more closely against him. Feeling bold in the one place outside his apartment where they could be themselves without fear of reprisals, Alberto pulled Benicio's shirt free of the waistband of his jeans and slid one hand beneath the fabric to mimic the way Benicio had touched him. He felt more than heard Benicio's sharp intake of breath and grinned. Benicio was responsive to his touch under any circumstances, but here, where anyone could see them, the illicitness of it all added to his reaction. Alberto knew the feeling well, even if the novelty had worn off some years ago. He wasn't above using it to his advantage now.

Benicio reached up and tugged at Alberto's head. Alberto followed his lead, thinking to lure him into a kiss, but Benicio surprised him, bypassing his mouth for his ear. The flutter of his breath sent sparks zinging over Alberto's skin, and when Benicio sucked Alberto's earlobe into his mouth, the sensation knocked Alberto's breath from his lungs. He'd never thought of his ears as particularly sensitive, but on the dance floor with Benicio pressed against him in what was resembling a dance less and less with each passing second, Alberto discovered a direct link between his earlobe and his cock.

Benicio noticed too, because he did it again, only this time with teeth. Alberto moaned helplessly. He was supposed to be the seducer in their relationship, the one with the experience to guide Benicio along unfamiliar paths, but once again, Benicio had turned Alberto's expectations on their ear with his boldness. Determined not to be outdone, he turned his attention to the dance and to all the moves he'd perfected over the years to drive a partner wild. This time, he'd even follow through on those promises, just as soon as he got Benicio home and into bed.

He spun Benicio in his arms so his chest rubbed against Benicio's back as they moved. He nuzzled Benicio's nape, pleased when Benicio lifted his arms to reach for Alberto's head. It gave a delectable arch to Benicio's chest that Alberto had no intention of resisting. He kept his hands on the outside of Benicio's shirt, but only because it would tease Benicio more.

Benicio's fingers tightened on Alberto's neck as Alberto ran his hands over Benicio's torso. He didn't linger anywhere yet, wanting to prolong the pleasure of both the dance and the seduction for as long as he could. Benicio turned his head enough that he could reach Alberto's jaw. Alberto tipped his own head to give Benicio easier access. The butterfly kisses Benicio pressed to his skin tickled almost as much as they aroused, leaving his skin hypersensitive to each touch. When a sharp nip replaced the light kisses, Alberto bucked forward against Benicio's ass as a surge of lust hit him. He had to stop thinking of Benicio as some clueless innocent when his lover had more tricks up his sleeve than Alberto had given him credit for.

Benicio arched back against him, rubbing provocatively, and Alberto gasped at the contact. Benicio had been dropping hints, but Alberto had been ignoring them. He wouldn't be able to ignore them much longer. He wasn't sure he wanted to ignore them much longer.

He glanced at the men surrounding them, but no one was paying any attention to them, so Alberto ran his hands down Benicio's chest again, one of them lingering over his nipples while he worked the other beneath the hem of Benicio's shirt. The motion bared Benicio's stomach to anyone who cared to look. More than one of the other dancers had discarded their shirts, so no one would be shocked at seeing skin, but the thought of Benicio half undressed, half hidden added to the feeling of illicitness. Alberto only hoped Benicio was as aroused by the thought as he was.

Benicio moved his hands from where they gripped Alberto's head, one of them coming to rest on Alberto's wrist above where the shirt touched. He stretched the other between them, closing his fingers around the bulge in Alberto's jeans. Alberto's knees trembled as he fought to keep his balance and his coherency. Benicio was all but jacking him off on the dance floor. He swallowed hard and tried not to lose it right there.

He looked around frantically, sure everyone would see what Benicio was doing to him, but they were still lost in the crowd of anonymity, so he relaxed into Benicio's touch and set about taking his lover apart as well.

He tweaked Benicio's nipple through the fabric. Alberto felt the rush of air escape Benicio's chest. He started to bring his other hand up to join the first when Benicio spun in his arms.

"What—?"

Benicio cut the question off with an incendiary kiss, leaving Alberto mentally scrambling to catch up. Yes, he'd started the seduction, but he'd planned on drawing it out until they got home. The way Benicio was kissing and touching him, Alberto wasn't sure he'd make it home before he lost all semblance of control.

His carefully constructed plans out the window, he threw himself into the kiss. If Benicio wanted a fumble in a dark corner, Alberto wasn't averse to the idea. Benicio pressed a leg between Alberto's, all but rutting against his thigh. Before Alberto could do more than gasp into the kiss in response, Benicio grabbed Alberto's shoulders and turned him around so he could rut against Alberto's ass instead. Ever since that night when Benicio had taken him apart with his fingers, Alberto had imagined what it would be like to let Benicio take him in truth. He hadn't expected tonight to be that night, but maybe he'd underestimated Benicio again.

"Are they watching us?" Benicio asked into his ear as he ground against Alberto under the guise of dancing. "Are they wishing they were in my place?"

If anything, they were wishing to be in Alberto's place, but he couldn't say that. Benicio wouldn't hear him with the music pounding around them.

"When we get home tonight," Benicio continued, "you're going to fuck me."

Alberto inhaled sharply. He could imagine it so easily, taking his time, opening Benicio up, slipping into his tight heat. Sensation shattered up his spine when Benicio cupped him boldly.

"This is going to feel so good inside me."

It was more than Alberto could stand. He imprisoned Benicio's wrist with his hand, pulled it away from his groin, and used it to drag Benicio off the dance floor. He didn't have condoms or lube in his pocket—why would he? He'd come to the Queen to dance, not to fuck—but he didn't think either of them would make it home without some relief.

He found a dark corner and pinned Benicio to the wall, then nearly lost it right there when Benicio wrapped one leg around his hip to pull him closer. He needed… he couldn't…. His brain shorted out on him, leaving him with nothing but the insane need for Benicio. Their mouths crashed together, though he couldn't have said who initiated it. He jabbed his hands beneath Benicio's clothes, one up his shirt, the other under his waistband. He needed contact. He needed skin. He needed….

A wolf whistle broke the spell, sending an icy shiver through him. He broke the kiss and pulled back, panting hard as the haze of lust dissipated enough for him to think about what he was doing. Dread settled in the pit of his stomach, warring with the desire that still danced along his nerves. He couldn't do this to Benicio. He couldn't make a public spectacle out of them when this actually meant something. Benicio deserved better than that. "We're going home," he said into Benicio's ear. "We're going somewhere with a bed and supplies and no audience, and then I'll give you what you want. But I won't do it here with people watching."

Benicio nodded and lowered his leg slowly, reluctance clear in every line of his body. Alberto understood. Benicio had pushed him past his breaking point. Only the thought of anyone else seeing Benicio's body or the look on his face when he climaxed held him back.

They pushed their way through the crowd to the door. The unexpectedly cool night air stung Alberto's overheated cheeks as they hurried toward his apartment. Fortunately his building was only a few blocks away. They managed to keep their hands to themselves as they walked. They weren't really dressed for the chilly breeze that gusted down off the mountains, so if anyone noticed their rush, hopefully they'd attribute it to the sudden drop in temperature that nightfall had brought. He had no desire for a confrontation, tonight of all nights.

They reached his building and took the stairs two at a time. Alberto's heart pounded in his chest as he fumbled for his key. He'd made promises he intended to keep, but that didn't make him less nervous.

Benicio waited only until they were inside and Alberto had locked the door again before grabbing Alberto and pulling him into another incendiary kiss.

"Now," he demanded when he finally let Alberto up for air. "I'm tired of waiting."

Alberto nodded, not sure where he'd lost his voice, and let Benicio pull him toward the bed.

Benicio started stripping as soon as they rounded the decorative screen. When Alberto didn't immediately follow suit, Benicio sent him such a pointed look that Alberto nearly squirmed from the power behind it. He undressed swiftly and tried to figure out how to regain control of the situation. Benicio, though, apparently had no intention of letting that happen. He grabbed the lube from the drawer and pushed Alberto back onto the bed before climbing on top of him.

"Condoms," Alberto squeaked out. "In the bathroom."

"Get them," Benicio said as he moved to the side so Alberto could get up. "Hurry."

Alberto did as Benicio said and fetched the box of condoms as quickly as he could. He was beginning to think one wouldn't be enough, not with the hungry way Benicio was eyeing him. He felt a little like a vicuña caught in the sights of a puma, but unlike the vicuña, Alberto would enjoy being devoured.

Benicio pounced the minute Alberto returned to the bed, pushing him back down again and straddling his waist. Alberto reached up and pulled him down for a kiss. He was willing to let Benicio control their interactions since he seemed to need it so much, but he wasn't willing to forego kissing him in the meantime. Nor was he willing to let Benicio do all the work of stretching himself when Benicio grabbed the lube and coated his fingers.

"Use that on me," he said as he brought Benicio's hand to his eager erection. "Let me take care of you."

Benicio looked about to protest, but Alberto had caught Benicio's urgency. He didn't waste any time beginning to prepare Benicio. Benicio rocked back on his fingers, two to start because neither of them had the patience for slow now and this was hardly the first time Alberto had fingered him. Benicio moaned when Alberto hit his prostate, sending another jolt of need up Alberto's spine.

Fuck, he loved the noises Benicio made when they had sex: all whines and moans and mewls, just begging Alberto to keep going. Tonight Benicio would get his wish because no matter how much Alberto had wanted to be careful and take his time, all his good intentions had flown out the window at the first sign of this new, more aggressive side of Benicio's personality.

"Now," Benicio begged, but Alberto shook his head. He wouldn't delay much longer, but he wouldn't hurt Benicio if he could help it. He pressed a third finger in next to the first two and reveled in the way Benicio's back arched in pleasure. When he'd allowed himself to imagine this moment, their positions had been reversed as he gently pressed Benicio into the mattress and made sweet, tender love to him. He hadn't expected this raw passion, but if this was the view he'd have, he wasn't about to complain.

"Please," Benicio choked out. "I need you."

Alberto shuddered at the desperation in his voice. He wasn't going to last a minute with Benicio like this, and that wasn't what Benicio deserved for his first time. There wasn't any stopping this now, though, so Alberto would just have to make it up to him later. He rolled a condom on quickly and settled one hand on Benicio's hip to steady him.

Benicio sank down on him with a grimace.

"Easy." Alberto grabbed Benicio's hips to keep him still. The urge to thrust even deeper into the furnace surrounding him left him trembling, but he wouldn't cause Benicio pain if he could help it. "You'll hurt yourself."

"Don't care," Benicio whined. "I want this."

"And you have it," Alberto said, "but I want you to be able to walk tomorrow too."

He moved one hand from Benicio's hip to his cock, intent on stroking it back to full hardness. Benicio gasped at that and shifted on Alberto's lap. Alberto gritted his teeth to keep from losing control and flipping Benicio beneath him so he could pound into him until they both lost their minds.

Slowly, so slowly Alberto thought he might lose *his* mind, Benicio started to move above him, little rocking movements at first that barely stirred Alberto's cock inside him. Alberto groaned at that. He needed so much more, but until Benicio could adjust, he had to hold back and give Benicio control over their interaction. He couldn't take over, no matter how much he wanted to.

Fortunately Benicio had no more patience for waiting than Alberto did, and before long, he had elongated his movements so that he caressed the whole of Alberto's length as he rose and fell. Alberto matched the strokes of his hand to Benicio's rhythm. He kept his touch light, teasing instead of driving for release, even if his desperation grew with each rise and fall of Benicio's body above him. He met Benicio's downward stroke with an upward stroke of his own and relished the groan that tore from Benicio's throat. All hint of discomfort had disappeared from Benicio's face now, leaving only pleasure in its place. Alberto wanted a comparable desperation for release to replace it, but he would wait. He would make this moment as perfect for Benicio as he could.

Benicio rode him with increasing speed, and soon all thought of control fled. Alberto let his body take over, let Benicio's actions guide his own. The clench and release of Benicio's tight passage was driving him mad with need, all tight heat and constant pressure around his cock. He gasped for air, his grip on Benicio's cock tightening as he fought to stave off his release a little longer. He couldn't leave Benicio hanging like that. He wasn't the virgin with no experience to teach him control.

He focused on Benicio's face, looking for the signs that he was close. He thrust up harder to meet Benicio's downward slide, and Benicio convulsed around him, rapture suffusing his features as he found release. Alberto's gut clenched at the sight. He pulled Benicio toward him, into a kiss, as he rolled them to switch places. All semblance of control abandoned, he thrust once, twice, three times more until his own orgasm bubbled up his back and exploded in his head. He collapsed on top of Benicio, panting against his neck.

Benicio's breath tickled his shoulder as they lay there. Alberto kept waiting for his heartbeat to return to normal, but it didn't seem to be happening anytime soon. Finally he lifted his head enough to kiss Benicio again, tenderly this time.

Benicio returned the kiss, tracing his tongue along Alberto's lower lip. Alberto sucked it into his mouth languidly, enjoying the way Benicio clenched around him reflexively. It prolonged the glow of release that much longer. He rocked slightly against Benicio to return the favor.

"Too much," Benicio groaned.

Alberto pulled back instantly, not wanting to hurt Benicio in any way.

That elicited another groan. Benicio rolled to his side and pulled Alberto down next to him. "Perfect," he said with a contented sigh.

Alberto thought that was a pretty damn good description of the moment. He dropped one more kiss on Benicio's forehead before settling down to snuggle. He'd have to get up and deal with the condom and the mess on his stomach before long, but not yet.

TWENTY

"I SHOULD just leave everything packed," Benicio grumbled as he searched Alberto's apartment for his paperwork. "It would be easier than having to pack every time we get ready to go on a hike."

"Your clothes might get a little rank if you did that," Alberto teased from his spot on the couch. Much to Benicio's annoyance, his pack and the duffel for the porters were already sitting neatly by the door, waiting for them to head out in the morning.

"I didn't mean my clothes," Benicio said. "I meant all the little stuff. Snacks, poncho, ID, water bottle, coca leaves, the stuff I actually carry with me instead of the pack I give to the porters. Other than replacing the snacks and coca leaves, it's not like any of it changes from week to week. One of these days I'm going to forget something and be stuck borrowing from you or having to buy something new at the last minute."

"So leave your pack here," Alberto said with a shrug. "It's not like it takes up much space. You can take the duffel home to get a change of clothes and wash the dirty ones."

"Yeah, I'll start doing that," Benicio said. He grabbed his wallet and frowned when he didn't see his INAC ID card where he usually kept it. He pulled everything out and sorted through it, but aside from a few *soles* and his personal identification, it was empty. "*Maldita sea*. I should have kept my mouth shut."

"What?" Alberto said.

"I don't have my INAC card. I must have left it in Pisac. I'll have to go back to get it. I'm sorry. I'll have to pass on football this afternoon." He hated to do that. He and Alberto hadn't had as much time together as usual between their last trip and the one that would start in the morning. One of the city guides had come down with the flu, and Alberto had agreed to cover for him on his days off. It was late to be catching the flu, with spring in full force in October and summer coming on, but Pablo was in the hospital, so Benicio could hardly argue with the severity of his illness. He didn't know what Miguel would do when they left on the trail tomorrow, but that was Miguel's problem. Benicio's current problem was his missing ID card. Without it, he wouldn't be allowed past the checkpoint at Piskacucho.

"We'll miss you, but the guys will understand," Alberto said. "I guess it's a good thing we went dancing last night instead of waiting for tonight."

Benicio grinned. They'd done a whole lot more than just dancing last night. He'd been hoping for a repeat before the meeting with the tourists at seven and then going to his cousin's to sleep. That wasn't going to happen now.

"Maybe this way I'll actually be able to walk tomorrow," Benicio retorted. He'd finally broken Alberto of his unnecessary insistence on always being gentle.

Alberto grinned at him wickedly and pulled him in for a swift kiss. "And here I was thinking it was your turn to make it hard for me to walk tomorrow."

Benicio flushed at the thought. He could never decide which he enjoyed more: taking Alberto or Alberto taking him. Fortunately Alberto was content with both options, so they switched around regularly, freeing Benicio of the necessity of choosing.

"Maybe the meeting will be short tonight and we'll have some time before I have to go to my cousin's," Benicio offered. Alberto nodded, but they both knew how unlikely that was. In the five months they'd been working together, they had only finished the meeting in less than an hour once. Most weeks it took closer to two hours, and with a 4:00 a.m. meeting time in the morning, that barely gave them time to sleep, much less do anything else.

He grabbed his wallet and keys. "The sooner I leave, the sooner I'll get back. I'll come by the football field if I get back in time, so we can at least have dinner together before we go. If not, I'll meet you at the hotel."

He missed the bus by a matter of minutes when he got to the station in the Plaza de Armes and had to sit twiddling his thumbs until the next bus came. Fortunately the weather was good, sunny and not too hot with a breeze coming off the mountains, so waiting was only miserable because he wanted to be elsewhere. Preferably playing football with his friends prior to making love with Alberto, but even on the bus to Pisac would be better than sitting here doing nothing.

He couldn't believe he'd left his INAC identification at home. Of all the things essential to the trip, that one was the most important. Without it, he couldn't clear the checkpoint and go onto the trail, and without him, Alberto couldn't take a group of more than eight people on the trail. Since tomorrow's group was fifteen, Benicio couldn't even bow out and let Alberto go without him. Nor could Miguel replace him with another guide. Benicio's name was already on all the paperwork.

Splitting his life between two cities and two apartments was getting harder and harder, but while Alberto never blinked when Benicio stayed, he always accepted it when Benicio said he needed to go back to Pisac. He always made room for whatever Benicio brought with him or even what he left there, but he never suggested Benicio bring anything back with him. Today's comment about leaving his backpack in Alberto's apartment had been the first explicit offer of that kind.

The time finally passed and he was able to catch the next bus, but it was full to bursting, leaving him standing in the aisle and clutching the overhead railing like a lifeline so he didn't take a tumble and end up in pain on the trail because of it. The press of bodies around him and the bright sun outside made the interior of the bus sweltering despite the open windows. Benicio groaned. He'd need a shower when he got back to Cusco or he wouldn't be presentable for the meeting tonight. He could take one at Alberto's apartment if he got back in time and could catch Alberto before he left for the hotel, but it was just one more frustration on top of all the rest in what was supposed to be a fun and relaxing day.

His shirt was soaked through with sweat by the time he pushed his way through the crowd going on to Ollantaytambo to get off at his stop in Pisac. He trudged through town to his one-room apartment and flopped on the bed to stare up at the ceiling. At least the room was cool compared to the bus or outside. The thick mud-brick walls had that advantage. He stripped out of his shirt and decided to shower there. Hopefully it would be cooler on the ride back, if only because the sun wouldn't be as high in the sky. If he waited and caught the five o'clock bus, it would be setting, and maybe he could make it through the meeting without needing another shower first. And if he didn't, well, the tourists likely wouldn't consider October temperatures high enough to face the cold water of the showers, so they'd be a lot dirtier than him by the end of the trip. Seventy degrees Fahrenheit—he'd gotten pretty good at doing the conversions in his head after five months of tourists looking at him blankly when he used Celsius temperatures—was hot for the Andes, but for most of the tourists, it was still on the cool side of spring or fall weather.

With a muffled groan, he dragged himself off his bed and into the shower. When he was clean and dressed again, he rummaged through his dresser until he found his INAC ID in the pocket of the shorts he had worn when they were in Machu Picchu a week ago. He heaved a sigh of relief that it had survived being washed. He'd have been in real trouble if it hadn't.

He didn't want to take the bus back in the heat of the day, but he didn't know what else to do with the time. He looked around the apartment blankly, trying to remember how he'd spent his time before he started hanging out with Alberto and their friends. With a wrench, he realized he hadn't done anything, really. He'd sat in his apartment and read whatever he could find about the Inca Trail, but he hadn't made any real effort to know his neighbors or to make friends in town. He still read whatever he could find about the Inca Trail. He just did it with Alberto now, and he knew Alberto's neighbors better than he knew his own. He'd slipped into Alberto's life so completely that it was now his own as much as it was Alberto's.

The only thing in the entire apartment that set it apart from any other place like it was his quilt on the bed. Everything else was as nondescript as any hotel room in any town in the area. This wasn't home. It was a place to keep his stuff, and not even a convenient one.

He didn't know how to broach the subject with Alberto, but if this day had taught him anything, it was that he didn't want to live in Pisac any longer.

ALBERTO SIGHED in relief when they finally got the tourists settled in their tents at Ayapata and could retire themselves. He hadn't gotten more than a moment alone with Benicio since he'd left for Pisac yesterday afternoon, and that was entirely too long to go without a kiss. The meeting had, as predicted, gone long the night before, and Benicio had rushed away when it was over so he didn't get to his cousin's house too late. They'd arrived at the hotel early, but some of the tourists were already in the lobby waiting and Domingo was outside with the bus, so he hadn't been able to sneak a kiss then either. He'd tried at lunch, while everyone was resting after eating before resuming the hike, but every time he thought they were alone, someone had come looking for one or the other of them. It had gotten beyond frustrating, especially when Benicio came out of the shower block at Ayapata, long hair dripping water down his back. Alberto wanted to drag him into the tent right then, but before he could, Arturo had called him over to ask him about plans for the morning.

Then it had been time for dinner and explaining the next day to the tourists, and now he was exhausted and ready to sleep, but he had to talk to Benicio first. Yesterday had driven some things home to him, and he needed to share those with Benicio.

His heart pounded in his chest and he wiped sweaty palms on the legs of his jeans as he bent to open the tent flap. He could see the reflection of Benicio's flashlight against the tent wall, so he knew Benicio was in there. The tourists were asleep or would be soon, and the porters were busy with their cleanup and setting everything in order for the morning. He could duck into the tent right now, get the kiss he'd been aching for since Benicio left for Pisac yesterday, and then talk to him. He could ask him to move to Cusco like he'd wanted to do for weeks but hadn't done because Benicio had all but moved in with him anyway. He could make it official.

And Benicio could shoot him down.

He didn't really think that would happen. Benicio hadn't been happy about having to leave yesterday. He'd made the occasional comment about it being easier to leave things at Alberto's place. Alberto didn't think they were hints so much as simple observations, observations that ought to give him hope. None of that stopped the nerves assailing him as he unzipped the tent flap and ducked inside.

He barely managed to get the flap shut behind him before Benicio grabbed him and pulled him into a kiss, a far more passionate one than they usually indulged in when not at home. He returned the kiss fervently, unable to completely silence the moan evoked by the feeling of Benicio's tongue running along his lower lip. He only hoped it was muffled enough no one else heard it or, if they did, that they assumed he was moaning over stiff muscles, not this suddenly wild kiss.

When Benicio finally let him go, panting nearly as harshly as Alberto was, Alberto slumped back on his sleeping bag. He'd been prepared for a number of things when he entered the tent, but even after several months, he was never quite prepared for the moments when Benicio decided to take charge. "Not that I'm complaining, but what was that for?"

"I missed you," Benicio said. "I know it was my fault, but we had yesterday all planned, and then I didn't get to spend any of it with you after all, and I've hardly seen you today with the way the group spread out along the trail."

Benicio couldn't have handed him a better lead-in to what he wanted to say if he'd tried. Alberto tried to pretend the tingling in his fingers came from the kiss, not from the adrenaline rush of fear as he worked up the nerve to say what was on his mind. "About that," Alberto said. He had to swallow hard past the lump in his throat. "I got to thinking yesterday… is there a reason for you to stay in Pisac? I mean, I know when you first started working, the rent was cheaper and Cusco was too big for you, but things are different now."

"The rent isn't any cheaper and Cusco isn't any smaller," Benicio said, but Alberto could see the grin on his face.

"It would be if we shared it," Alberto said, drawing hope from Benicio's expression. He hadn't said no. Maybe he needed some convincing still, but he hadn't said no. "The rent, that is. If you moved in with me, or even if we moved into a slightly bigger place together, the rent wouldn't be any more than what you're paying in Pisac and possibly less. I hate the nights you have to go back to your apartment, and if we lived together, you wouldn't have to worry about forgetting something in Pisac like you did yesterday. Everything would be right there and—"

Alberto didn't get to finish his list of reasons why moving in together was a good idea—and he'd prepared a long list in case Benicio needed convincing—because Benicio was kissing him. Then again, if the way Benicio was kissing him was any indication, he didn't need the rest of his arguments. Another surge of adrenaline left his skin prickling, from excitement this time. He shifted them around until Benicio was lying next to him. The hard ground wasn't a replacement for his bed, and the sounds of the porters moving around outside was a damper on their ability to go beyond kissing, but Alberto couldn't complain when he had what he'd hoped for since Don and Shaun's anniversary trip.

"What will we say if people ask about it?" Benicio said when he finally ended the kiss.

"We'll say it doesn't make sense for you to live in Pisac when you work out of Cusco, but that rent is too high for you to afford a place of your own," Alberto replied. The question sobered him somewhat. He had assumed the kiss was an acceptance of his proposal, but maybe he'd gotten ahead of himself. He could do this, though. He'd thought about this yesterday. He'd planned answers to Benicio's likely concerns. "We'll say we spend more nights together on the trail than apart anyway, so sharing an apartment is easy after that. Other than Joaquin, none of the guys has been to my apartment. They won't know there isn't really room for a second bed. And Joaquin won't say anything where the others can hear. What do you say?"

There. He'd laid it out as bluntly as he knew how. Now it was up to Benicio.

"Yes," Benicio said against Alberto's lips. "God, yes."

Alberto's shoulders slumped with relief as the tension of wanting and waiting fled in the wake of Benicio's answer. He'd said yes. Benicio had said yes. They'd be living together as soon as they got off the trail and could make it happen. "Thank God." He had to kiss Benicio again. He desperately wanted to make love to him, but they were on the trail. Other than a few kisses, they'd kept to their promise to behave professionally, and he wouldn't go back on that now, but oh, he wanted it. He lingered over the kiss, dragging Benicio's shirt up so he could run his hands over the bare skin of his back. The contact wasn't enough, but it was already more than they'd agreed to allow on the trail. He pulled back grudgingly, although he didn't loosen his grip on Benicio's shoulders. He couldn't make love to him like he wanted to, but he'd take what he could get.

"We'll go to Pisac as soon as we get off the trail and move all your stuff. How much stuff do you have?" His voice sounded hoarse in his own ears, proof of how profoundly this had all affected him even now that Benicio had said yes.

"Clothes and a few sundries," Benicio replied. "Nothing that will take up much space."

"I wasn't thinking about space in the apartment," Alberto said. He'd turned to practicalities as a way to keep from jumping Benicio despite their agreement, but he didn't want Benicio to think they were anything other than the steps necessary to get what they wanted. "Only about carrying it back on the bus."

"If the bus isn't crowded, we'll be fine," Benicio said. "If it's busy, it might be a little difficult. We could do it in more than one trip if necessary."

"Or we could see if Leonardo would help us, since he has a car," Alberto said. "One friend helping another one move and all that. If we treat it like it's no big deal, everyone is less likely to think anything of it."

"It is, though," Benicio said softly. "I mean, nobody else will know, but between us, it means something, right?"

"Yes, it means something," Alberto assured him. "Whatever I might say in public, I'm not just looking for a roommate or trying to make things easier on you. I'm asking you to move in with me because I want you there with me."

Benicio snuggled closer to Alberto on their mats and rested his head in the crook of Alberto's neck. "As long as you want me there."

Alberto couldn't imagine ever not wanting him there. He kissed the crown of Benicio's head, all he could reach in their current position, and wondered if he could find sleeping bags they could zip together at night so they wouldn't have to sleep apart on the trail.

"OKAY, I think that's it," Miguel said as they wrapped up their meeting to prepare for the next trip. "Unless there's anything else?"

"I just need to give you this," Benicio said, handing Miguel a piece of paper with Alberto's address written on it. "I got tired of the trip back and forth to Pisac, so I moved."

Miguel took the paper with a nod and glanced down at it before looking back up at him, eyes narrowed. "You're sharing a place with Alberto?"

"He offered," Benicio said with what he hoped was a casual shrug. "We spend half our time together anyway, and living in Cusco will certainly make things easier. It seemed like the perfect solution."

Miguel turned that sharp look on Alberto. Benicio could feel him trying not to squirm. "I suppose," he said slowly. "As long as I don't get any complaints."

"Why would you get complaints about where Benicio lives?" Alberto asked innocently. "When the tourists even ask, we never tell them more than the city we live in."

"That's not all the tourists sometimes ask," Miguel replied pointedly.

"We're professionals, Miguel," Alberto said sharply. "Have you ever gotten a complaint about either one of us?"

"No."

"Then I don't see how a change of address will matter," Alberto replied. "We'll see you at the hotel tomorrow night to get the paperwork for the trail."

TWENTY-ONE

THE RAIN started as they passed the checkpoint at Wayllabamba. Benicio put his cover over his backpack, pulled his hat down over his ears, and hoped the waterproofing on his boots held up. It was too hot to put on his poncho, even as thin as it was. He'd just have to be wet now and dry out when they made it to Ayapata. Besides, at this time of year, the light drizzle would probably blow past in a matter of minutes.

An hour later, he had to revise his opinion. The drizzle had turned into a pounding rain that had darkened the sky early and forced them to pull out their flashlights well before they reached Ayapata. He overheard the worried whispers that passed among the porters, but they wouldn't be sleeping at Pacamayo tomorrow. They would push on to Chaqulqocha as always, so they wouldn't have to worry about flooding, even if the rain continued.

"It's only early December," Alberto told the tourists at dinner. "Rain in this season can be hard, but it doesn't usually last long. It will blow itself out before long and tomorrow will be a beautiful day, I'm sure."

Benicio did his best to look reassuring, but he knew better than to make promises like that. Yes, it was a month before the rainy season was supposed to begin, but he'd lived in the mountains all his life. He'd long since learned the futility of predicting the weather. If it was raining, it would rain until it stopped. If it was dry, it would be that way until it started raining again. Trying to predict anything more specific than that was pointless.

Alberto's words eased the tension among the tourists, though, so Benicio left it alone and focused on helping him keep the conversation flowing.

Arturo brought the main course in just as one of the tourists—Benicio hadn't learned all their names yet—asked if they were married.

"Only to each other," Arturo said in Quechua. Benicio froze. He knew the head porter understood some English, even if he rarely spoke it, so he'd obviously heard and understood the question. It was the answer that worried him. Alberto either hadn't heard or didn't understand Arturo's answer, because he didn't blink as he replied that neither of them was married or had a girlfriend. Benicio summoned a smile and tried to pretend he wasn't reeling from Arturo's comment.

If Arturo knew, who else had figured it out? Miguel wouldn't fire them just because the porters knew, but if they started complaining or if the tourists figured it out and said something, he would be within his rights to separate them at work. Benicio dreaded the thought of working with another guide. He and Alberto had formed a seamless partnership since they started working together in May. They knew each other's cues, each other's strengths and weaknesses. They complemented each other on the trail as much as off it, and it showed in their evaluations, but if it caused problems, Miguel would have to address it.

Dinner seemed to drag on forever, but once they finished eating and Alberto gave his speech about the plan for the next day, no one lingered. They all wanted dry clothes and warm sleeping bags as much as Benicio did.

"See if Arturo needs anything?" Alberto asked. "I'll do a final check of the camp and meet you at the tent."

Arturo was the last person Benicio wanted to talk to right now, but he couldn't very well explain that to Alberto with the porters still milling around washing dishes and preparing for the night. He nodded and sought out Arturo.

"Do you need anything else tonight?"

"For the rain to stop and the trail to be dry tomorrow," Arturo said with a shrug. "Beyond that, nothing."

"About what you said in the tent...." Benicio didn't even know what he wanted to say.

"It wasn't a criticism, just an observation," Arturo replied.

"Do the others know?" Benicio didn't want to hear the answer, but he had to know what they were dealing with.

"Most of them," Arturo said. "They don't care. You treat them fairly. You value their work. You speak Quechua with them and ask about their families. Luis and I dealt with the ones who might have had a problem with it months ago. There are plenty of guides to work with at Huaman Travel. They don't need to work with you."

"You told Miguel?"

"I told him they weren't a good fit for our team," Arturo said with a shrug. "He trusts me to put together a team that can work together and do what needs to be done. A man who can't work with our guides doesn't belong on our team."

"I never expected…."

"That's part of why they like you," Arturo said. "You don't expect them to do anything you aren't willing to do. They see enough of themselves in you to ignore the parts that are different. You're a good guide, Benicio, and Alberto is one of the best out there. That makes up for a lot out here."

"Thank you," Benicio said. "I… thank you."

"You're welcome. Get some sleep. If this rain doesn't pass, tomorrow will be a long and miserable day."

"You too."

He left Arturo and headed for the tent. Alberto was just ducking inside when Benicio reached it. He pulled his boots off and climbed in after Alberto.

"Are you all right?" Alberto asked when Benicio started stripping off his wet clothes.

"I'm… flabbergasted," Benicio said after a moment. "Arturo knows about us. He's been picking porters who don't care that we're together and transferring ones who do to other teams. I don't know what I thought would happen if they found out, but it wasn't that."

"I knew there'd been some turnover on the team, but I trusted Arturo's judgment and didn't ask why," Alberto replied slowly. "I never imagined he was protecting us."

"He said we're good guides. Well, he said I'm a good guide and you're one of the best guides on the trail, but he said it was worth going to the trouble for us."

"That makes us incredibly lucky men," Alberto said. He changed into dry clothes and stretched out on his mat. "I don't like the sound of the rain. It isn't lessening. Everything is going to be wet in the morning. Day two is hard enough without adding wet rocks to the mix."

"We'll deal with it," Benicio said. "We already have a head start over most of the other groups. We'll just have to push through. One step at a time, right?"

"One step at a time," Alberto agreed. He pulled Benicio into a kiss.

Benicio relaxed into the embrace, letting it chase away the chill from the rain.

"How'd you figure out Arturo knew about us?" Alberto asked eventually.

"He made a comment at dinner. The woman asked if either of us was married. Arturo heard her and said 'only to each other' in Quechua. You must not have heard him because you didn't react at all, but I nearly dropped the platter he'd just handed me."

"So much for being discreet. Did he say how he figured us out?"

"I didn't ask," Benicio replied. "I was too worried about him knowing to go beyond the fact that he didn't care. None of the tourists have ever said anything, have they?"

"Not to me, and not in their evaluations," Alberto replied. "We'd have seen them even if Miguel chose not to say anything. So now what do we do?"

"We go to sleep," Benicio said. "We can't do anything about them knowing now, and honestly, I don't know that we need to. Tomorrow is going to be an early morning and a long day. Everything else can wait until we reach camp tomorrow night or even until we get home."

MORNING DAWNED, if he could call the near-black misery of the morning dawn, much the way the day had turned to dusk the night before, with heavy rain and low-hanging clouds that obscured the light almost completely. Alberto had hiked the trail enough times to expect twilight when they first woke up at Ayapata, but usually it was light by the time they were ready to start the hike. He wasn't hopeful for it this morning.

"Take your time today," he ordered Arturo while Benicio and the porters woke the tourists. "However slowly you go, you know the tourists will be twice as slow. It doesn't help anyone if you get hurt or if we lose a pack. If the weather clears, you can hike faster then and get the tents set up to dry before night. If it doesn't, getting to the site early won't help anything anyway."

"Yes, boss," Arturo said with his usual easy smile. Alberto wasn't sure how he managed to be cheerful so early in the morning with weather like this, but he wasn't going to complain. If nothing else, it was one less grumpy face to deal with.

Alberto started to turn away, but Benicio's revelation last night lingered in his memory. "Oh, and Arturo?"

"Yes, boss."

"Thank you. Benicio told me what you said."

"Nothing but the truth," Arturo replied. "You just proved it again this morning. If I have to be out on the trail in weather like this, I want to be here with a guide like you who actually cares about us, not just one who's there for the tourists."

"Miguel drove that lesson into my head from the first time I stepped foot on the trail with him," Alberto said. "I'm not likely to forget it, especially not now." Behind him, he could hear the tourists beginning to shuffle toward the dining tent. "Let's get moving. We're going to need every second of daylight today."

They ate breakfast mostly in silence, passing around the hot water for coca tea, coffee, or hot chocolate without prompting. Luis had switched the meal, choosing to serve the hot quinoa porridge instead of the crepes they usually had on the first morning. It would warm everyone from the inside out and provide an extra dose of calories to help keep them warm until lunch. A doctor who had traveled with them once had calculated they burned six thousand calories a day on the trail. With the rain added to the mix, both in terms of making the hike more difficult and in terms of stealing body heat, Alberto wouldn't be surprised if it was even higher today. When everyone was finally settled and eating, Alberto decided the time had come to address the weather and the rest of the day.

"Buenos días, amigos," he said. "I'd hoped for better weather this morning, but Illapa is still in a bad mood, it seems. The god of rain is like that sometimes. He is known to be vengeful at times."

"Couldn't he have waited until next week?" one of the men asked.

"Who can predict the moods of the gods?" Alberto said. "The rain will make the rocks slippery. Rely on your walking sticks to brace you. The rubber tips won't slip even on the wet rocks. It's more important than ever to take your time and place your feet carefully. Yes, we have a long hike today, but we don't want anyone getting hurt. That will be far more difficult to deal with than hiking the last kilometers in the dark. The approach to Chaqulqocha is flat once we come down from Runkurakay, so it will be no problem to hike it with flashlights if we have to. Benicio will take the lead today. He grew up in the mountains. He knows the signs of danger and won't lead us wrong. I'll bring up the end of the line to help anyone who falls behind."

"Is it really safe to hike in this kind of weather?"

"The Inca Trail is open during the rainy season. It is only closed during February for maintenance and training for the guides and trail cooks. We have hiked in worse weather than this."

He didn't mention that even in the rainy season, it rarely rained this hard for this long. He didn't want to worry them unnecessarily when the rain could clear at any second. Thunder rolled across the mountain peaks. Or perhaps in a few hours, Alberto corrected his thoughts. It was never a good idea to tempt the gods.

"Are you sure you want me in the front?" Benicio asked when the tourists left the safety of the dining tent to gather their gear for the hike. "You know the trail better than I do."

"If I thought it would work, I'd insist everyone stay close enough together that I could keep you in sight no matter what," Alberto replied, "but we saw yesterday how they don't hike at the same speed, and while the rain isn't good, it's not so dangerous that we have to slow everyone down for a few stragglers. We'll go on as always until there's a reason not to. Then we'll see what our options are."

"You sound worried."

Alberto looked pointedly at the roof of the dining tent, where rain continued to beat in a steady rhythm. "This is February rain, not a brief shower in December. I don't like it."

"Realistically, what options do we have?" Benicio said. "We can't stay here because another group will be here tonight. We could hike back out, but if we're wrong and it clears in an hour, we'll have disgruntled tourists for no good reason. Our only other option is to hike on and make it as far as we can, whether that's to Pacamayo or on to Chaqulqocha as planned."

"Pacamayo isn't safe in this weather."

"I know it's not, but neither is hiking in the dark," Benicio replied. "We'll do what we can with what we have and pray that the gods are kind. It could still clear up. Even in February, I've seen rains like this hit, stay for a few hours, and clear up like they'd never come."

"We'll hope you're right," Alberto said, because what else could he say? Benicio was right. They had no choice but to push on.

TWENTY-TWO

THE RAIN had eased up a little by the time they reached the lunch site, but it did little to brighten the mood. Everyone was wet and miserable, and the fact that it wasn't freezing was the only good thing Benicio could think to say. The porters nodded along with him when he said it, all of them having lived through this kind of rain at more extreme temperatures at least a few times in their lives, but the tourists took no consolation from it.

"Our evaluations are going to leave something to be desired this time," Benicio murmured to Alberto as they huddled in the lee of the dining tent while the tourists washed up or used the restrooms before lunch.

"Probably, but we can't change the weather, and Miguel knows it. As long as no one gets hurt, he'll overlook the complaints," Alberto said. He rubbed his hands together in an effort to warm them, to little avail. "Even my gloves are wet. It makes it hard to stay warm."

"I'll warm you up tonight," Benicio promised in a low voice. Arturo could say the porters knew and didn't care, but Benicio didn't think it wise to flaunt it.

"Just thinking about it will keep me warm all day," Alberto quipped back. "Come on. Let's get inside the tent. Luis's soup will be a godsend right about now."

"What kind is it today?"

"Chicken vegetable, usually, but I didn't ask," Alberto replied, "but it will be hot. Nothing else matters."

Benicio could hardly dispute that, so he checked once to make sure their group was all in the tent and then followed Alberto inside. The propane lamp illuminated the dim space and gave off enough heat that the inside of the tent was warmer than outside, but it wouldn't dry any of them out while they broke for lunch.

"The hardest part is over," Alberto said after they passed the bowls of soup down the table. "We have another pass to climb, but it's not as high or as steep as Dead Woman Pass. Runkurakay is only at thirty-nine hundred meters and only about four hundred meters above us now. Then it's a quick descent to Chaqulqocha, only three hundred meters below the Runkurakay pass."

"Is there any chance of the weather clearing up?"

"Is always a chance," Benicio said, "but is hard to predict in the mountains. Weather changes in minutes or in days. Is no telling which until it happens."

"I guess there's no way but forward," another tourist commented.

"Not really," Alberto agreed. "Not unless we turned around and hiked back out the way we came, but then you wouldn't get to see Machu Picchu, and isn't that the whole reason for being here?"

"Not the whole reason, but a very big one."

"We're more than halfway through the trail," Alberto added. "Tomorrow is a short day, and then just a few hours the morning after to get to Machu Picchu. Yes, it's wet, but you can do this. You *are* doing this."

"Do groups ever get this far and then turn back?" someone asked.

"Not often," Alberto replied. "Is easier to go forward than back from here. If someone can't make the hike, a guide might send them back at the end of the first day, but if they make it to Pacamayo or Chaqulqocha, is easier to finish than to go back."

"And if someone got hurt and couldn't go on?"

"It would depend on the injury," Alberto said. "We carry a stretcher. If necessary, two porters could carry the person between them. It wouldn't be easy or pleasant, but we could get them out."

"How fast could they get someone out if it was really an emergency?"

"Some years ago, the Peruvian government sponsored a race from Piskacucho to Machu Picchu. Was to predict how fast Inca runners could get messages from Machu Picchu to Cusco. The distance is same as a marathon. People from all over the world entered. A porter won the race.

He did the entire trail in three hours forty-five minutes, carrying nothing but water to drink. We're in the middle of the trail. If we had to get a message out, we could get someone there in a matter of a couple of hours."

"That's actually reassuring."

"The controllers at Wayllabamba and Wiñay Wayna have satellite phones," Alberto explained. "So we wouldn't have to go all the way to the trail ends."

"That's good."

BY THE time they reached Chaqulqocha, Benicio was ready to climb into his sleeping bag and not move for a week. He was wet and tired and sore, and he was pretty sure he'd rubbed a blister on his heel in his wet socks. He pulled out the first-aid kit and sat in the dining tent, because if he went into the tent he shared with Alberto, he wasn't sure he'd come out for dinner, and he needed the food.

He unlaced his boot and eased his foot out. He frowned when he saw blood on the heel of his sock. It was worse than he'd thought.

"What's that?" Alberto asked.

"A really bad blister," Benicio said with a sigh. "My sock rubbed today, apparently."

"Stay here," Alberto ordered. "I'll get a basin of hot water so we can clean it up."

Benicio started to protest, but Alberto had already left the tent. He returned a few minutes later with a basin of steaming water and a towel. "Soak your foot in there if you can," Alberto said. "The hot water will get your circulation going again and hopefully draw out anything in the blister."

Benicio eased his foot into the water. It was almost painfully hot on his chilled skin, but Alberto was right, and the alternative was picking wool fibers out of his heel with a pair of tweezers. He'd take the hot water over tweezers any day. He soaked his foot for several minutes, until the tingling from the heat of the water faded and the stinging subsided. He pulled his foot from the water and crossed it over his knee, but the angle was awkward.

"Here, let me do that," Alberto said. The angle wasn't any less awkward for him, but Benicio relaxed into the touch. Alberto examined the blister carefully, rubbing at it from time to time with the towel.

"It looks clean to me," he said after a few minutes. "I think we should put ointment on it, bandage it up, and keep an eye on it until it heals. There's not really anything else we can do on the trail."

"Go ahead," Benicio said. "It doesn't hurt nearly as much now."

The ointment Alberto smeared across the open wound stung, but Benicio bit the inside of his cheek to hold in the hiss that threatened to escape. Alberto covered the area with a wide piece of gauze and wrapped a strip of medical tape around his ankle to hold it in place. "Okay?"

"Yes, thank you," Benicio said. He'd leaned forward, intending to give Alberto a quick kiss, when he heard Arturo calling their names. "Later," he whispered as they separated, and Alberto opened the tent flap to draw Arturo's attention.

Arturo joined them in the tent with a grave expression on his face. "A porter from the group ahead of us just came into camp. They're spending the night at Phuyupatamarca because the trail to Wiñay Wayna is blocked by a landslide. A couple of the porters went to check if the optional trail around to Intipata is passable, but they hadn't come back when it got too dark for the group to continue."

The words sent ice down Benicio's back. He'd grown up with a healthy respect for the mountains, and earthquakes were the only thing he feared more than landslides.

"Was anyone hurt?" Alberto asked.

"Not in the group this porter was with," Arturo said, "but there were groups ahead of them on the trail that must have gotten through before the landslide hit, because only about half the groups that were supposed to sleep at Wiñay Wayna tonight are in Phuyupatamarca now. They're doubling up in tents and sharing supplies and trying to make the best of it, but I don't know that there is such a thing."

"What are we going to do?" Benicio asked Alberto. His heart pounded in his chest, making his fingers tingle. He took a deep breath to dispel the adrenaline rush.

"I sent Javier to Phuyupatamarca," Arturo said. "He'll wait until news comes, either tonight or in the morning, and bring it back as soon as he can. If the optional trail is passable, we can still get to Wiñay Wayna tomorrow as planned."

"Don't say anything to the tourists," Alberto directed. "We'll tell them once we know more."

"Talking to the tourists is your job, boss," Arturo said, although his attempt at levity did nothing to lessen the tension in the tent. "This is bad," Benicio said when they were alone again. "Really bad. Landslides are dangerous."

"It's not good," Alberto agreed, "but if the optional trail is open, it's not as bad as it could be. Let's see what news Javier brings back before we panic."

"I'm not panicking," Benicio insisted. "Just weighing our options."

"Push our way forward, stay here and wait to be rescued, or head back," Alberto said. He squeezed Benicio's hand in reassurance. "Those are our options. Which one is the best will depend on what Javier finds out. For now, the best thing we can do is eat. Whatever Javier finds out, being hungry won't help."

Benicio nodded and pulled his boot back on over the bandage. He could do this. Alberto wouldn't steer them wrong. He just had to have faith in him. "I'll gather the tourists. Hopefully by the time we've eaten, Javier will be back. What are you going to tell them if they ask about tomorrow before then?"

"I'm going on the assumption that the optional trail is open," Alberto said. "We'll plan to get up and leave at our usual time. If Javier hasn't returned by that time in the morning, we'll wait for him and make a decision then, but hopefully he'll be back tonight."

Benicio hoped Alberto was right. The more time they had to consider options, the better, especially if going forward ended up not being a choice.

THE PORTERS had started serving dessert when Arturo appeared at the tent flap and tipped his head toward the mountain pass they would have to cross in the morning if they could continue. Alberto nodded and leaned over to Benicio. "Javier's back. I'm going to talk to him. I'll be back as quickly as I can."

"Okay," Benicio murmured in reply. Alberto could hear the nerves in his voice, and he didn't blame him. This was Benicio's first emergency on the trail, and that was nerve-racking enough without it being as serious an emergency as a landslide that had possibly cut off their easiest way off the trail.

Alberto ducked out of the tent and muttered a curse as rain went straight down his back. "Where's Javier?"

"In the cooking tent warming up," Arturo said. "He's soaked to the bone."

"And the news?"

"Bad," Arturo said. "I didn't get all the details, since I figured you'd want to hear it too, but forward isn't an option. I know that much."

"Okay," Alberto said. "Let's go hear what he has to say, and I'll decide what to do from there."

"Whatever you decide, we'll do everything we can to make it as safe and simple for the tourists as possible," Arturo said. "You can count on us."

"Thanks," Alberto said. "That means a lot."

They ducked into the cooking tent, where Javier sat wrapped in a blanket with a cup of something steaming in his hands. Alberto took that as a sign of how cold he truly was, since the metal cups got nearly as hot as the tea or coffee inside.

"What's the word from Phuyupatamarca?" Alberto asked as he took a seat on one of the campstools that a porter—he didn't see which one—vacated for him.

"Bad," Javier said hoarsely. "Two porters from another agency tried the optional trail to see if they could get through. Only one came back. They weren't even three feet apart when the trail gave out. The one in the back managed to jump back to safety. The other one fell. Some of the porters will go in the morning to see if they can find him… or his body."

Alberto crossed himself immediately. They knew the risks when they signed on to work the trail, but after so many trips with no real problems, it was easy to become complacent. "Did you know him?"

Javier shook his head. "Not by name. I might recognize him if I saw his face. We speak in passing on the trail without necessarily getting to know people beyond that unless we work for the same agency."

"I know," Alberto said. "It's the same with the other guides. Did they say what they were going to do with their groups?"

"Come back this far, at least," Javier said. "They aren't really in a campsite where they are. No water, no facilities. They made do for the night, but they can't stay there for an extended period of time."

It made sense, but it complicated Alberto's decision, because the influx of extra groups would put a strain on the campsite here if everyone currently there stayed as well. "Thank you for going to find out what was going on for us."

Javier smiled, but the expression didn't reach his eyes. Alberto patted his shoulder and stepped away. "Has anyone gone to tell the other groups?"

"Not yet. I wanted to hear what you had to say first. I'll tell them as soon as we're done here."

"We have enough food for four more meals if we make hiking-size portions," Luis said as he joined them. "If we made smaller meals, we could double that, probably, although we might run out of propane before we run out of food. That's still only enough for three and a half days."

Alberto nodded. "I have to think. If this had happened last night, it would be easy. We'd just turn around and head back down, but turning around now isn't as easy. It's two long days back out with tourists who are already wet and exhausted. Now they're going to be scared on top of that. Turning around isn't as easy as it sounds."

"Whatever you decide," Arturo repeated, and Luis seconded it.

"I know. I just have to decide."

"Morning is soon enough," Luis said. "Whatever you decide, it won't change what we do tonight."

"I know, but I have to decide what to tell the tourists. If we're staying here, we don't need to wake them at four thirty tomorrow morning."

"Give yourself time to think," Luis urged. "Make the right decision for us. The other guides will do the same for their groups."

Alberto took a deep breath and nodded. "I'll let you know what I decide."

He left the tent and headed back to where he'd left Benicio and the tourists.

"I sent them off to bed," Benicio said when Alberto ducked back into the dining tent. "They were all falling asleep at the table, practically. I told them we'd wake them in the morning and could go over the day's plans then. They all seemed fine with that."

"Thanks," Alberto said. "We can't get to Machu Picchu. Both paths are blocked, and there's been at least one fatality. One of the two porters who went to see if the alternate trail was open lost his footing and fell when a section of the trail there gave way." Just saying the words made him sick to his stomach. This wasn't a case of someone not being careful. This was a porter, someone who was as adept at surviving in the mountains as anyone, and he had been helpless to stop his fall. If he couldn't make it, what chance did the rest of them have?

"So what are you thinking?"

"I can't stop visions of the porter being swept away," Alberto admitted. "I don't even know who it was. Javier said he didn't know the man by name, so I probably didn't know him either, but he was still one of us. And now he's gone. Am I crazy to even consider trying to go back?"

"I don't know," Benicio said. "There are certainly risks to going back, but how long would we survive out here if we don't try? We have limited food and propane, which means we have a limited supply of safe water. I might be able to drink the water without getting sick, but the tourists will all be sick in a matter of hours if we start giving them water straight from the springs. I'm not sure staying put is really a better option."

"There are no good options," Alberto agreed. "I'm trying to figure out which is the least bad. We've used up enough supplies that we could shift loads around and send two porters back with nothing to carry but water. They'd make it to Wayllabamba by tomorrow night if nothing slows them down. There's a phone at the checkpoint. They could call Miguel and have him send supplies in to us, whether it's here or to meet us part of the way back. As long as there isn't a landslide behind us too, we could get supplies in on foot, and if he knows where we are, they could even fly supplies in if they had to. We could get around the limited supplies with time and planning."

"Yes," Benicio agreed, "but our guests have flights home. They're not going to want to stay here indefinitely, waiting for the trail ahead to be cleared. That could take weeks."

"Months, even," Alberto said. "I wouldn't stay indefinitely, but we could stay a day or two while they recover their strength and while the weather clears. Even if we have to hike all the way back out to Piskacucho, doing so after a day or two of rest would be less daunting than doing it tomorrow. They won't make their flights home, but Miguel will help get them rescheduled."

"You're assuming the weather will clear," Benicio said. "I know it's early for the summer rains, but if this is the start of the wet season, the storms could be here to stay, which would make it harder to fly in supplies too."

"You think we should start the hike out tomorrow."

"Staying here doesn't feel safe to me," Benicio said. "I can't explain it more clearly than that or put my finger on why I feel that way, but I do."

Alberto took a deep breath. "Then I guess we need to figure out the safest way to get us all out of here and back to Piskacucho."

"You'd do that just because I said so?" Benicio asked in surprise. "You don't have to do that just because I've got an itch between my shoulder blades I can't explain away."

"You said it yourself. We can't stay here indefinitely, and if we're going to move, we may as well move now," Alberto said. "There aren't any safe choices. Whether we stay or try to hike out, it's going to be dangerous. If your instincts are telling you it's more dangerous to stay, I see no reason to ignore that."

"If you say so," Benicio said.

"I do." Alberto leaned forward and kissed Benicio swiftly. "Get ready for bed. I'll tell Arturo and Luis what we decided and be there in a few minutes."

TWENTY-THREE

"Benicio and I talked," Alberto said without prelude when he walked back into the cooking tent where the porters had gathered to eat their dinner. Silence reigned even before he spoke, but after he did, he could have heard a pin drop.

"And?" Arturo asked after a minute.

"We'll leave in the morning to start back to Piskacucho. We'll take it as far each leg as we can, even if it means we don't make it all the way to Ayapata tomorrow. I hope we'll make it past Pacamayo, because I don't want to sleep there in this weather if we can avoid it, but pushing to the point someone gets hurt won't do us any good either. The tourists are tired, wet, and discouraged. Hearing they won't make it to Machu Picchu and that we'll have to hike back out the way we came in is only going to make it worse. Furthermore, I'm not getting spread out along the trail. We won't go any faster than the slowest person can go, no matter what. If I look back and can't see the end of the line, we'll stop and wait until I can."

"What do you want us to do?" Arturo asked.

"Pick two of your fastest hikers," Alberto said. "Divide the supplies we have left so they're only carrying water for themselves and send them ahead to Wayllabamba. We have to let Miguel know what we've decided. I expect he'll send supplies in to meet us, but no matter what he decides, he can't make a decision until he knows what we're doing. Luis, I hope he'll send us more supplies, but we need to stretch four meals into six, at least until we know we're getting more from Miguel. I'll leave it to you to figure out how to do that. I'll need everyone to watch for places besides established campsites where we can have lunch or sleep if we have to. I'd rather be in a campsite, but there's no guarantee we'll be able to make the usual distances."

"We can make do at any of the ruins," Arturo said. "The ground might be a little rocky in places, but there's always enough space to pitch tents. The problem will be water if we're not at a campsite."

"If this rain keeps up, it won't take long to fill a pot to boil," Alberto said. "It's not the way we usually do things, but I'll take what we can get at this point. I've never had a serious injury in a group I'm leading. I won't have it start now. Whatever precautions we have to take, we will, but we will get everyone off this trail safely."

"Yes, we will," Arturo said. "We'll figure out the packs and send runners as soon as it's safe in the morning. News of the landslides will reach Miguel before the runners get to Wayllabamba. He'll have a plan in place, just waiting on us to tell him what we're doing. You'll see."

"I know he will," Alberto said. "We just have to coordinate with him, and that's going to mean runners. Probably more than just the two tomorrow morning."

"We have runners," Arturo said. "We'll work in shifts, we'll carry extra loads, we'll leave things behind. One way or another, we will give you the support you need. We all want this to go right."

"I know," Alberto said. "Thank you. I don't know what's going to happen, but I know there's no better group out here. There's no one I'd rather have helping me through whatever comes than all of you. Get as much sleep as you can tonight. We'll need it come tomorrow."

Alberto ignored the snicker he heard as he left the tent. It didn't do any harm to let the porters joke about him and Benicio. They meant it in good humor, and Alberto had heard them tease each other about their girlfriends and wives. If they felt comfortable teasing him the same way, it could only help the unity of the team.

They'd need it with what they'd be facing tomorrow. His skin crawled just thinking about everything that could go wrong. He needed to take his own advice and get a good night's sleep, but he wasn't sure he'd be able to rest. The weight of his decision bore heavily on him, curving his shoulders and slowing his steps. He knew better than to second-guess himself. He'd made the right decision, but that didn't stop visions of landslides tearing down the mountainside from assaulting him. He took a calming breath before undoing his boots and climbing into the tent.

Benicio sat on his mat inside the tent, biting at his lip. Alberto reached up to stop him, only to find blood on Benicio's lip. "Benicio?"

"I'm scared," Benicio said. "I keep telling myself we're making the right decision and that we're better off trying to get out than waiting for rescue. My gut tells me that staying here is dangerous at best, but I'm still scared."

The vulnerability in Benicio's voice broke Alberto's resolve. He pulled Benicio into his arms and kissed him desperately. "I'm scared too," he admitted as he buried his face in Benicio's hair. "We've made the right decision. Arturo and Luis agree. But we've already lost at least one experienced porter to this weather and the capriciousness of the mountains. I know it could happen again at any moment and without any warning. We could get halfway back and get trapped again. We could get hit by another landslide and not make it back at all. And that terrifies me."

"So what do we do?" Benicio asked.

"We hold each other as tight as we can tonight, and tomorrow we go out there and do our jobs," Alberto said, "because however scared we are, our tourists will be a hundred times worse when we tell them. They're going to look to us for guidance and reassurance."

"Can we really give them any?"

"We can tell them we will do everything in our power to get them all out of here as safely and quickly as possible," Alberto said. "We can tell them that we have a lifetime of experience dealing with the mountains, and we will put all of that experience to work to make the best decisions possible at every turn."

"I'm not sure that's much consolation," Benicio said with a tremulous smile.

"It's no consolation at all," Alberto agreed, "but it's the best I have. Unless you have a better idea of what to tell them."

"I couldn't even come up with everything you did," Benicio said. "I certainly don't have any better ideas."

"The government doesn't want black marks from failing to respond to a crisis," Alberto said. "They'll do everything they can to help get people off the trail safely. And Miguel is a formidable voice on our side. He's not going to stand by and do nothing, and the other agency owners will rally around him. They'll get porters or llamas with supplies on the way to us, and if we can get to Wayllabamba, the villagers will help too. We just have to take it one step at a time."

"I'm not letting you out of my sight tomorrow."

"I wasn't planning on anything else," Alberto said. "For one thing, we can't help each other if we're all spread out. More importantly, though, I won't be able to concentrate on helping the tourists if I'm worried about you."

"I can watch out for myself."

"I know you can," Alberto said, "but it's natural to worry about the person you love when he's in a dangerous situation, even if he's perfectly capable of taking care of himself."

"The person you... love?"

"Yes," Alberto said. "The person I love. I don't know what tomorrow will bring. One or both of us could be dead by this time tomorrow night. I'm going to do everything I can to keep that from happening, but I can't stop a landslide. If the worst happens, I don't want to go without you knowing. You don't have to say the words back. I know it's sudden, but I had to say it."

"I'm glad you did." Benicio tightened his hold on Alberto. "I love you too, but I wouldn't have worked up the courage to say it first."

"If we make it out of this nightmare, I'm telling Miguel we aren't hiking the trail without each other ever. I don't want to ever be in a situation like this and not have you by my side."

"If we make it out alive, we can tell anyone anything you want," Benicio promised.

Alberto couldn't help but laugh. "Even your mother?"

"If I tell her you made sure I got home safely, I'm pretty sure she'll adopt you no matter what," Benicio replied.

"I can live with that," Alberto said. He stretched out on the sleeping mat and pulled Benicio down beside him. "I didn't think the first time I told someone I loved him would be on the trail where I couldn't do anything about it but kiss him."

"Until a few months ago, I didn't think I'd ever say to it anyone other than my mother," Benicio replied. "The fact that I can say it at all is a miracle I never looked for. I don't need to make love with you right this minute for it to mean something."

"We'll get through this," Alberto said fervently. "We'll get off the trail, even if it takes four or five days, and when we do, we're going home and not leaving for a week. They'll have to clear the trail before we can take any more groups, so it'll be weeks if not months before we can lead another group out there. Miguel won't mind giving us a few days off."

"What will we do? I mean, we earn our living out here."

"Depends on whether the roads and rail are open," Alberto said. "We can still take groups to Machu Picchu. We just won't hike to get there. We can also do things in Cusco and the Sacred Valley. The Inca Trail may be my passion, but it's not all I know. Even if we don't work together during the day, we'll be able to come home to our bed every night. It won't be all bad. It'll be good to give our knees a rest."

"Always the optimist," Benicio teased.

"Not really, but it's better than thinking about the next few days," Alberto replied. "If I think about that, I'll panic again."

"Yes, let's focus on other things," Benicio agreed. "We can save the panic for when we really need it."

"Let's pray we don't."

"Amen."

ARTURO PULLED Alberto aside as soon as he climbed out of his tent in the morning. "I've sent four runners ahead. Two of them will go to Wayllabamba or all the way to Piskacucho if necessary. They will get word to Miguel, no matter what. I also told them to take messages for any groups they pass on the way there. The other two are going to Pacamayo and to Llulluchapampa and coming back to tell us the condition of the trail. It'll give us a better idea of how far we can reasonably get today."

"Ayapata is out of the question," Alberto agreed. "We might be able to make it, but the tourists won't, not in this weather and after two days of hard hiking. Llulluchapampa would be ideal. It's pretty much halfway back, but as long as we make it past Pacamayo, I'll be happy with our progress."

"I'll be happy with any progress that gets us closer to home," Arturo said. "Even if it's just as far as Runkurakay. We'd be safer at the top of the pass than at the bottom."

"Best estimate, how long will it take the porters to get to Llulluchapampa and back?" Alberto asked. He knew the record for the fastest time over the length of the trail, but that didn't mean every porter could traverse the whole twenty-six miles in less than four hours.

"The one who went to Pacamayo will probably be back in two hours," Arturo said. "Barring problems, of course. Llulluchapampa will take longer, but he should make it back to us by lunchtime."

"I want to have lunch at Pacamayo if at all possible," Alberto said. "I don't want to sleep there tonight."

"No, I agree," Arturo said. "As long as the trail is wet but not blocked, it's a reasonable goal. We can see what time it is and how everyone is feeling at lunch and decide the rest from there."

"It's a plan," Alberto said. "Now to explain all of this to the tourists."

"They know something isn't right," Arturo said. "They may not know what, but you can see in the way they've been watching the sky and the mountains since they got up. Just knowing will be better than worrying aimlessly."

"Yes, you're right. I'll tell them over breakfast."

"WHAT?"

The chorus of exclamations from the tourists was deafening. Half of them, mostly the men, seemed to think yelling would change something. The other half sank in on themselves, pulling their coats more tightly around themselves for comfort.

Alberto rode out the tide of displeasure, waiting until the noise level settled before he started again. "There have been two landslides on the trail ahead. Two that we know of, that is. There may have been more. One of those landslides has already claimed one life. We can't go forward. Staying here would only prolong the time until we get out."

"But… shit, we've hiked how far to get here, and now we're exhausted. We don't have dry clothes. And what about our flights home?"

"I know," Alberto said. "I don't have any more dry clothes than you do. I hiked the same distance. But I know staying here won't help anything. The only solution is to get off the trail, and that means turning back. We'll spread it out more if we need to. We'll hike as far as we can and stop. On the way here, we had assigned campsites we had to reach each night. We won't have that on the way back. We'll get as far as we get and we'll stop."

"And if there's another landslide?"

"Then we'll deal with it," Alberto replied. "For now, we need to get started. Porters have gone ahead to make sure the trail is safe. We'll have lunch in Pacamayo and then decide where we're camping for the night. Trust us. We'll get you out of here safely."

His words only appeased them marginally, but it was enough to get them out of the tent and shouldering their packs. Alberto caught Benicio's eye and gestured for him to take the front of the line. He'd grown up in the mountains. Hopefully he'd see any warning signs fast enough to avert a catastrophe.

BENICIO TURNED back to look up the trail behind him, as he had done every few minutes since they left Chaqulqocha, when the sun wasn't even above the horizon yet. The rain had tapered off to a fine drizzle instead of the torrents from the previous days, but Benicio was no less soaked and miserable for it. His heel hurt from the blister, and he was ready for a hot bath and dry clothes. He wouldn't get his wish today, or for at least two more days if their current pace was any indication. They had made it back to Runkurakay early enough that they'd decided to push on to Pacamayo for lunch. The porter who had returned assured them the trail was wet but stable all the way to the campsite.

The tourists didn't have the porters' confidence in the trail or their own feet, though, and the descent took its toll on their knees. It was nearly two o'clock by the time they made it to Pacamayo for lunch.

"There's only three hours of daylight left," Benicio said when he and Alberto found a few minutes alone while the tourists used the facilities at Pacamayo. "There's no way we'll make it to Llulluchapampa."

"I know," Alberto said, "but there's no way I'm staying here. With all the rain we've had, it's asking for trouble. We can camp at the top of Dead Woman Pass. We won't have running water, but Arturo thinks they can carry or collect enough to get us through the night and to Llulluchapampa tomorrow. Look around you, Benicio. You can see places where it flooded already, and it's still raining. Not as hard, granted, but until it stops completely, I don't trust it here."

"No, you're right," Benicio agreed. Puddles of water stood in almost all the campsites, and in places it was deeper than just puddles. If the rain picked up again, the campsite could be the victim of a flash flood, and Benicio didn't want to get caught in it. "Dead Woman Pass, it is. Even then, though, we're going to get there after dark."

"Everyone has a flashlight. We'll just have to make do," Alberto said. "Even if we only make it to Llulluchapampa tomorrow so everyone can rest, we'll still be halfway back, and by then, we should have news from Miguel."

"Good news, I hope," Benicio said. "I noticed breakfast was smaller than usual, but Luis can only stretch our supplies so far."

"He said he could get us through dinner tomorrow with the supplies he has on hand," Alberto replied. "After that, we'll have to hope Miguel comes through. Or else we hike hungry to Wayllabamba."

IT WAS nearly dark now, and they were only halfway up the mountain to the pass. Benicio itched to hike faster, but they'd agreed to stay within sight of each other, and since the sun had set, that meant staying even closer than before. He counted flashlight beams instead of heads now, because he couldn't distinguish Alberto's features at the back of the line. When he thought everyone was caught up, he started out again, eyes back on the goal of the peak ahead of them, barely outlined in the deepening twilight.

You can do this, he chanted to himself as he hiked. *You can lead them out. Alberto believes in you. He loves you. You can do this.*

It had been his mantra all day, but he clung to it now to fight the despair that threatened. They'd passed the detritus of various groups over the course of the day, things the porters or tourists had left behind to save weight as they struggled to get out. They'd passed other groups that had decided to hunker down and wait for outside help. Benicio almost envied them. They might not be any safer than he was, but they weren't exhausted, sore, and blistered on top of being trapped on the trail.

He pushed the negativity down. He couldn't think that way. He and Alberto had talked about it. They'd weighed their options and chosen the one they felt was the best for them and their group. If they'd had a different group of tourists, they might have made a different decision. If they hadn't been the first to hear of the demise of the porter from the group ahead of them, they might have clung to the illusory safety of the established campsites. As it was, though, they were making their way out, one slow, painful step at a time.

He had bruises all up and down his shins from where his feet had slipped out from under him at various times, sending him stumbling into the step ahead of him. He didn't think he was bleeding, but he wouldn't know for sure until they got to the campsite and he could check more carefully. From the various mutters and curses he'd heard all afternoon, he didn't think the tourists were faring any better. They'd have to pull out the first-aid kit when they got to camp and make sure everyone cleaned up any injuries they'd acquired. Everyone was still moving, so Benicio didn't think any of them were serious, but even a small cut could get infected without proper care.

He nearly cried with relief when they crested the pass at Warmiwañusca and saw the tents lined up and the porters bustling about.

"Stow your packs and come to the dining tent as quickly as possible," Alberto told the group as they stumbled into the clearing. "Everyone needs to check for cuts and other injuries, and that's easiest done in the dining tent with the lamp."

Benicio breathed a sigh of relief as he dropped his own pack into the tent and went to help the others. Arturo met him at the entrance of the dining tent with the first-aid kit. "I thought you might need this."

"Thank you. Any news from Wayllabamba?"

"No, but I didn't really expect any tonight. By lunch tomorrow, maybe. Even if they got to Wayllabamba by lunchtime, they had to make decisions before sending someone back, and since they didn't know how far we would get today, I expect they'll wait until morning to start out."

"That makes sense. I'd just hoped for something to tell the tourists," Benicio said. "Their spirits are pretty low."

"Theirs aren't the only ones," Arturo said, "but we're safe for the night, and there's enough food for dinner. We'll worry about the rest tomorrow."

Benicio took the first-aid kit and ducked into the tent. Basins of steaming water waited along the table at intervals. Benicio took one of the towels that sat in a stack in the middle. It was a little damp but not nearly as wet as he'd feared it would be. He dipped it in the water and began washing away the mud that coated his legs so he could make sure none of the smarting spots were cuts instead of painful bruises.

One of the tourists—Patricia from New Orleans, Benicio reminded himself—came in and sat down next to him. "Towel is there," he said. "Clean up if you can."

She nodded and took a towel to begin her own ablutions. "Do you really think we'll make it out of here alive?" she asked after a minute.

"I think Alberto, Arturo, the others, they do everything possible to make it so," Benicio replied slowly. "Is scary for us too. The mountains, they no care who you are when earthquakes come or mountainsides collapse. Porter, guide, tourist—it no matters. But I learn something growing up in the mountains. You no can worry constantly. The *apus*, the mountain gods, they do as they please. We have to keep living no matter what they do because floods, earthquakes, landslides, they are going to happen. We get up again, clean up again, rebuild again, and go on until the next time. Is one reason Andean villages use mud bricks. Cheap, easy to rebuild if the *apus* are vindictive."

"It's hard not to worry, though. I have children at home. They're with my mother right now, but if we didn't come home…."

"I no know porter who died, but he likely had a wife and children too," Benicio said. "Is the same for us." He didn't mention Alberto or their relationship, but he understood her fear.

"We're all in the same boat. Is that what you're telling me?"

Benicio took a moment to parse the English expression, but once he had, he smiled. "Yes, is what I want to say. Guides, porters, we have families to go home to. We want to get home safely too. If we make decision, is best one for all of us. Trust us."

"I do," she said. "It's just easy to get scared."

Benicio patted her hand. "For all of us. Clean cuts on your legs. Is no good if they get infection. Walking will be even more hard then."

She smiled a little and turned back to the task of tending her injuries while Benicio did the same.

TWENTY-FOUR

THEY WERE a few hundred meters down the mountain the next morning when Benicio heard it: the telltale rumbling that too often preceded disaster in the mountains. Heart pounding, he searched the ridges above them for signs of impending collapse, but everything seemed stable. The sound rattled through the valley again. He turned to look out over the gorge and flinched as the mountainside across from them gave way. Rocks and mud tumbled from the top of the peak, gaining momentum and picking up more detritus.

Benicio braced himself against the mountain face, even knowing the landslide would not reach him where he stood. He wanted to look away from the destructive flow, but he couldn't tear his gaze from it. Behind him, he heard gasps and cries from the tourists and knew he should say something to reassure them, but words failed him. What could he say in the face of such vivid proof of the very real dangers they would face until they could leave the trail?

"Keep moving," he heard Alberto shout over the din. He waved an acknowledgment and pushed himself to standing again. His knees shook with the strain of the descent, made worse by the adrenaline surging through him, but he leaned on his walking stick and made his body obey. He had to be strong for the tourists.

As swiftly as the noise had started, it ended, the collapsing morass finding level ground at the base of the mountain. Benicio looked down at the chaos in the valley below. Llamas and alpacas bleated as they milled around, trying to put as much distance between themselves and the landslide as possible. Benicio didn't blame them. He wanted to put as much distance between himself and the landslide as he could too.

They hiked another ten minutes until they reached a wider section of the trail. Benicio gestured for everyone to take a break. If their peaked faces were any indication, they needed it as badly as he did. Alberto came to his side as soon as everyone was settled. Benicio squeezed his arm in reassurance. It wasn't what he wanted to do, but with the tourists gathered around them, he didn't dare do more. Alberto caught his eye, and Benicio could tell he felt the same. That would do for now.

"Are you all right?" Alberto murmured.

"Shaken but otherwise yes," Benicio said. "It was on the other side of the valley."

"And it could just as easily have been this side," Alberto said, finishing Benicio's unspoken thought.

"It could have been, but it wasn't," Benicio said. "If we're lucky, the next one won't be either."

"If we're lucky, there won't be a next one," Alberto corrected. "I'd planned on staying at Llulluchapampa even though we'll probably get there close to lunch, but I'm not sure anyone will sleep tonight if we do. It's close enough to see the site of the landslide."

"We could try to push on to Ayapata," Benicio said, "but everyone's dragging already. Let's see how we feel after lunch. Hopefully we'll have news by then, and that might change our decision too."

Alberto nodded and turned back to the group. Benicio regretted the loss of his heat immediately. "See those buildings down there?" he said to the tourists. They all looked toward the end of the valley and the cluster of buildings at its mouth. "That's Llulluchapampa. That's where we'll have lunch. Once we get there, we'll decide if we want to try for Ayapata or if we want to stay there for the night."

"Is it safe after that landslide?" Will asked.

"It's in a flat area at the end of the valley," Alberto said. "Even if we had another landslide, the chances of it reaching all the way to the campsite are almost zero. You'll see better when we get down there. Rest another five minutes, and then we'll keep going."

THEY HAD almost finished lunch at Llulluchapampa when a shout went up from the porters. Alberto shot out of the dining tent before anyone else could react.

"Stay here and finish lunch," Benicio directed. "Is happy shout, no danger." Then he followed Alberto outside.

The porters had gathered into a knot around someone Benicio couldn't see, but they parted to let him through when he approached. Two porters he recognized as being part of one of the other teams at Huaman Travel stood in the center of the ring, talking to Alberto.

"What's going on?" Benicio asked.

"The trail is clear all the way back to Piskacucho," one of the porters said. "Miguel is sending supplies for two more days. He says to stay here tonight, to hike to Hatunchaca tomorrow, and the rest of the way out the day after that. He's making arrangements to change flights for the tourists so they can get home two days after we leave the trail. He thought they might like time to rest before traveling home."

"That is good news," Benicio said, nearly sagging in relief. "Do we know when the supplies will get here?"

"The other porters were sorting the last of the supplies when we left this morning. They should have left no more than half an hour behind us," the other porter said. "They'll hike slower because of their gear, but they should be here before dark. If not, they will meet us at Ayapata for lunch tomorrow."

"Miguel also said the storms had passed. Maybe a little more rain this afternoon and then the sun will come back out."

Benicio looked skyward and saw that the clouds did indeed seem less threatening than they had in the previous few days. They weren't quite the misty wisps Benicio was used to seeing over the mountains here, but definitely an improvement. "We should go ahead and set the tents up," he said. "That way they'll have time to dry out before tonight. After we finish eating, of course." He knew the porters frequently ate after the tourists were done, finishing up any leftovers along with the hearty stews they prepared for themselves.

"We've eaten," Arturo said. "We'll get the tents up and then deal with any leftovers and the dishes. You tell the tourists. Hopefully the good news will settle them."

Benicio hoped so as well. He'd done everything he could to stay calm and reassuring for their sakes, but the constant tension was taking its toll. An afternoon free of worry would be a boon to them all.

They went back to the dining tent to tell everyone the news and what decisions had been made. "The rain has stopped," Alberto said when he had answered everyone's questions about the plans for the next few days. "I would suggest laying out your wet things to dry. We will all be more comfortable in dry clothes. Usually I tell people not to leave anything outside the tent, but under the circumstances, I think it will be okay this time. There may be other groups who make it this far before tonight, and if that happens, you may want to bring your things in then. For now, though, feel free to spread out."

The tourists scattered at that, going to search for their bags and follow Alberto's advice.

"I suppose we should do the same," Benicio said.

"It would be sensible," Alberto agreed.

"But?"

"Alberto, Benicio, I set your tent up," Arturo called. They turned to find him coming from the opposite side of the campsite. "Over there," he added as he pointed to the far edge of the campsite. "I thought you could use a break without everyone right on top of you. If other groups come, we may have to move you closer, but for now, enjoy the privacy."

"You don't have to play matchmaker," Alberto told him. "We're already together."

"The first thing I do when I get home, whenever that finally is, will be to kiss my wife, and then kiss her again and again, until I lose the fear of never seeing her again. If you're not feeling the same way, something's wrong with you both. You can't do that in the middle of camp with all the tourists milling around. Over there, you don't have to worry about every little sound carrying. Get some rest. You've earned it."

"And you and the others haven't?" Benicio asked.

"We have, and we'll take our rest too, as soon as the dishes are done," Arturo promised. "We won't do anything more strenuous than hanging out our wet clothes until it's time to make dinner. You should do the same."

Benicio didn't need to be told twice. The blister they'd tended before they realized the trail ahead of them was closed had gotten more painful, and being off his feet for the afternoon sounded like heaven.

He traipsed across the campsite to the tent. Now that he knew he could rest, his exhaustion nearly overwhelmed him. He debated trying to take a shower just so he'd be clean, but even that seemed like too much effort. He slumped down in front of the tent and pried his boots off his feet. If he never had to wear them again, it would be too soon. He peeled away the bandage they'd replaced this morning. It was already sticky with pus and blood. He'd be glad for the week off and some easier trips until it healed completely.

"Here," Alberto said. "Wash it out again. There's running water here and with supplies on the way, we don't have to worry about running out of propane for the camp stoves. Get it as clean as you can with the rag and then soak it for a while. It'll hurt, but it will keep it from getting worse."

"It's bad enough as it is," Benicio said. "I'm pretty sure it's infected."

"We'll go to the doctor when we get back to Cusco," Alberto said, "but soak it for now. It might not get rid of the infection, but it can't hurt."

Benicio scrubbed at his heel as thoroughly as he could stand before easing it into the basin of hot water. He hissed at the contact, but after a moment, the pain faded and the heat relaxed the tense muscles.

"When we get back to Cusco, I'm going to take a hot shower until the water runs cold and then I'm going to lie in bed for a week," Benicio said. "Every muscle in my body aches."

Alberto looked around for a moment, but no one was anywhere near their tent. "Give me your other foot," he said. "Let me see if I can help."

Benicio leaned back on his elbows and stretched his other leg out in front of him. Alberto cradled his foot in his lap and dug his fingers into the arch. Benicio hissed at the sharp pain, but when Alberto stopped, he shook his head. "No, keep going. It's going to hurt, but it feels good too."

Alberto returned to his massage. Benicio could practically feel the muscles unknotting as Alberto's fingers worked their magic. He raised an eyebrow when Alberto moved from his feet to his calves, but Alberto just smiled. "Don't tell me it's only your feet that are sore. I know better than that."

"I wasn't going to," Benicio said. "I just wondered how far you were planning to go out here in the open where anyone could see."

Alberto shrugged. "The porters know, and if you think they aren't speculating about what we're doing over here with our tent so far away from everyone else's, think again. If the tourists do come over, I'm helping you out. You're clearly hurt, even if you've managed to hide it from them, and we're friends."

"I don't know many friends who go around massaging each other's feet and legs," Benicio said, "but I'm not going to worry about it if you aren't."

"No, not going to worry about it," Alberto said. "Not today, not tomorrow, maybe not ever. That landslide this morning could have been on the other side of the valley. We could have been a day ahead of where we were and caught in the one between Chaqulqocha and Wiñay Wayna. I'm done worrying about things I can't change. We're here, we're safe, and by some miracle you love me back. Nothing else matters."

Benicio's breath caught in his throat. The last two days had been so stressful and so busy that Benicio hadn't dwelled on the words they had spoken in the darkness of their tent. He reached for Alberto's hand on his leg and squeezed tightly. "You're right," he said. "Nothing else matters."

EPILOGUE

AS TERRIFYING as the two days after the landslide that closed the trail to Machu Picchu had been, the final two days of the trek out were strangely anticlimactic. To Benicio's surprise, Miguel had shown up with the porters and supplies, and with him there, the weight of managing the trip shifted away from Alberto and Benicio. Miguel had sent them ahead when he saw the state of Benicio's foot. Benicio went to the doctor as promised and got medicine for the infection. And today, he'd gone back and returned with a clean bill of health.

"Do you still want to go to Cancha Cancha for Christmas?" Benicio asked. He'd written his mother frequently since the landslide had reminded him of how short life could be. He'd refrained from telling her the true nature of his relationship with Alberto, but he hadn't held anything else back. His mother's responses had been full of warmth and insistence that Alberto join them for Christmas if Benicio could manage the hike.

"If you're up to the hike," Alberto said. "I don't want to set back your recovery."

"The doctor cleared me this morning. As long as I wear a bandage to keep it from rubbing a new blister, we can go home for Christmas."

"What will your mother say?" Alberto asked.

"She'll say thank you for taking care of me out on the trail," Benicio said. "And if I'm wrong and she says anything else, we don't have to stay."

"I don't want to come between you and your family," Alberto insisted.

"We've had this conversation once already," Benicio said, "but I'll repeat myself again just to be clear. If they can't accept you, that's their choice. Mine is to stay with you. I know you think I'll change my mind if it comes to that, but I won't. You're stuck with me."

"I can think of worse things that could happen to me," Alberto teased.

Benicio laughed and went to gather the presents he planned to take to his family for Christmas.

"HOW'S YOUR foot?" Alberto asked for the fiftieth time since they'd begun the trek up to Cancha Cancha. Benicio rolled his eyes.

"It's fine, just like all the other times you asked me that."

"Sorry, I know I'm worrying for nothing, but I want you ready to go back on the trail with me when it opens again," Alberto said.

Benicio pulled him in for a quick kiss. "I will be. Come on, we're almost there and this pack is getting heavy. I'm not used to carrying my own load anymore. Arturo and the porters have spoiled me."

"Do you want me to take it?" Alberto asked immediately.

"No," Benicio said with a huff. "You have your own pack. I just want to get to Cancha Cancha so I can set it down. If we hurry, we can be there in twenty minutes. Come on."

Benicio knew Alberto didn't believe his insistence that if it came to it, he'd choose Alberto over his family, but Benicio had thought long and hard about this visit before telling his mother they would come as long as his foot was up to the hike. He truly didn't believe his mother would make him choose. She had been bemused by Shaun and Don, but she hadn't looked at them like an abomination. More like a curiosity. Or like something made sense that had never made sense before. He couldn't explain it to Alberto when it was little more than a feeling he'd gotten from that last visit and from her letters, but he knew she wouldn't turn them away.

"Benicio!" Señora Quispe exclaimed when they came in. "And Alberto. I didn't know when to expect you, or even if you would be able to come."

"Thank you for inviting me to come, señora," Alberto said politely. "I don't have any close family left, and it means a lot to be included in yours."

"As if I would turn away a friend of my son," Señora Quispe scoffed. "Benicio, you take Alberto in your room and get him settled. I didn't put out a mat. I thought you wouldn't mind. You spend half your nights in the same tent and the rest of them in the same apartment. But if you want one, I can get it."

Benicio smiled and kissed his mother's cheek. "No, we don't need a mat."

He went into his room to set down his pack and waited for Alberto to follow. As soon as Alberto shut the door, Benicio pulled him into a tight hug and kissed him firmly.

When they separated, he grinned and pulled Alberto's pack from his shoulder.

"I told you so."

ARIEL TACHNA lives outside of Houston with her husband, her daughter and son, and their cat. Before moving there, she traveled all over the world, having fallen in love with both France, where she found her husband, and India, where she dreams of retiring some day. She's bilingual with snippets of four other languages to her credit, and is as in love with languages as she is with writing.

Visit Ariel at her website http://www.arieltachna.com or on Facebook, https://www.facebook.com/ArielTachna, or e-mail her at arieltachna@gmail.com.

Exploring Limits Series

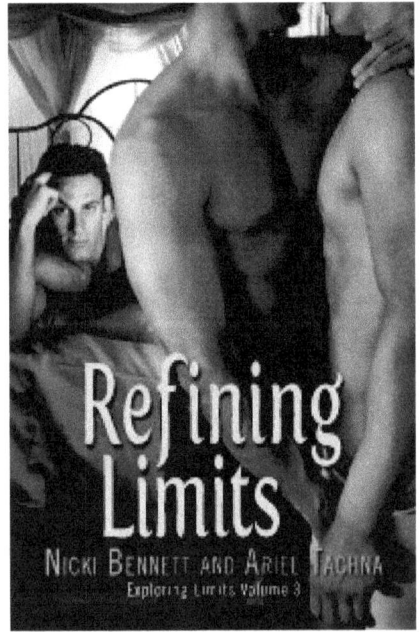

http://www.dreamspinnerpress.com

Exploring Limits Series

http://www.dreamspinnerpress.com

Hot Cargo Series

http://www.dreamspinnerpress.com

Lang Downs Series

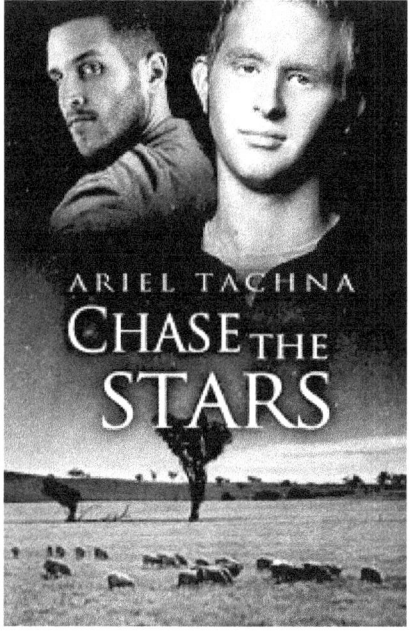

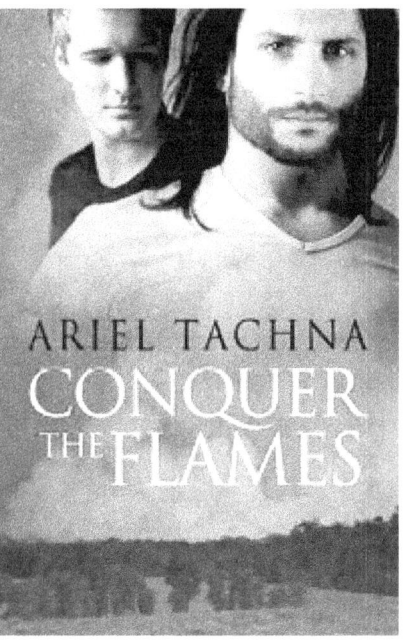

http://www.dreamspinnerpress.com

Partnership in Blood Series

http://www.dreamspinnerpress.com

Partnership in Blood Series

http://www.dreamspinnerpress.com

http://www.dreamspinnerpress.com

HER TWO DADS

ARIEL TACHNA

ARIEL TACHNA

the Inventor's Companion

the Matelot

Ariel Tachna

Once in a LIFETIME

ARIEL TACHNA

http://www.dreamspinnerpress.com

http://www.dreamspinnerpress.com

http://www.dreamspinnerpress.com

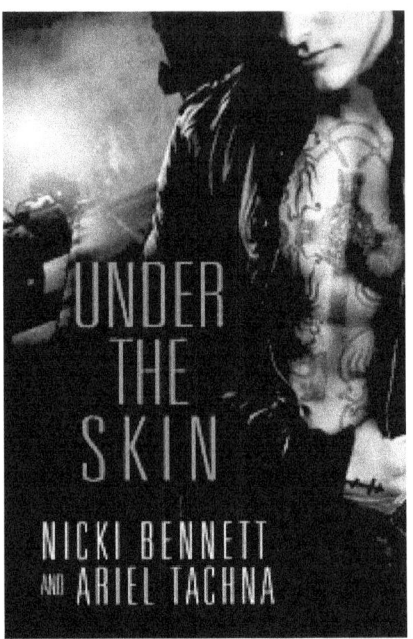

http://www.dreamspinnerpress.com

BRU BAKER

FINDING
HOME

BOOK 2 IN THE DROPPING ANCHOR SERIES

http://www.dreamspinnerpress.com